THE WOMAN
HE LEFT BEHIND

BY PHILIP ANTHONY SMITH

GET A FREE BOOK BY VISITING:
WWW.PHILIPANTHONYSMITH.COM

INSTAGRAM: @PHILIPSMITHFICTION
FACEBOOK: PHILIPSMITHFICTION
COPYRIGHT © 2024 PHILIP ANTHONY SMITH

CONTENTS

PROLOGUE 1
DEATH 11
THE FOOL 27
THE LOVERS 43
THE HANGED MAN 58
WHEEL OF FORTUNE 74
THE TOWER 94
THE SUN 111
THE EMPEROR 128
TEMPERANCE 145
THE MOON 161
STRENGTH 177
THE MAGICIAN 194
THE HERMIT 206
THE CHARIOT 222
JUSTICE 237
THE HIEROPHANT 253
THE STAR 268
THE HIGH PRIESTESS 286
THE WORLD 300
JUDGEMENT 313
EPILOGUE 330

TRIGGER WARNINGS

This book does contain some challenging themes and references that some readers might find distressing. In order to preserve the mystery of the story, these have been listed at the end of the book. If you wish to check them before continuing, feel free, and please practice self care during and after reading.

For my angelic daughter Alyssa,
Although you are under one year old, you have just begun taking your first steps, and it's an amazing feat to behold. As I am typing this, you have just crawled over to me, with an almost apparent eagerness to read what I have been typing.

Not a chance.

Try again in 18 years.

PROLOGUE

AMELIA - BEFORE

I touched the old oak doors delicately with my shaking hand and stroked the grain with my fingertips. Every single moment of what was about to happen had been planned meticulously, and every single detail was studied and prepared. Each possible eventuality was also precisely calculated. I'd spent so long thinking about this moment that it had occupied my every waking moment for over a year. I kept telling myself I needed to be present and not dwell too much on the past or the future, but there was a level of finality to what I'd agreed to do. Was I making the right decision? I hoped so. I never thought I would find myself here, in this very moment, touching the door to destiny. The choice to open the door or not was seemingly a simple one, although it was the last chance I would get to change the course of my entire life. What would my life look like if I didn't go through with this? The anxiety hit me like a stinging slap in the face, and my breathing became shallow and laboured.

Remember, *breathe*.

A familiar hand touched my arm, and I turned to look at him. He was smiling, trying to be reassuring, but it did little to calm my nerves. I reciprocated with a feigned half-smile, and his smile widened in response. I turned back to the door; its indifference to my situation was warmly welcomed. In a moment of impulse, I pushed it slightly, but the door was heavier than I anticipated, and it remained stationary. His hand gripped my arm lightly to get my attention.

"You can do this," he whispered.

I was on the precipice; those four words were all I needed to spur me into the decision. I pushed the door with conviction, and it creaked open ominously. The man I came here for was waiting for me patiently with his hands clasped together, his back to me, and completely unaware I'd just entered. I took a single, measured step over the threshold, and I was almost knocked off my feet by the dramatic blasts of an organ echoing off the walls. The melody made him turn, and his eyes locked dramatically with mine.

Harry.

His eyes brightened, and the signature cheeky smirk he was famous for spanned his face; it was infectious. I smiled back in an explosion of butterflies and warm blushes. Of course, it was the right decision, and I felt ridiculous for even questioning it for a single moment. I was in love with him, more in love than I had ever thought possible. Every anxiety and insecurity instantly evaporated the moment I laid my eyes on him. My stride grew quicker and longer in a subconscious effort to be with him as fast as possible, but the hand on my arm held me back slightly. I turned to its owner, Dad, and he didn't have to utter a word. He was right. I should slow down and savour every fleeting moment; this would be the first and last time I ever did this.

The church looked exactly how I'd dreamt it would be. Each pew was adorned with bouquets of bright white flowers, each petal leaning into the intense sunshine beaming through the stained-glass windows. I'd dreamt of this moment since I was a little girl, though the identity of the man waiting for me at the end of the aisle had always been a mystery, which made me wonder whether he really existed at all. But I'd found him, against all odds, and he found me. With each step forward, my anticipation grew, and every fibre of my being wanted to be with him forever. I reached Harry, and he leant in to give me a passionate kiss, but I turned my cheek, and he giggled slightly.

"You look absolutely breathtaking, Ames," Harry whispered to me as I arrived.

"You don't scrub up half-bad either," I smirked.

"John, thank you so much for welcoming me into your family," Harry said to Dad with a handshake.

My Dad rejected it and plumped for a hug instead, which incited cheers from the rest of the guests. I was so transfixed on Harry that I didn't even realise they were there. I took my place at the altar, and Harry grasped my hands firmly, still gazing deeply into my eyes. I'd looked into them before, of course, but that day, I could see everything: our past and the future we would eventually build together as man and wife. The celebrant was talking, but we were so enraptured by each other we didn't hear the words. She tapped me on the shoulder comedically to get my attention, and the rest of the wedding guests burst into laughter at our blunder.

And the laughter continued heartily.

The flawless day gave way to the perfect evening as the beer and wine flowed freely. Harry effortlessly moved around the room, mingling with the guests. He had this boyish charm that just took everyone he met by surprise. To look at him, you could be forgiven for thinking that Harry was a bit of a rascal, but he was the most loving, caring person I'd ever had the pleasure of knowing, and he was mine forever. Most brides may have been annoyed that their new husband was socializing with guests to this extent on their wedding day, but I was quite content simply admiring him from a distance. Harry caught me looking and shot a smile my way, followed by an awkward grimace aimed at the couple who were talking at him. He gestured over to me and made his escape.

"I'm shattered. They won't leave me alone!" Harry laughed, slumping on the chair next to mine.

"Me too. Can't we just ask them to leave? Or is that a bit too much?" I joked.

"I think your new mother-in-law might have something to say about that, Ames."

"Harry, I've actually been counting how many glasses of wine she's had. The amount she's knocked back could easily kill a horse."

"She's had a lot of practice," Harry chuckled.

"My feet are killing me," I said, kicking off my heels, "is it bad I just want to go to bed?"

"Let's get out of here, then."

"What?"

"It's our wedding. Screw it. We can do whatever we like. If you want to get out of here, let's do it."

"But the guests—"

"Sod the guests. I need to save my energy for what I have planned anyway," Harry smirked.

"Oh? And what plans are those?"

"Well, it is customary, after the wedding, for the bride and groom to—" Harry ended his proposition with a suggestive whistle and insinuating wink.

I faked disgust, but truth be told, I could hardly wait either. We both fled out of the room giggling, much to the bewilderment of my new mother-in-law, Yvonne, who probably expected us to beg for her permission to leave. Strangely, or perhaps not, it was one of the most vivid memories I had of our wedding day, his mischievous face as he excitedly led me up the stairs to the honeymoon suite. I had never felt as connected to someone as I did that night. Our very souls had melted into each other, and the emotions of the day built into a crescendo that absolutely blew my mind and body.

I used to think that my wedding day would be the pinnacle of my love for Harry, but it wasn't. Every day that passed, I felt myself feeling even stronger for him. Harry knew me better than I knew myself; he understood and saw me like nobody else did or anybody else would. It didn't take much to lure him away from the sleepy seaside village of Filey to my home city of Manchester, much to the dismay of Yvonne. Without wasting time, we rented a small flat in the city centre whilst we searched for the home of our dreams. We quickly found it and moved into a semi-detached house just outside of the city. The house was amazing, and I was so happy. I could hardly conceal my overflowing joy. We loved big city living; just being able to find a shop open past 8 pm was enough for Harry to want to move from Filey. We didn't even seriously entertain the idea of staying in there. We needed enough distance between us and Yvonne for a start.

Wedded bliss was all I ever wanted, and I'd found the perfect man to share it with. However, Harry wanted some little Harry's running around. Not that I was against the idea in principle, but I'd never planned on having kids. When he asked me if I wanted children in the future, I always responded with a 'firm maybe.' Yes, I know, pleasing your partner isn't the best reason to have offspring, but for Harry, it was a deal breaker. I just hoped that the maternal instincts would kick in afterwards and I could become the mother of the children he had always wanted.

We decided to start trying about six months after we got married. It sounds rushed, I know, but I wasn't getting any younger, and as ridiculous as that may sound, I could hear my biological clock ticking away. However, months and months of constantly trying to conceive ended in failure. Despite the fact that Harry remained positive, I still felt like I was broken inside. Once I realised it would be a lot more difficult to have a baby than we originally anticipated, my apathy turned to obsession, leaving me wanting to conceive more than anything, just to prove that my body was capable. I thought my constant breakdowns would end up perturbing Harry, but luckily, they didn't. He was so seemingly understanding and supportive; it gave me the resolve to continue trying. If anything, the struggle made me feel even closer to him.

After weeks and months of me crying in the bathroom while gripping a negative pregnancy test, we finally made the decision to get outside help. We went the holistic route at first; we had a cupboard full of herbal remedies and disgusting teas made from God knows what, and most of our evenings consisted of Harry frantically searching for the latest fad to boost our chances of conception. Still, after sustained disappointment, he convinced me to go down the scientific route, and I agreed with him.

After two failed IVF attempts and thousands of pounds later, we were still left with no prospect of a child. We had a follow-up appointment at the IVF clinic to see if the third attempt had finally stuck, and I was pregnant at long last. The doctors had assured us that if there wasn't a 'positive outcome' after three attempts, we would have to start looking at other options. I didn't think Harry would accept that and he would want to continue trying. What option would we have if not? That appointment was out of the ordinary because Harry wasn't going to be there with me. He had planned a trip back to Filey, and I would be following him up there the day after. He did offer to rearrange it a number of times, but I insisted he should go without me.

"Not having any breakfast, Ames?" Harry asked, shoving a fistful of toast into his mouth.

"I can't. I feel sick," I responded.

"Amelia, whatever happens, we will deal with it," Harry started, "do you not want to try the old-fashioned way one more time before I leave?"

"Funny. No, I feel like I'm going to throw up."

"I didn't know I had that effect on you."

"It's just nerves about today."

"Are you sure you don't want me to cancel? We can always go up together tomorrow. I don't mind waiting."

"No, it's fine. I can't bear to see Yvonne's face if I robbed her of an extra day with her precious son."

"What's this?" Harry asked, pointing to a small, insulated bag on the counter.

"Just a little survival kit in case you get hungry. A few drinks and snacks."

"You really are the most amazing wife in the entire world, you know that?"

"I can't have my man going hungry, can I? Or eating questionable service station sandwiches. When do you need to set off?"

"I thought I'd go now; the car is already packed. I'm going to try to avoid the morning rush. Is that okay?"

"Of course. I love you; I'll see you tomorrow," I smiled, leaning in for a kiss.

"I love you, Ames. Let me know how it goes."

Harry grabbed his bags and made his way out of the front door to the car, and I followed him so I could see him off on his drive. He opened the car window and waved at me as he reversed down the drive. He liked to play this little game where he would pull a stupid face just before he peeled out onto the main road. Every time, I thought he would run out of faces and repeat one, but somehow, he managed to keep it fresh.

"Au revoir!" Harry shouted with his eyes crossed, lifting his top lip to expose his teeth. Unfortunately, the image of him pulling that stupid face is seared into my memory forever.

It was the last time I would ever see Harry alive.

DEATH

AMELIA

With each strike of the shovel, piercing the mountain of earth beside him, my unwillingness to accept his death grew inside me. Thud. The collected shovel full of dirt is cast into the void. I felt every wet-slapping noise the soil made when it fell on the coffin as if it were punching me in my stomach. Thud. Every blade of grass around the grave shuddered under the force of the shovel hitting the ground. I still hadn't shed a single tear yet, not that I didn't want to; I just wasn't capable. I know how I should have felt; beside myself, hysterical. Still, I felt none of those emotions. Numb probably describes it most accurately. I felt as if I was having an out-of-body experience, watching myself through third-person eyes. 'Why isn't Amelia crying?' I thought about myself. I became increasingly agitated when I could no longer hide the absence of facial expression and the lack of emotion I was experiencing. I kicked myself internally to try and get it together.

His mother, my mother-in-law, who was wailing like a banshee being dragged over hot coals, glared at me in between the dabbing of her eyes with a handkerchief. It's worth noting that her excessive eye make-up was still intact; it must have been immune to the effects of crocodile tears. Just cry, I thought to myself, just one single tear, to show everyone how much he meant to you. I pushed myself to picture his cold and lifeless body in the coffin below to try and force some kind of emotional response, but I remained numb. I loved this man more than I'd ever loved anybody in my life, and he was gone, and yet I couldn't bring myself to accept it. I was half expecting a trademark Harry-style prank, and he would spring from the loose earth and scare us to death. As much as I would have loved for that to happen, it never did.

The coffin was now completely obscured, covered by the dirt. The gravedigger carried on piling the dirt on top of it without relenting, and the rest of the cavity filled up quickly. In my left eye a tear finally started to form, but quickly retreated when I saw my mother-in-law shoot more daggers at me. She looked as if she was working up to saying something scathing to me. 'Not here, not now,' I thought on repeat, but tact wasn't a word she ever had in her vocabulary.

"You could at least try to look upset, Amelia," She scolded, being held tightly by her latest husband, John.

"Look upset? I *am* upset, Yvonne," I uttered in response, barely looking at her.

"Just leave it, love," John said, delicately restraining her.

Yvonne and I never got on, so it came as no a surprise that she would be like this at my husband's funeral. To her, I was just the woman who swept her son off his feet and dragged him back to Manchester. She never forgave me for that. Although Harry had never implicitly said it to me, Yvonne blamed me entirely for our bad luck in conceiving, too, not that we even had a chance to. She continued to stare pure venom in my direction; she couldn't even hold it back for a few hours out of respect for her son.

Half of the mourners looked genuinely upset, whereas the other half were either waiting for the sandwiches or secretly amused by Yvonne's outburst. Stripped of the context, Harry would have found his mother saying that to me hilarious. He would have given me that knowing look that said, 'I've had to put up with her longer than you have.' I'd have to avoid her at the wake. It wasn't worth the inevitable argument. The last shovel of dirt was placed on top of the mound, and it was done. The earth beside Harry had entirely depleted and had been returned to the grave. The digger gently patted the mound flat and turned to the celebrant conducting the ceremony with a nod.

"The family would like to thank you all for attending and warmly invite you to enjoy some light refreshments and swap some stories about Harry at the 'Ox and Plow.' Anyone who would like to pay their last respects are welcome to stay behind for a few minutes," the celebrant announced.

The hungry ones left immediately. One by one, the rest of the mourners visited the grave and whispered some words into the soil. I wanted to hear them, but I was still submerged in a trance of disbelief. It was only weeks ago that we were trying our hardest to start a family, and then all of a sudden, I was burying him. I wanted to claw at the earth violently to save him, but what was left of my inhibitions, in my deeply fragile state, deterred me from actually going through with it.

A group had formed in front of me, waiting patiently for me to snap out of my trance. Each mourner greeted me individually, mostly stereotypically expressing their sorrow for my loss. Yvonne stood a few feet across from me, still glowering at me disapprovingly with her particular flavour of intense disdain. I did think about pulling a funny face at her, but the resulting scene wouldn't have been worth it. I was certain that Harry wouldn't have been able to resist; he had a dark sense of humour, and to him, it would have definitely been worth the repercussions. Part of me did feel for Yvonne, but to put it bluntly, she lost her son over a decade ago. Despite being very vocal that it didn't bother him, I never managed to find out if Harry was actually secretly upset about not having a decent relationship with her. When his father died, he and his mother kind of just grew apart, and Harry moving away from Filey was the final nail in that coffin.

Only one mourner remained. I didn't recognise her. She was still standing at the grave, delicately laying a single flower on it whilst carefully whispering something into the dirt. It was plain to see that she had been crying. The profound sadness on her face led me to infer she must have been close to Harry at some point. The jealous part of me thought she could have been an ex-girlfriend, not that it mattered, given the circumstances. I could see Yvonne was rather irked by her presence at the grave. She was now turning the poisonous glare she had been exclusively aiming at me throughout the funeral to the unknown woman.

"Who's that? One of your... friends?" She quipped bitterly.

"Not a clue."

"I'm going to ask who she is."

"Yvonne, just leave her, she's obviously upset."

Yvonne, determined to find out who the mysterious mourner was, shuffled over to her and tapped her gently on the shoulder. I followed her, mainly just to diffuse her anger in case Yvonne saw red again. Not that she saw any other colour.

"I'm sorry, but I don't seem to recognise you. How'd you know Harry?" Yvonne enquired.

"Just an old friend. I'm Kim. I'm so sorry for your loss," Kim replied.

"Don't be sorry, Kim," I began, "I'm sure Harry would have wanted you here."

"I hope so," Kim smiled through the tears welling up in her eyes.

"You'll be joining us for the wake, I assume?" Yvonne asked matter-of-factly.

"No, sorry, I have to get back. I'm glad to have met you both," Kim responded awkwardly.

"You too," I uttered as she briskly walked off in the direction of the car park.

"That was a bit strange, wasn't it?" Yvonne remarked.

"Not really. I'd say most people don't enjoy being at a funeral."

"Well, I thought she was being odd."

I didn't care about Yvonne's ramblings. I just wanted to be alone with him. He was there, and I could still feel him, barely. I was desperate not to appear petty or rude towards Yvonne, but internally, I just wanted to scream at her until she left. I kept my calm, obeyed social convention, and took a deep breath.

"Can I have a minute alone with Harry, please?" I asked gingerly.

Yvonne hesitantly placed her hand on my arm before leaving to give me some peace with my late husband. I watched her disappear into the distance, and I stood above the grave, staring down at the dirt that had been left there. I was half expecting Harry's hands to slide around my waist from behind at any moment and for him to tell me it was all okay. But it wouldn't be okay ever again. Without an audience, the floodgates finally opened, and the tears gushed down my cheeks and soaked into the loose ground beneath me. I wanted to let out a single, ear-shattering scream. I had everything I ever wanted, and it was taken away from me at the height of our love.

"Harry?" I wept, "I just want you to know I'll never stop loving you."

Harry remained uncharacteristically silent.

"You were everything to me, and now I'm lost without you. I'm so sorry for what happened."

I had no option but to accept that I now had to navigate this world without him. He was my best friend, my soul mate, and I didn't know what I'd do without him by my side. I thought we had so much more time together. We'd made plans, and we had a future to look forward to. But all of it was ripped away from us in the most devastating way I could ever imagine. Grief is a strange emotion, and admittedly, I hadn't encountered it often in my life. What I felt stronger than anything else was the guilt, the world-shattering pit of inescapable guilt. I didn't know if my response was the typical one. I just kept thinking about every decision I'd ever made, no matter how seemingly insignificant it may have been. Maybe if we'd conceived naturally, it would have made a difference, diverting the course of fate just enough for Harry to still be with me. I replayed in my mind every insignificant and frivolous argument we'd ever had. Perhaps if I'd conceded blame to a few, he would still be here. Or we would both be gone. At that moment, at Harry's final resting place, either option was preferable to the truth.

"I miss you, Harry," I whispered.

I turned my back on Harry and started the long walk to the car park. I wasn't in any rush to get to the wake. Surely, I would be allowed some lateness, given the horrific circumstances.

The accepted story was that Harry had driven down to Filey and arrived safely. He met some of his old friends at the pub, as he often did. They tended to overdo it a little because they didn't see one another as frequently as they used to. When the pub called last orders, they decided to continue drinking back at Steve's house. He lived at and ran the caravan park right near Filey Brigg. Steve was Harry's best friend growing up, and they were as thick as thieves. When the booze had run dry, Harry decided to call it a night and made his way back to Yvonne's house but took the scenic route. In his drunken state, he somehow lost his footing at the top of the Brigg and plummeted from it. The coroner said Harry wouldn't have felt any pain. He fell from quite a height onto the rocks below, so it was near instant. I didn't find any solace in the coroner's words; he shouldn't have died like that, regardless of how quick it was.

Yvonne had been adamant that she wanted Harry buried in Filey; 'It was his home', she protested. I didn't put up much resistance. It was best to let her win that one. In the end, he had turned his back on the village, but he still loved it there. The 'Ox and Plow' was a traditional public house in the centre of Filey. Harry had often regaled me with many stories of his misspent youth inside its walls. It was a dingy, little pub with wonky exposed beam ceilings and dimly lit walls. Locals would describe it as a 'charming little boozer', albeit to me, and putting it politely, it was a shithole. The walls were decorated with black and white photographs of the men who had wasted their lives in there since it had opened; I now wondered if Harry was featured in one of them.

Regardless, it was certainly a fitting place to send him off. It was his local, and anywhere else wouldn't feel quite right. I was the last to arrive there, and the mourners were already a few drinks deep. They were laughing and joking, and I heard snippets of the stories they were telling one another as I meandered through the mass of people. I knew deep down that this was exactly what Harry would have wanted to see happening, but it grated at me. How dare they laugh and joke at a time like this.

"Whiskey, please. Double," I said to the barmaid.

"Pace yourself, dear," Yvonne interjected, appearing almost in a puff of smoke in the crowd of mourners at the bar.

"You're one to talk," I muttered under my breath.

"Sorry?" She replied.

"Nothing," I smirked.

My whiskey arrived quickly, along with an unrequested look of feigned sympathy from the barmaid. Harry constantly lectured me that alcohol harmed the chances of conceiving, so I'd been trying to cut back. 'Bottoms up,' I thought. The amber liquid burned my throat as it coated my stomach; I puffed out my cheeks and held my mouth to prevent it from making an instant return.

"How are you feeling?" A voice behind me asked.

It was Harry's older sister, Penelope, but everybody called her Poppy. I actually got on with Poppy, but we were very different people. Poppy was somewhat of a hippy and had this tendency to shoehorn spiritualism into every conversation she had. She frequently wore a carefully curated selection of crystals and vehemently claimed they all had specific spiritual powers. But not today; she was dressed in a floor-length black dress. I thought it was a respectful gesture. Harry never believed in any of that and called it nonsense. Given the choice, I'd have to agree with him.

"Amelia? Sorry, that was a stupid question," Poppy asked.

"Sorry, Poppy, I was lost in my thoughts. Not great, to be honest," I responded.

"I know, love. Great turnout, though. Harry would have loved to see the old gang back together again. We haven't all been together properly since your wedding."

"I know."

"You know, at times like these—"

Here it comes.

"—There is some comfort in knowing that he isn't really gone. He is all around us. You should speak to my medium, James. He's very good. He might even be able to contact him."

"*Contact* him? He is dead, Penelope."

The hustle and bustle of the pub immediately fell silent once I'd raised my voice. All eyes were locked on us, waiting for Poppy's response. She was more of a crier than a fighter, and I don't know why I picked on her so readily. My emotions got the better of me, and her ridiculous comment had tipped me over the edge.

"I'm just saying he can help—"

"No, Poppy, this is not the time to be preaching. My husband is dead. Your brother is dead. He died in this pathetic town, and we're never going to see him again."

Poppy, shocked by what I'd said, elected to walk away from me instead of trying to respond. I have to say, it was the right decision. Yvonne replaced Poppy in her position in front of me. She was clearly going to use my outburst to cause a scene. I downed the rest of the whiskey left in the glass, waiting for the inevitable.

"Come on, love, let's go outside for a minute," Yvonne said softly, ushering me outside. She walked me through the staring mourners, opening the door and signalling me to step through it. I went outside and exhaled loudly, expecting a loud argument.

"What now?" I asked abruptly.

"I know what it feels like. When we lost Harry's father, I felt like my whole world collapsed. Whatever you need to do to try and move on from that, do it. But shouting at Poppy won't help."

I was shocked. Yvonne was actually being nice, or at least something that resembled nice. The sheer personality change I had just witnessed before my very eyes was strong enough to make the anger evaporate instantly. I'd never seen this side of her. Maybe she did have genuine empathy and wasn't the heartless mother-in-law I'd always pegged her for. We'd barely exchanged any niceties since I'd met Harry, but maybe she did understand how I was feeling. She'd lost her son, after all, and I kept forgetting that.

"I know, but she always comes in with that psychic bull—" I started.

"And don't reject anything that could help you," Yvonne interrupted.

"Fine. You're right. I'll tell Poppy that I'm sorry."

"You don't need to. Come on, let's go back inside."

"Give me a minute. I need some fresh air."

"Whenever you're ready."

Yvonne left me alone, and I looked up and down the streets aimlessly. I never understood the allure of this place. Sure, it had its charm in the summer, maybe. If you visited when it was warm and people flocked here to see the beach, it was a totally different place. But we were in the off-season, and Filey had returned to hibernation. In every direction, you could see a guesthouse or a pub, each donning a brightly illuminated 'Vacancies' sign in the window. Even though I detested it, I did feel closer to Harry here. I could almost see him stumbling out of the pub with his friends, and it made me feel closer to him.

"How're you feeling, Amelia?" A man emerging from the pub asked.

It was Steve, Harry's best friend. I hadn't seen him for at least a few years, and I barely recognised him. He had really packed on the pounds since and lost quite a bit more of his hair. My skin used to crawl whenever he was near me. Around Filey he was known to be a bit of a lech and for not being able to keep his hands to himself. Harry always defended him to the hilt, though, and I never could see why.

"Why do people keep asking that?" I replied.

"Sorry. It's hard to know what to say. Great turnout, though. Harry would've loved this."

"Yeah, he certainly would."

"You should come back in; we're swapping stories about Harry," he suggested, touching my arm gently.

I wondered whether I should go back inside or not, but I knew deep down that I had to. Part of me just wanted to go home, and for Harry to be waiting for me when I arrived. But it wasn't home anymore, not without him there. Against my better judgment, I reluctantly returned inside and immediately saw Poppy weeping in the corner like a wounded animal. I didn't regret what I had said in principle, but I suppose I could have said it more delicately. She had as much of a right to grieve as I did.

"Poppy, I'm sorry. I didn't mean what I said," I tenderly said.

"I know you didn't. I'm not upset with you. It's just all the emotions coming at once."

"Listen, if you think that medium will help, I'll give it a shot. Thank you for trying to help."

Poppy smiled slightly. "I'll text you his number."

Yvonne heard the amicable exchange and almost smiled at me. Poppy rose to her feet to give me a gripping hug, which I clumsily accepted. She took out her phone to send the number, and mine beeped.

"There you go," Poppy said.

"Thanks," I replied.

"Right, come on. Let's have a drink for Harry. He wouldn't want to see us all bickering like this," Poppy smiled, putting her arm around me.

"You're right."

And she was right. Harry loved his sister; she was the one member of his family that he had a decent relationship with. They went through a lot together, and with their mother essentially being absent their entire childhood, he badly needed that bond. Harry wouldn't have accepted a bad word said about Poppy, even if she was talking about spiritualism or psychic powers.

I don't remember much about the evening; I'd gotten myself into a bit of a state by the end. I thought it was expected of me, but I did get carried away somewhat. The booze did little to make me forget, although it was nice to swap stories and remember Harry for the man he was before everything that happened. The pub emptied slowly, leaving only the closest family and friends. Eventually, we all parted ways, and I vaguely remember stumbling back to my guesthouse at around midnight. Yvonne did invite me to stay the night at their house, but regardless of the fragile ceasefire I couldn't bear the thought of sleeping in Harry's old room or under the same roof as Yvonne.

I regretted not accepting her offer bitterly. I'd underestimated just how alone I would feel sitting in that room at the guesthouse. I sat on the edge of the bed, scowling at the walls. That day was the first day I had truly accepted that Harry was gone, and I'd barely made it through. I remember thinking that every day after would feel like that, which I found utterly soul-destroying. Would I ever feel any better than this? I remembered what Poppy had said about James in my drunken stupor, and in a moment of weakness, I decided to send him a text.

> *James, this is Amelia, Poppy's sister-in-law. She said you could help me.*

As soon as I clicked send, I instantly wanted to take it back. Harry would be laughing his head off right now if he had seen me do it. But Yvonne was right; even though it was most likely nonsense, I shouldn't reject anything that could make me feel better, and there was an admittedly slim chance that there could be some truth in it. I fell backwards onto the bed, and the alcohol-induced headache was already starting to rear its ugly head. I dizzily tried to get to sleep, but thanks to the combination of the unfamiliar room spinning and the deafening silence of Filey, sleep felt almost impossible. Just as I was about to defy the odds and finally drop off, my phone lit up and produced a single beep. I fumbled to reach it on the bedside table, my eyes squinted in the dark, trying to decipher the message.

> *Amelia, I'm so sorry for your loss, but I can see your husband's death wasn't an accident.*

THE FOOL

AMELIA

I glared at the text message, which was instantly sobering. Any hope that I held of falling asleep was shattered immediately. What did he mean it wasn't an accident? How could he know that? The longer I looked at the message, the more I felt sick, the kind of visceral nausea that usually accompanies a shock of this magnitude. I'd texted him on a drunken whim, looking for some bland words of encouragement or an off-the-shelf sentiment. I wasn't expecting a response so soon, let alone something so ominous. I remained staring at the blinding screen of my phone, my thumbs hovering over it as if poised to respond but unable to form any words to text him back with.

He couldn't have known anything about Harry's death. It wasn't possible. It was simply a wild stab in the dark, trying to bait me into some kind of emotional response. The nausea subsided and was quickly replaced by outrage. I didn't know this man, and he didn't know me. What gives him the right to spout such unsolicited nonsense to a grieving widow? Poppy had clearly spoken to him, so he knew a little about my situation, but to start sending messages like that was a step too far. I only started replying out of sheer anger that he dared to speak about Harry's death like that. He was clearly spewing rubbish.

> *What are you talking about?*
> *James?*
> *How dare you say that.*
> *Answer me.*
> *James?*

Roughly ten minutes had passed without a response when my rage built. It was like James was playing with me. The dots appeared on my screen, indicating James was typing, but they kept stopping and restarting. Eventually, they stopped altogether, and I was left looking at my frantic, unanswered messages. I must have waited an hour for a response at least, but eventually I fell asleep, still tightly gripping my phone in my hand.

I woke up the next morning, and the hangover had hit me like a freight train. Every drop of moisture in my mouth had evaporated overnight, an unfortunate but expected effect of drinking spirits until midnight. I staggered to the bathroom, desperately in search of water to quench my intense thirst. I looked into the mirror; I'd never seen myself in such an appalling state. What little makeup I was wearing the day before was smeared all down my cheeks, my normally straight hair pointing in every direction. I splashed the cold water onto my face to try and bring myself back to life. Harry rarely got hungover; he had this ritual where he would drink two bottles of water before bed, and he claimed it stopped hangovers. I only had to look at a glass of wine incorrectly, and I'd feel rough the next day. Harry would be up at dawn, whistling and frying up bacon and eggs. I missed that.

I checked my phone; James still hadn't been in touch. Hopefully, my rapid and aggressive barrage of text messages let him know I wasn't the fool he thought I was. It was clearly a mistake ever contacting him, and he was obviously a fraudster who knew nothing about Harry's death other than what Poppy had already told him in her sessions. It was very uncharacteristic of me, but I decided to let it go and make my way back to Manchester. I couldn't bear to be stuck in this sleepy seaside town any longer. I yearned for the noise of the city, where I would be able to drown out my own thoughts, if anything else. Filey couldn't be any quieter if you placed the whole town in a vacuum, and it made my skin crawl.

I stumbled down the guesthouse stairs; they creaked and splintered as I took each step. Like most of the guesthouses in Filey, it was operated by an adorable old couple who had been inexplicably married for over a hundred years. They'd moved to Filey to live out their retirement dream. Joan, the woman who ran the ironically named 'Coastal Bliss' guesthouse, seemed to be glued to the front desk at all times. She really was a lovely woman who couldn't do enough for her guests. Whenever Harry and I visited Filey together, we would always stay here rather than at his childhood home. He said it was for my benefit, but in reality, I don't think he ever wanted to stay at his mum's house either—too many bad memories.

"Morning, Joan. I'm checking out," I hoarsely announced.

"It's been a pleasure to see you again, dear. Was everything up to scratch?" Joan asked.

"Yes, thank you."

"And I'm so sorry about young Harry, so tragic."

"Me too."

"Cuppa tea love?" A voice came from the kitchen.

"Yes, please," Joan replied, "do you want one, Amelia?"

"No, thank you. Sorry, I need to get going."

"No worries, love."

I stood at the front door for a minute and saw Joan's husband bring her the cup of tea he had promised. If I had been asked a few months ago if I wanted that to be my life in the future, I would have laughed my head off. But now Harry was gone, I would trade anything for the possibility. As much as I despised this place, I would give up my life now for the chance of spending my twilight years with my husband, like Joan was. I could taste the bitter tang of jealousy on my tongue. Joan and her husband were some of the nicest people you could ever meet, but it didn't stop me from feeling intense envy. I averted my eyes and walked outside. The polar opposite of wholesome Joan, Yvonne, was standing there with her lips glued to a cigarette and waiting for me to emerge.

"Leaving so soon?" She asked.

"Yes, I've got to get back."

"You can stay at ours for a few days, you know? Get your head together?"

"I think it's going to take more than a few days."

Yvonne extinguished her cigarette against the garden wall and took a few steps closer to me. I didn't know if she had been drinking again or if it was just last night's booze I could smell on her clothes and breath. She was definitely struggling to walk in a straight line, though, which wasn't all that unusual for her, thinking about it.

"You can always pick up the phone for a chat. If you need to talk to someone," She offered.

"I'm sorry, Yvonne, but why would I do that? You've never liked me."

"That's not true."

"It is," I insisted.

"Yes, we haven't got on in the past. But I know exactly how you are feeling. Harry would have wanted us to get along."

"I don't think he would care."

"Of course, he would. It breaks my heart knowing what you are going through. I went through it, too."

She didn't know how I was feeling, and I resented the comparison of her situation to my own. I knew every sordid detail of their family dynamic when Harry was growing up. His father, Paul, desperately tried to hold their family together whilst Yvonne went out drinking and sleeping around. Paul pretended not to know what was going on, but in fact, he did. That's why he did what Yvonne had been trying to do for years: drink himself to death. I didn't know what Yvonne's game plan with me was, but I was looking forward to not having to deal with her again. I even toyed with the idea of telling her exactly what I thought of her, but I decided it would be in bad taste. I found it almost unbelievable that Harry had become such a well-rounded adult after his tumultuous upbringing. I could have told her some home truths and burnt those bridges forever, but Harry would have thought it was cruel. I simply faked a smile and brushed my way past her with my suitcase in hand.

"Are you not even going to at least say goodbye?" She asked.

"Goodbye, Yvonne."

I threw my suitcase in the back of my car and got in. Yvonne was already lighting another cigarette before I got the engine started. Once the cigarette was lit, she began clumsily strolling down the promenade. I fervently hoped it would be the last time I ever saw her. I'd tolerated her for so long, but there wasn't anything holding me back anymore. I had no intention of taking her up on her offer of a chat. She would only use it as an excuse to belittle me. I saw through her overused 'I know how you feel' routine. I loved and honoured my husband, and she would never know what that is like.

It was a good three-hour journey back to Manchester; I'd always hated driving long distances on my own. Harry and I used to take these little road trips when we first met, driving down to Bristol for the day or up to Blackpool for the fish and chips. We were so free-spirited back then; we barely planned a thing and just went wherever the mood took us. I knew I'd never take one of those trips with him ever again, and I cried almost the whole way home. I didn't know how I was going to survive without him by my side.

I stood at our front door. I put the key in the lock, but I couldn't physically turn it. I needed to prepare myself; the house was full of reminders and memories of Harry, and I was petrified of my own reaction to seeing them.

After a few minutes of reflection and deep breathing, I turned the key. The house was so eerily quiet that front door creaking as it opened almost shocked me. I don't think I'd ever heard it before. It was somehow colder without him here; all colours had faded to grey by his absence. I abandoned my suitcase at the bottom of the stairs and dragged myself into the kitchen.

We had a speaker plugged into the wall, and Harry had an old MP3 player that he always left connected to it. I'd always hated his taste in music. To wind me up, he would be playing cheesy rock classics all hours of the day. I pressed play; it was still halfway through a song from the last time Harry had listened to it. I slumped down onto the kitchen floor, listening to the music I claimed to hate for years, but it was so comforting to hear it again. It made me fantasise Harry was just in the next room, cooking dinner or working from home. I took out my phone to make my daily call; it had become a ritual of mine every time I returned home.

"Hi, this is Harry. I can't come to the phone right now. Please leave a message," the phone played.

Just hearing his voice again was just enough to keep me going, at first for a few hours, but I'd begun to become immune to its effects. I'd called his phone every day for the last two weeks since his death. It had been recovered by the police, but the phone itself was smashed to pieces. Harry's number was still active. I didn't have the time or inclination to cancel it. It remained as a ghost, a piece of Harry that I could summon with a tap of my phone. I knew it was an unhealthy habit, but I couldn't help myself. I could feel it slowly becoming an addiction. One day, I knew I was going to ring his number, and I wouldn't hear his voice. It would be like losing him all over again. The short-lived respite from misery had faded, and I was alone again, a pathetic bag of emotions languishing on the kitchen floor. I called him again and again. I was desperate to avoid actually dealing with the grief and the endless stream of emotions that came with it.

It wasn't just the emotional side I was ignoring. There was also a mountain of paperwork to go through. The sheer number of ridiculous things you need to sort out after losing someone you love is torturous. The paperwork and letters lay stacked on the kitchen counter island. Whenever I imagined the sheer mundanity of sorting through them, it filled me with dread. Under normal circumstances, I was a planner, and I constantly had a plan in place for everything in my life. But, for the first time, I was adrift. I had no idea what to do next and no clue where I was going. In a way, Harry had spoiled me with years of looking after every facet of our lives. There was even talk about me giving up my job at the pharmacy. I'd always been fiercely independent, and I was reluctant to give it up. Harry thought that if I went into early retirement, our chances of conceiving would be more favourable. I touched my stomach gently; I wished

I could have given him what he so desperately wanted whilst he was still here.

There must have been some alcohol in the house somewhere. Something to at least take the edge off. Anything. I urgently moved from cupboard to cupboard, searching, but there wasn't a single drop. Harry had symbolically removed it all when we moved into our new home, and he was keen to abstain with me, too. I felt absolutely hopeless. Everything good in my life had vanished. I returned to the cold kitchen floor on my back, banging my head lightly against the ceramic tiles. Harry's playlist had ended, and I was left there, broken and in silence.

This is exactly what I had feared my life would be like when I was younger: a spinster. I'd always struggled in relationships, mostly never making it past the first date. I never could put my finger on why they had ended before they even started. I just chalked it up to bad luck, but as I got into my thirties, the dating pool began to dwindle to almost nothing. I found myself rejecting almost everyone whom I met under the flimsiest of pretences. I had this primal need to find a partner quickly, but I was also terrified of wasting my time on a relationship that wouldn't go anywhere.

When I met Harry, he changed that. He changed me. I first met him a few weeks after my 30th birthday. Before our paths crossed, I'd already convinced myself that love and marriage were just something other people had. As ridiculous as it sounds, and given my age at the time, I never thought it was on the cards for me. Despite my growing lack of hope, Harry bounded into my life and truly swept me off my feet. After years of loneliness, I'd become accustomed to being on my own, but once I had a taste of the good life, there wasn't any feasible way I could go back. I never even had any friends to speak of. I'd devoted my life to Harry, turning down every social invite in favour of spending more time with him.

My period of reflection was interrupted by my phone violently vibrating on the countertop, and I strained to reach it.

> *I can see you have calmed down now. Are you ready to begin the journey to the truth about Harry?*

I hadn't calmed down. I was in a perpetual state of anxiety, dread, and rage. James clearly was in the wrong profession, but I needed to talk to someone nonetheless. Anyone. Even this fraudster was using my grief as some kind of angle. I don't know why I replied. In truth, it was either to just feel some kind of human interaction or to mess with him to make myself feel better. What he had said the night before was playing on my mind, too. If there was even a slender chance that he knew something about Harry's death, I needed to find out exactly what it was.

> *What did you mean when you said my husband's death wasn't an accident?*

> *Harry didn't fall. I can sense that you will cross paths with a young woman today in the park. Be there at 3 pm. She will start you on your quest and help you.*

I didn't know what to make of his message; it was vague, but there was some specific information in there, at least. I still thought he was a charlatan, trying to reel me into some kind of swindle, but I'd be lying if I said I wasn't curious. There was another explanation, of course, that he was indeed psychic, but the odds of that were slim to impossible. In truth, it felt good to have some direction in my life for the first time in weeks. I still didn't believe he truly knew anything about Harry's death, but I would dip my toe in the water and see what came of it.

Harry and I would often take walks in the park, which was a rare green space in the city. Also, an exceedingly popular spot for dog walkers and parents, we used to wander amongst the trees and flowers, imagining what it would be like when we had children of our own. I hadn't been here since Harry's death; I'd rarely left the house. Being around so much happiness and glee when you feel nothing but dread and anxiety doesn't help. It makes the profound sadness more concentrated if anything. I sat on a bench overlooking the playground, and a young couple were playing with their daughter on some swings. It made me smile for a brief second before I remembered it would never be us. James was wrong, and he was proven a fraud. I waited until almost ten past the hour, and I still hadn't met anyone.

I rose to my feet, satisfied that James didn't 'know' anything but admittedly disappointed it didn't lead somewhere. My little foray to the park had only made me feel worse. I briskly started to make my way back home. The couple's laughter and children's gleeful screams felt like needles being inserted into my ears. I needed to get away from it, and I quickened my pace. I pulled my phone out to start composing a scathing message to James but collided with another parkgoer.

"Watch where you're walking!" I snapped, retrieving my phone from the dirt.

"Amelia?" They asked.

I looked up to see a young woman wearing exercise clothes and holding a yoga mat. Her curly blonde hair was tied up in a messy bun, the loose hairs being splayed out of her face by her glasses. We both stood there, staring at each other, with a scrunched-up facial expression you can only reproduce when you vaguely recognise someone. It clicked who she was, and I stood up.

"It's... Kim, isn't it?" I asked.

"Yes, oh god, I'm so sorry, I wasn't paying attention," Kim apologised.

"Me either, don't worry about it," I replied, returning to my feet, "what are you doing here?"

"They do yoga in the park on Fridays."

"No, I mean in Manchester."

"I live here."

"Oh, for some reason, I thought you lived in Filey."

"No, I moved here a few months ago."

Kim looked extremely awkward, obviously not expecting to bump into me again. Was Kim the woman that James was speaking about? It must have been a coincidence, surely, but if it were, it would have been a pretty far-fetched one. It made me feel quite strange being told that I would meet someone in the future, and then, voilà, there she was. The whole thing made me feel really anxious, but I'd gone that far, and I needed to explore it.

"Listen, you are clearly on a bit of a health kick, but do you fancy going for a drink?" I asked.

"Er, sure. When?" Kim uttered anxiously.

"Now. I could use somebody to talk to."

"Of course. I'd... love to," Kim answered awkwardly.

We made our way through the park to a small bar on the opposite side of the road. I had been there once or twice with Harry after a previous long walk in the park before. It was typical for a bar in Manchester. It was very trendy and sold incredibly overpriced drinks. Overhead were exposed steel vents and lots of mood lighting, giving the place a very industrial yet modern feel. It was filled to the brim with hipsters and people in suits having working lunches. We sat at a table near the window, and Kim nervously looked at the drink's menu.

"What can I get you, ladies?" The waiter asked.

"I'll have a glass of Merlot, please. Kim?" I replied.

"An orange juice, please," Kim requested.

"Yoga? Fruit juice? You really are on a health kick," I jested.

"Alcohol doesn't really agree with me."

"That's the point, isn't it?"

I didn't fancy myself as a body language expert, but never before had I seen someone look so awkward in my company. Kim had her arms folded tightly across her stomach and could barely look me in the eyes. I stared at her intently, but she remained looking down at the table. The drinks arrived, and she took a single sip when I caught her eye.

"You don't look too comfortable, Kim. Is something bothering you?" I asked.

"No, I'm just like this."

"Fair enough. How did you know Harry again?"

"An old friend."

"From where?"

"Filey."

I was starting to get a tad annoyed at Kim's inability to hold a conversation, and her drip-feeding of information was starting to exhaust my patience. It was glaringly obvious that she was holding something back. If James wasn't a fraud, there was a reason he had led me here. I gripped my glass so hard that I thought it might shatter in my hand, but I kept the painted-on smile across my face so as not to scare her off.

"Do you want to elaborate on that?" I added hastily.

"We were friends back in the day, but we lost touch. That's about it, really."

"Sorry, but you seemed very upset at the funeral, way too distressed to just be an old, out-of-touch friend."

I don't know whether it was the content of what I said or the constant barrage of questions, but Kim stopped looking down at the table, and her eyes met mine with unexpected intensity. I could see she was finding the courage to say something. My patience returned, and I maintained eye contact until she was ready to speak.

"I *loved* him," Kim blurted out.

THE LOVERS

HARRY - BEFORE

Should I ring the doorbell again? I don't want her to think I'm some kind of pest. I checked my watch. She did say 8 pm, and I'd already waited an extra five minutes in the car just to make sure she would be ready. My palms were sweating. Why was I so nervous? Ringing this doorbell in itself wasn't unusual for me; I'd been left standing in this doorway many times. But this time, the context was wildly different. We'd been friends for years, and I'd only recently plucked up enough courage to actually tell her how I truly felt. I heard fumbling behind the locked door, and my anxiety spiked. I started to incessantly rub my palms on the back of my jeans to dry them. I was expecting my date, but instead, her father, Malcolm, opened the door with an intimidating grimace.

"Ey up, Malcolm. Kim in?" I said with pseudo confidence.

Malcolm didn't utter a word in response, and he just kept on giving me an incredibly menacing look. After approximately thirty seconds, just when it had become unbearably awkward, he started laughing manically and dragged me inside by the scruff of my neck. It felt like a silverback gorilla was tackling me. Malcolm had been a steelworker his entire life, and you only had to look at the size of his tattooed arms to know. There was no way I was wriggling out of his grasp; I decided almost to play dead as he swung me around like a rag doll.

"I can't believe you finally grew a backbone and asked our Kim out! What took you so bleeding long?" He laughed. I couldn't muster a response whilst he was bouncing me off the walls of their hallway.

"Hi, Harry," a voice said from up the stairs.

Malcolm and I stopped our jovial skirmish, and I stared up at her. She was so beautiful; how I'd never noticed it, before recently, was totally beyond me. She was wearing a short, silky, floral-print dress that was so vibrant that it lit up the room as soon as she appeared. Her long, slender legs were finished in a pair of black high heels. Kim looked absolutely incredible, and she knew it. She swayed slightly as a huge smirk grew even bigger on her face in response to my obvious ogling. Malcolm's grasp tightened on my neck slightly. He was about half a second from picking up my jaw off the floor himself. He finally released his grip and threw his arm around me.

"Hi, Kim," I smiled.

"Are you ready? Or are you and Dad having a moment?" Kim joked.

"No, we're all done."

"You aren't going out like that, love," Malcom lectured sarcastically.

"Sod off, Dad," Kim laughed.

"And you," Malcolm said, turning back to me, "make sure you look after her."

"I will," I replied.

"Back before midnight!" Malcolm boomed as he walked into the sitting room laughing.

I'd met Kim at high school almost 15 years prior to our first date. What can I say? I'm a slow burner. I'd say I always fancied her at some level, but I was young and way more interested in chasing skirt than settling down with a girlfriend. Whenever I finally decided to act on those feelings, she always had a boyfriend. I assumed the same thing happened to her; the timing was just never right. When the stars finally aligned and we were both single at the same time, I took the plunge and told her how I felt. It sounds brave, I know, but I took the coward's route and did it over text message. Once I realised she felt the same way, we quickly decided to arrange a date.

I'd spent my early twenties how most Yorkshire lads at a city university probably spent them. I had countless one-night stands and spent most of my years at university either drunk or hungover. I'd developed a bit of a tolerance over the years, and once I hit my mid-twenties, that former life had finally lost its appeal. I wanted to settle down, and once I'd got back to Filey, I'd found the perfect woman to settle down with. And there she was, right in front of me the entire time.

Kim led me out of the door, walking a few paces ahead of me. She had her golden blonde hair effortlessly tied up in a messy bun, and she twirled as she walked, clearly excited for our highly anticipated first date. As I watched her waltz and tango underneath the streetlights, I couldn't believe how lucky I was.

"Sorry about my dad. He was only joking," she said.

"I know. He's got quite the grip on him," I joked.

"He's done that with every single boyfriend I've ever had. I think it helps him cope with it or assert his dominance or something."

"Boyfriend?"

"You know what I mean," she smiled with a blush.

We continued sauntering down the seafront. I'd booked a table at the fanciest Italian restaurant in Filey. Well, I say that, but it was kind of the only Italian restaurant in town. It won by default. I desperately felt the need to impress her. I had a degree now and a promising future, which was actually a rarity in that neck of the woods. Most of my friends had barely left the town in their entire lives, but I'd actually escaped, and I was keen to show Kim what I'd learned about how to treat women on my sabbatical. She knew me as the idiot of the group growing up, always getting into some kind of trouble, or pulling pranks. I needed to show her that I'd grown up, at least.

"Why do you keep looking at me like that?" Kim asked.

"Like what?" I laughed.

"I'm not sure. I've never seen that look in your eyes before."

"I'm just happy we are finally doing this."

Kim smiled. "Me too."

We arrived at the restaurant, and I remembered all those stereotypical things my mother had always tried to instil in me when I was growing up. Always walk on the outside of your lady friend. Pull her chair out. The sheer number of things to remember was making me clumsy and awkward. Kim giggled at my attempts at chivalry but allowed me to continue the act until we were seated at our table.

"Just relax, Harry! You don't have to try and impress me," Kim laughed.

"Oh my god, Kim, I'm so nervous, and I've no idea why," I confessed, laughing.

"We're just two old friends having dinner."

"It's more than that, though, right?"

"Yes. Now shut up and order us something to drink."

Her admission made me feel at ease; she felt the exact same way as me, but she was simply better at showing it. My palms started to dry, and I began to relax. I still wanted to make a good impression on her. I just had to do it with my natural charm rather than force it. I was a city boy now, and I scanned up and down the wine list, hoping for one to jump out at me as an impressive choice. The waiter was coming towards us at speed, and I still hadn't selected. Kim, still smirking at me at my inability to even order a drink, chose to go first.

"Pint of lager, please. Anything on draught. Harry?" She said.

"Same," I grinned.

"You don't have to impress me, Harry. You've spent a decade and a half doing that. Even my dad likes you. Just chill."

We spent the evening talking about anything and everything that sprung to mind. What old acquaintances were up to, or funny things that had happened to us at school. I even carefully discussed my time at university, opting to leave out certain lifestyle choices. I'd been on hundreds of dates in the last few years with only one goal in mind, but this was different. I'd never had so much fun on a date with my clothes still on, and Kim was so different from all the other women I'd ever met. Regrettably, I'd barely got to know women before we started the physical side of a relationship, and I always thought we could be friends later. But with Kim, that was in reverse, and we had been friends for many years. Without even realising it, I had been laying the foundation for this to happen for over a decade, and it instantly felt right.

Six months went by in the blink of an eye. We laughed and joked, and we got to know each other on a much deeper level than just friendship. I could feel myself falling for her, and who would have thought, after all those years, we would finally end up together? For the first time in my adult life, I felt like I was ready to commit to a woman, and we'd started looking for little houses in Filey to move in together. We did debate moving away from there, but we loved our sleepy seaside town too much to leave it behind. I would have thought we would have run out of things to talk about, considering the length of time we knew each other, but it turned out that I'd barely scratched the surface.

Apart from work, we spent every waking second together. Every weekend, we would walk up and down Filey Beach, debating what breed of dog we would get when we had a house. We shared our hopes and dreams with each other, and all our wants and desires aligned perfectly. Kim was the best thing that had ever happened to me, and sharing the transition into fully-fledged adulthood with her was amazing. It was a totally distinct experience from my other relationships. I felt like we were on a long journey, exploring what our lives could be together.

I got a job at a little office above the butchers on the high street. They offered financial services to the residents of Filey. It wasn't the busiest job or even the highest paying, but I was finally using my degree in finance. The job mostly consisted of giving pension advice to retirees, but I still loved every minute of it. Kim worked at a local café, but she had dreams of opening her own one day. And I'd be there, right beside her, to help her do it.

We even spoke about children, and our thoughts on that perfectly aligned, too. We decided on two children, a boy and a girl. The boy definitely had to be first, so the girl had an older brother to intimidate any bullies away. Everything was going even better than my wildest expectations, but I still hadn't introduced her to my family just yet. I wanted to keep those two worlds apart. They knew of her from school, of course, but I hadn't told them we'd started a committed relationship. It was the only sticking point between us, to be honest. Kim was getting a bit impatient and kept asking me when I was planning to introduce her to them, but she didn't know them like I did. Dad had way too much on his plate, and my mother would just drive her away if she thought it was possible.

I'd just finished work on the evening of my birthday. I had planned to meet Kim at the very same Italian restaurant where we had enjoyed our first date. We were trying to start a new tradition; every birthday and anniversary, we would make an effort to go back to that same restaurant. The tradition, however, was broken on the first hurdle. I'd definitely say it was my most memorable birthday; I was about halfway down the promenade to meet Kim before my phone started ringing.

"Love, I'm so sorry. It's your father. You need to come home," my mother said.

The most vivid memory I had of that night was the phone call, and the rest was faded, clouded by confusion, rage, and plain disbelief. I remember turning around on my way to the restaurant and running in the opposite direction back to my childhood home to find my mother standing outside chain-smoking, with a blank expression on her face. I ran over to hug and comfort her, but she barely noticed I was even there because she was that numb.

Massive coronary event. That's what the doctors described it as. I remember thinking the term didn't do it justice. Dad died an hour after complaining of chest pains, clutching his chest on the cold garage floor. He was alone. The ambulance arrived in good time, but he lost his life on the journey to Bridlington Hospital. There were so many things left unsaid between us and so many lessons I still had to learn. The first emotion I felt was denial, but it quickly gave way to anger. It was undirected at anyone at first, but the more I thought about it, there was only one person I could conceivably blame. No matter what the doctors wanted to call it, we all knew how he died; we just never spoke about it. He couldn't go a single night without drinking a bottle of whiskey, mainly because of how my mother had treated him their entire marriage.

For as long as I could remember, she had spent most evenings making increasingly unbelievable excuses to go out when, in reality, we all knew she was down at the pub, trying it on with any man who gave her even a modicum of attention. Dad was deeply ashamed, but he didn't summon the courage to step up and do something about it. She treated him like dirt, and everyone in town knew it. To most people, least of all me, it wasn't a surprise that he had died the way he did. My mother and I hadn't enjoyed the best relationship anyway, but after my Dad's sudden passing, I couldn't even stand to be near her most of the time. I blamed her bitterly for his death, and if she hadn't acted the way she did for so many years, he would have still been with us. When I was a little older, I looked back at my childhood, and I didn't approve of a lot of the decisions he made, but I knew he was just desperately trying to keep the family together.

Kim was understanding at first. I'd not only ignored her calls and messages that evening but for days after, too. She heard about my dad's passing through a customer at the café. I couldn't imagine how that would have made her feel, but I just couldn't stand to tell her myself. She regularly sent me messages expressing how sorry she was and offering her shoulder to cry on, but I ignored them. I didn't have the capacity to reply to her. I was so wrapped up in my dad's death I couldn't think about anything else. As the weeks passed, her messages became less and less frequent. I felt so guilty about not replying to them. We had this one-of-a-kind blossoming romance, and she didn't deserve to be dragged into my pit of depression.

Filey was a small town, and it didn't take long for me to start seeing Kim around with someone else. I didn't blame her. Even given the circumstances, I knew that I'd treated her unfairly. She looked happy, and I didn't want to ruin it for her. Kim and I could have made it, but once again, we were foiled by horrific timing. Subconsciously, I think I just forced anyone out of my life who could conceivably ask me how I was doing because, truthfully, I didn't know how to answer the question.

The whole thing made me look at my own life closely. I thought I wanted to settle down and get married, even have a few children, but when I looked at my parents' marriage, it made me change my mind. I reverted to my old ways, getting blind drunk and waking up next to some woman I barely knew. My best friend, Steve, was ecstatic; he had his old drinking buddy back, but he was totally ignorant of the void of depression I had been imprisoned in. We repeated the same behaviour, week in and week out, but the emotion-numbing effect started to lessen. We found ourselves drinking even more and started travelling beyond our beloved Filey to get our fix. I would get the train down to Manchester, drink the entire way there, end up in some club, and then wake up in a cheap hotel room. Or, if I was lucky, in a woman's bed whose name I didn't know.

I'd love to say it made me feel better, but made me feel worse more often than not. I kept telling myself if I just ignored my grief and numbed it with casual sex and alcohol, it would go away, but it didn't. With each month I put my body and mind through this torture, I became immune to it. I was going through the motions, pretending to have the time of my life when, in reality, it was the darkest time I'd ever endured. It got to the point where we would get off the train in Manchester, and I'd barely feel tipsy. All I cared about was getting drunk enough to not have to face my own demons.

Once again, I found myself on the dancefloor in a nightclub in Manchester. Staring across the sweating throng of people at Steve at the other end of the room, making a futile attempt to take some woman home who was way out of his league. Witnessing Steve embarrassing himself to this extent kindled a moment of extreme lucidity within me. It was like gazing into a mirror. I was using alcohol and sex as a crutch, limping through life the same way Steve and my dad did. If I continued down this path, I would likely end up the same way he did. It largely happened without me even realising until it was too late.

It wasn't a surprise that I'd behaved the way I did; both my parents had similar vices and never even attempted to hide them. My sister, Poppy, and I had spent most of our childhoods trying to be nothing like them, so it was so frustrating for me to stand on the exact same path of destruction as that of our parents. I couldn't even blame them for it, particularly. Poppy had always been quirky, but she stayed on the straight and narrow; she was a few years younger than me but decades wiser. I knew what she would say if she found out how I'd been behaving the past few months, and that's why I'd intentionally stayed out of touch. I hadn't even asked her how she felt about Dad passing because I was so selfishly wrapped up in my own emotions.

I threw down the crutch. I had to get my life back on track, and Dad wouldn't have wanted me to end up like him. I needed to show everyone, including myself, that I could make it through this and become stronger for it. The same feeling I had in my mid-twenties came back: the resolve to aspire to be something better than I was. In a single moment, I recalled every single drop of alcohol

I'd numbed myself with. Every woman I'd slept with and not bothered to learn their name. I felt despicable. I'd been behaving like a twisted concoction of the worst parts of both my parents. I was already half drunk, and I just wanted to flush it all out of me and start afresh.

I meandered through the clambering hordes of people, up to the bar, and as the clubbers parted to let me pass, I spotted a woman standing at the bar on her own. She was standing on her tiptoes, leaning over the bar, trying to capture the barman's attention. She didn't look at all like the other clubbers; she had long, glossy chestnut hair, its curls delicately resting on her shoulders. Not the usual sweat-ridden recreational drug user that came ten a penny in a place like this. She was wearing an elegant but sexy black mini dress, barely covering her body as she continued to stretch over the bar and wave her arms furiously.

When I reached the bar, she turned to look at me and smiled alluringly. Her sage green eyes lit up as we held intense eye contact for a second. She was a little bit older than me and had this air of sophistication about her in the way she held herself and even the way she'd done her makeup. If I believed in any of that nonsense, I would have put it down to fate that we met just after my epiphany. Whilst our eyes were still locked, the barman finally came over to serve her, but I met his gaze first.

"Bottle of water, please," I asked. He nodded in response.

"Unbelievable," she uttered.

"What's that?"

"Do you realise how long I have been waiting for you to just appear out of nowhere and ask for a bottle of water?"

"Sorry. I'm thirsty."

"Buy me a drink, then?" She smiled.

I looked her up and down, and I loved what I saw. The temptation to continue my lecherous and laddish behaviour was strong, but I immediately snapped out of it and made myself promise it wouldn't be like that with her. Maybe if I treated her with some respect and actually got to know her, it could amount to something more than a quick one-night stand.

"Sure. I'm Harry," I smiled.

"Nice to meet you, Harry. I'm Amelia," she said.

IV

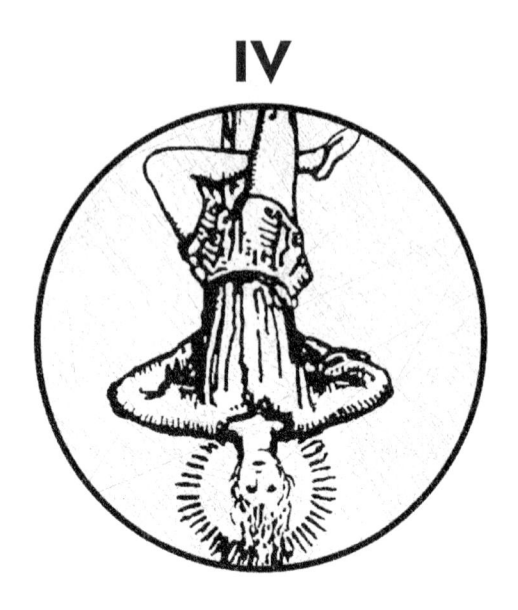

THE HANGED MAN

AMELIA

And there it was. My instincts at the funeral were bang on. I knew there was more to Kim's story than just being an old friend. An surprising pang of jealousy washed over me, as Harry had never even mentioned her name to me. I curiously found myself examining her closely and comparing myself to Kim. She was pretty, a lot prettier than I was. Kim was closer to Harry's age, too, about five years younger than me, at least. Above all else, Harry had always told me he went for brunettes.

I did suffer from a great deal of paranoia in our marriage, primarily because I thought that Harry was such a good catch. My worst nightmare was someone snatching him from me, and I did have my moments when I couldn't help it and I let those feelings escape. Harry was always very defensive, denying any wrongdoing, but the fact that he had omitted to tell me about Kim felt a little shady. I fully admit I would make a mountain out of a molehill on occasion, and I could understand why he chose not to tell me about her, but married couples were supposed to be completely open and honest with each other, right?

"When?" I asked bitterly.

"A while ago," she said.

"Was it serious?"

"It could have been. We were seeing each other for about six months."

"What happened?"

"His dad died."

"What's that got to do with anything?"

Kim sighed deeply, and I could see the lingering hurt across her face.

"He just shut himself off from everybody, including me. I waited for him for a few months, but I heard he'd moved on, so I did the same."

Kim resumed her nervous state, this time shuffling a beer mat backwards and forwards incessantly. I thought I knew all about Harry's past, but there must have been a reason for his secrecy. Maybe he just wanted to spare me from the jealousy. I met Harry almost a year after his father died, which would make Kim his most recent ex. It explained why Kim was so upset at the funeral, at least. As irrational as it was, I couldn't shake the feeling that he had somehow gone behind my back with his lies of omission. It wasn't like I could call him up and ask him straight; it was just another mystery I had to bury for the rest of my life.

"Did he ever mention me?" Kim asked quietly.

Any pity or understanding I'd felt only moments before quickly vanished. I couldn't believe her audacity. It sounded like she was trying to compare my profound grief to her own and likening her six-month juvenile relationship to my marriage. It took every shred of strength I had to stop myself from dragging her across the table by her cute, messy little bun and screaming in her face.

Breathe.

I wasn't known for holding my tongue. But as much as it turned my stomach, I had to keep her on my side nonetheless. If I wanted to know what happened to Harry in his last moments, I'd have to. She clearly had information that I wasn't privy to, and if I wanted it, I'd have to play nice.

"No. Never. Sorry," I said abruptly.

"Oh," Kim solemnly whispered, "excuse me a minute."

Kim rose from her seat and made her way to the toilets, leaving her phone and bag behind. I picked up her phone, but obviously, it had a passcode on it. I didn't know what I was expecting to find, maybe a picture of them together on her phone wallpaper or something. I couldn't bear the thought of Harry with another woman, regardless of how long ago or the duration. I did have an unhealthy sense of ownership of him. I fully attest to that. But we were married, after all. I locked her phone again with a disappointed huff and returned it to the table. I could feel the paranoia and jealousy building up, and I resisted the urge to surrender to it further. I kept reassuring myself that Harry was gone and their relationship, or whatever it was they had, was a long time ago. I should not lose sight of what was important. I just needed to find out what she knew about his death.

I was reluctant to tell her about James; she was clearly skittish in general, and if I started talking about mysterious text psychics and suspicious deaths, she would grab her yoga mat and sprint out of the door. I necked a mouthful of Merlot, took a deep breath, and got my phone out. I needed to play this very carefully.

> *Is Kim the one that can help?*

> *The woman you have met will be your guide down the path of truth.*

He could have just said yes, I thought. Kim returned to the table a minute or so later and as expected started to drink her orange juice tensely again, and she still wouldn't meet my gaze after the awkwardness brought on by her confession. I needed to be calm and diplomatic if I wanted to pry any information out of her. It would require a delicate hand, and unfortunately, that wasn't something I possessed. I sat across from her, deliberating what approach to use, and decided to try and be understanding.

"Kim, you are clearly upset about Harry, and I get it. But I need you to tell me what you know about his death," I said softly.

"What do you mean?" Kim asked, looking worried about my line of questioning.

"Do you think it was suspicious?"

Kim returned her drink to the table and refolded her arms. She made intense eye contact with me for a few seconds as if she were trying to pre-emptively weigh up my response to what she was about to tell me.

"He didn't fall. He barely drank anything," she announced.

Silence. Total silence. Kim sat there, immediately itching for me to say something. Anything. But I couldn't. Not when my whole world was unravelling. What she had just said had left me mute, and I didn't know how to react. I wasn't there when Harry died. I'd only seen him in the morning, but I'd been told the stories of how he died by his kith and kin. The general consensus was that he drank too much and fell off the Brigg. Even the police accepted that version of events, after conducting an extensive investigation into his death. Kim was now gripping the table tightly, almost stripping the varnish with her fingernails. The coroner's report said that Harry had alcohol in his system, so he'd indisputably been drinking. At least a few beers. Kim could be lying outright just to hurt me, although I really couldn't put my finger on why she would. If Harry wasn't drunk when he fell, it raised a whole host of other questions.

"Amelia?" she said abruptly.

"How… how could you possibly know that?" I asked bemusingly.

"Because I was there."

"You were there?"

"At the pub and Steve's party, yes. But he was on non-alcoholic beer. His mates didn't know."

"Why?"

"I think he might have been worried he'd have to drive home if you had bad news from the clinic. He thought the boys would tease him if he said he wasn't drinking."

Harry had never mentioned this woman's name to me in his life, but she did know intimate details of mine. I was furious. She wasn't an 'old flame' from back in the day, and she still had some kind of friendship with him.

Worse than that, he had confided in her about our conceiving woes, which in itself felt like an emotional betrayal. She'd confirmed what James had already insinuated to me: the people around Harry were suspicious of his death, but why wouldn't they come to me about it?

I inexorably pictured Harry sitting with Kim and discussing all of my most closely guarded secrets. I would never divulge the darker details of our marriage to anyone. They should be kept between a husband and wife. I thought Harry felt the same way, and he respected our privacy. I didn't like the idea of another woman being privy to the fact that I struggled to conceive. It made me feel less of a woman than her. The whole thing was making me jittery, and my first reaction was to just up and leave to avoid further embarrassment.

"Amelia?" She asked.

"Just tell me what happened," I ordered.

"Harry was weird all night. All evening, he'd been trying to make a phone call that went unanswered. He walked off, still trying to get through, and that was the last time I saw him."

"Do you happen to know who he was trying to call?"

"I don't know," Kim explained, letting out an exculpatory sigh, "but he was agitated."

"Who do you think it was?"

"Well, to be honest, I thought it was you," she confessed.

"Why me?"

"He said you had been anxious about the IVF results."

"Well, it wasn't me. The last time I spoke to him was when he left for Filey."

Kim looked vexed by my total lack of information and exhaled dramatically.

"I don't know then. The only thing I'm certain of is that he didn't slip, let alone fall. He was stone-cold sober when he left Steve's house. There's only one explanation in my eyes."

"What?"

"He stepped off the Brigg intentionally."

Kim genuinely believed Harry had done away with himself. Is that what everyone secretly thought? As selfish as it may sound, the first thought that sprang to mind was that she was implying he wasn't happy with me, or we had marriage issues. I refused to believe that my husband would take his own life. He never had a suicidal thought in his life, even after everything he had been through with his family. Harry was tough as nails and resilient, which were some of the qualities that attracted me to him in the first place. The mere suggestion that people thought he would end his own life was so insulting to me. It almost insinuated that I had something to do with that decision. I couldn't afford to have her spreading this around, and I immediately needed to correct her.

"He did not step off the Brigg. He wouldn't do that. We were starting a family," I shouted.

"Okay. I'm sorry. But he wasn't drunk enough to fall, so something else must have happened," Kim asserted.

"He didn't commit suicide, Kim," I insisted.

"Okay. But something else happened that night. Even if he were drunk, Harry could manage his drink better than any of us."

"So, what do you think happened?"

"What about money issues?"

"No. We've never had any issues with our finances."

"Are you sure?"

Harry worked as a financial advisor back in Filey, but when we moved to Manchester, he managed to get a much higher-paying job as an investment specialist. He was making more money than he had ever earned in his life. He was only there for about a week before he died, but the signing bonus alone was quite vast. There was no way that we had hidden money troubles. My part-time job at the pharmacy didn't contribute much, and Harry told me not to worry about it; he would provide for everything else. If we were in some kind of financial hardship, he was a dab hand at concealing them well. We'd just bought our dream house, and we were both driving brand-new cars around. Harry never seemed to be worried about going out for a meal or whenever we needed to buy something big. If anything, he seemed to have an endless supply of cash. But I was starting to presume that maybe Harry may not have been entirely truthful with me throughout our marriage. I hated white lies, and it seemed our relationship was plagued by them. Did he think I was so emotionally fragile that he felt the need to constantly shelter me from the truth?

That being said, I rarely got involved in our finances. Harry would often ask my opinion on things, but because of his profession and education, I largely left it to him. It sounded out of character for Harry to stretch us so thinly that it would leave us with money problems, but it would explain a lot. I thought the house we had bought was way out of budget, and when I saw him write the offer down, I went weak in the knees. But it all went through, so he acquired the money from somewhere. It never occurred to me to ask him where from.

"No, I'm not sure. What do you know?" I asked defeatedly.

"I overheard him telling Steve he owes money out to some bad people. Some brothers from Leeds," Kim said.

"He never said anything about that."

"I think he was embarrassed by it."

I couldn't take it any longer. A putrid mixture of shame and anxiety forcefully gurgled up my throat forcefully. I'd had panic attacks before, and I could feel a strong one coming. It started with a prickly sensation moving up and down the back of my neck, not alarming at first but growing in strength with each second. My heart lost all its rhythm; each beat was erratic and vicious, and my chest started to ache with every thump. Seconds later, my lungs started to falter, and my breathing became laboured and shallow. I fumbled in my bag for the tablets, but I'd lost all sensation in my fingertips. I could barely remove the cap from the bottle. Kim was looking at me with extreme concern, like I was some kind of drug-addled maniac. But I didn't care. I just needed the drugs in my system as soon as possible to mitigate what was happening to me. A thousand thoughts and questions aggressively collided with one another aggressively in my mind, and I still couldn't make head nor tail of them. I'd bitten off more than my mounting anxiety could chew, and Kim's revelations had pushed me over the edge. I placed two of the pills in my mouth and grabbed Kim's drink to wash them down with. I closed my eyes and concentrated on my breathing, as the doctor had taught me, and slowly, the sensations started to subside. When I opened my eyes again, Kim was half standing from her seat, not knowing what to do to help me. I rubbed my temples and exhaled.

"Are you all right?" Kim asked worriedly.

"I suffer from panic attacks," I confessed embarrassingly.

"Do I need to get help?"

"The tablets help. They are called Alprazolam; they are for anxiety attacks."

"I'm so sorry about all this, Amelia. It cannot be easy hearing all this, especially from a stranger, but you deserve to know."

"It's fine. Anything triggers them these days."

"Take my number down, just in case you need help with anything."

Kim unlocked her phone and showed me the screen. It had her number on it. I typed the number into my phone and rang her briefly so she had mine. I locked my phone and resumed eye contact with Kim. She had this look of pity across her face, and I hated being on the receiving end of it. Objectively, I could see why Harry remained friends with her; she obviously worked very hard to appear to be a really nice person, and I hated her for it. I needed to keep her close, though. Her insight would be invaluable in finding out what everyone knew about Harry's death. But I couldn't bear to sit with her any longer, and I needed to go home and sleep off the migraine that was brewing in my head.

"I need to go," I said offhandedly.

"Okay. If you need to talk, honestly, don't hesitate to get in touch."

"I won't. Thank you."

I stepped out of the bar, and I felt like the last hour was a fever dream. Just hearing someone else say all these things about Harry was enough to make me feel ill. Every fibre of my being needed to know what happened to him up on the Brigg; I wouldn't be able to rest until I did. Part of me wondered if he actually stepped off the cliff face purposefully, but I carried on telling myself that he didn't. He wouldn't do that to me, would he?

I walked back home like I was in a trance. The bright lights of the city and the passing cars blurred my vision as I barely even paid any attention to where I was heading. The hours following a panic attack were as bad as the attack itself. The skull-splitting headache was the worst complaint, followed closely by persistent nausea. I was in constant fear that it would return; just the fear of the panic attack itself was enough to induce one. The dizziness subsided by the time I'd got back home, but the anxiety was there to stay. My phone vibrated as I unlocked the front door; I knew who it would be.

> *I can see you are one step closer to finding out the truth.*

> *Where do we go from here?*

> *I see you will meet two men who will bring you closer to what really happened. But tread softly. They are dangerous.*

> *The brothers from Leeds?*

> *Seek out Harry's childhood friend. He holds the key to connecting with them.*

I didn't know what to make of James. He was certainly proving himself to be useful, but could he be trusted? I didn't know how I felt about the medium thing either. I'd always thought it was a bit of a con, but so far, he had been absolutely spot-on. Whatever his motivation, he was easing me closer to the truth, and I had to follow the path he had set. I trusted Poppy in principle, but I still wasn't sold on the whole psychic thing. Kim's admissions had taught me that I had to be suspicious of everyone involved in this, and for me to leave James out of that suspicion would be foolish. I needed to find out more about him and why he was so hell-bent on exposing the secrets around Harry's death. But above all else, regardless of the source of his information, spirits or otherwise, I needed to find out what he knew.

James had referenced Harry's childhood friend, which was likely to be Steve. I'd always thought he was a bad influence on Harry, and I often wondered how he suddenly became the owner of the most successful caravan park in Filey. At least that was one mystery quickly solved. If he had been involved with those criminals from Leeds, he must have gotten the seed money from them. Whenever Steve participated in anything, there was always trouble. Harry would claim he was going out with Steve for a few drinks, and I often wouldn't hear from him until the next morning. Steve wasn't married and spent most of his time drinking or trying to bed any woman who would have him.

I didn't have Steve's number; I'd never needed it before, and just the thought of him having mine always made me feel queasy. We weren't close, and I got the impression that he disliked me because he thought that I took Harry away from him. I preferred not to discuss this over the phone anyway; I wanted to look the man in the eye, and regrettably, I had to go back to Filey to do that. If he were as embroiled in the sordid side of Harry's life as Kim had suggested, he could lead me to the truth. James' warning to tread softly was playing on my mind, too. If Harry owed them a lot of money, they might look at me as an opportunity to collect the debt. I couldn't believe the mess that Harry had left me in. If these brothers were as dangerous as James warned, I'd need backup.

I didn't really want to bring Kim in on this, but I needed to keep her close, and I didn't know who else to contact. She seemed deadly serious about finding out what happened to Harry, and she could be useful if I kept her close. She was at Steve's party too, so it was the perfect way of getting in touch with him. I pulled my phone out to send her a text.

> *Kim, I'm going to see Steve this weekend.*

> *Why? Is everything okay?*

> *To find out more about these brothers. I'll let you know.*

> *I can come with you if you'd like. I'm not working this weekend, and I want to get to the truth, too.*

> *Okay, meet me at the park gates at 9 am. I'll pick you up.*

I didn't know what to make of Kim, but I decided to take her at face value until I had reason to think otherwise. I chose to ignore all the red flags and put aside my jealousy. Even though I felt like Harry and Kim had betrayed me somehow, I needed her, and she was a means to an end. If my paranoia was proven true down the line, then I would deal with it then.

"Hi, this is Harry. I can't come to the phone right now. Please leave a message," my phone played and beeped.

"Harry, what were you playing at?" I whispered.

WHEEL OF FORTUNE

HARRY - BEFORE

It's just not possible. There was no way we could afford it, but what was I supposed to tell her? Weeks and weeks spent on house hunting, only for her to find something wrong with every single one. Our budget, constantly being stretched to breaking point, was way higher than we ever agreed on. Money aside, I had to agree with Amelia. The place was absolutely astounding. It was the one. I could almost see the little Harrys or Amelias standing on little stools, brushing their teeth in the mirror. Or running around the hallways laughing. Maybe, just maybe, if I'd looked at my bank balance long enough, it would have magically grown another zero. I'd worked the hardest I had ever done in my life just to cobble enough money together for a deposit, but this was way outside of our budget.

Amelia wasn't in the know. She'd just gleefully arranged the viewings with almost no regard for the price tag, although she couldn't be blamed for it. If I had the courage to sit her down and explain our financial situation, surely, she would have understood, eventually. But I didn't have the stomach for it. I'd built up this perception with her that I was this amazing provider and exemplary husband, but it was mostly bravado. I didn't wish to shatter her illusions of me and deeply upset her, and I desperately wanted to live up to the image she had of me in her head.

But this house. It had everything we ever wanted, even down to Amelia's obsession with bi-fold doors in the kitchen and blackened chrome plug sockets. There was also plenty of space for children, and if I'd had my way, we would have filled the house with them. I couldn't let her down, and I needed to find the money somewhere. I was due to start my new job at the investment firm a few weeks later. If I asked for an advance, would that be too cheeky? Probably. The only thing I knew for sure was that if I told her that we couldn't afford it, she would be distraught, and I hated making her upset.

"Are you all right in there, Harry? The estate agent has another viewing to get to," Amelia shouted through the bathroom door.

"Yeah, coming," I replied.

I flushed the toilet and ran the taps. When I opened the door, Amelia was standing there with an accusatory grin on her face.

"Don't tell me. I don't want to know," she laughed.

"I wasn't doing anything! I'm just nervous, Ames, it's an awful lot of money. I just needed a minute."

"Oh my God, Harry. I'm in love with this house, it's incredible. Are you sure we have enough to cover it?"

"Yes, I think we can do it. All I need is to move some money around, before we sign on the dotted line," I insisted.

"I love you," Amelia said, leaning in with a kiss.

"I love you, too," I replied.

We made our way down the stairs, and the estate agent was waiting for us at the bottom with a huge smile on her face. She clearly knew she was about to make a sale. I awkwardly reciprocated the smile, but there was a lump in my throat the size of an overpriced house brick. This was the single biggest purchase I'd ever made, and I knew the bank wouldn't stretch the mortgage to accommodate it.

"It's a marvellous house, isn't it?" The estate agent beamed.

"Just beautiful, Sally. We think we're ready to make an offer right now!" Amelia responded.

"Well, we've had some other offers, so it'll have to be over asking, I'm afraid. But it's so worth it!" Sally replied.

"Over the asking price, you mean?" I quivered, the lump in my throat doubling in size by the second.

"Yes, she means over the asking price, Harry. Don't be stupid," Amelia interrupted.

"Yes, but the sellers aren't in a chain, so you'll be in before you know it!" Sally enthused.

"A chain is when the sellers are waiting for their house purchase to go through," Amelia explained to me.

"I do know what a chain is, Ames," I said.

Sally tapped the form lightly on the table in the hallway and clicked her pen, handing it to me. I looked at Amelia, and she was radiating glee. If there was a way that we could afford this, I had to find it by hook or by crook. Amelia grabbed my free hand; I could feel her fingernails digging into my hand in anticipation. She was urging me to write the offer. Screw it. I hastily wrote down £480,000 in the offer box, and Amelia's eyes widened. I handed the pen back to Sally, who received it with a fawning smile.

"I think the sellers will be more than accommodating for that offer, congratulations! I'll let you know as soon as I hear anything," Sally beamed.

"Thank you so much!" Amelia effused.

"Thanks," I uttered half-heartedly.

Amelia's grasp loosened on my hand as Sally led us out of the house. Our house. If only I were able to scrape together the funds to make it happen. I hadn't realised I'd been sweating so much, but the cool Mancunian breeze dried the mist on my forehead. We both turned, and Amelia put her arm around me tightly. It truly was an amazing house, one that we could fill with cherished memories, but it didn't stop me from feeling sick at the thought of actually handing the money over. Sally shook both of our hands and returned to her hatchback to complete some paperwork.

"We did it, Harry!" Amelia said excitedly.

"We did!" I responded insincerely.

"Do you think they'll accept the offer? Or should we have gone higher?"

"I hope so. We can't really go any higher, Ames."

"Of course we can. Just look at the place. It's beautiful. And nothing needs to be done to it; it's perfect."

I got back behind the wheel, and my hands were shaking. Amelia didn't seem to notice; she was so caught up in the adrenaline of buying her dream home. But in reality, it wasn't ours until I'd shifted heaven and earth to come up with some more money. The mortgage offer we had wouldn't even cover half of that, and by the time my new salary kicked in, this house would be snapped up by someone else. I needed to borrow some money from somewhere, anywhere, just for the short term.

"Listen, when we get back to the flat, I need to take care of a few things. Are you going to be all right on your own for a while?" I asked.

"What things?" Amelia asked.

"I just have to drop some paperwork off at my new office. I won't be too long," I fibbed.

"What paperwork?"

"Just some contracts and other bits and pieces."

"I thought we could get lunch together. You know I don't like being without my husband."

"I know, but we can celebrate later! I'll be looking forward to it."

"I just wish you'd said sooner. I'll miss you."

"I'll miss you, but it's important."

For the rest of the journey home, I could barely stop quaking with trepidation. I put on a brave face for Amelia, and she seemed like she was none the wiser, which made me feel awful. I needed to speak to Steve. He always knew where to get a few quid when he was feeling the pinch. He'd managed to raise enough to buy that caravan park, and he must have been doing well for himself. It would only be for a month or two, a quick remortgage, and we'd be back on track.

I dropped Amelia off on the street outside our flat. It was a huge block with hundreds of flats inside. You could smell whatever was cooking from the floor below, and the walls were paper-thin. Our neighbour must have had allergies because she spent most of the day sneezing and it sounded like it was right in your ear.

"I'll see you later, Ames. A few hours, tops."

"If you say so," Amelia said plainly.

"What's the matter?"

"I just don't like you dropping these things on me at the last minute. We should be celebrating."

"We can when I get back, I promise. I love you."

"I love you too," Amelia replied as she walked into the block of flats.

I loved Amelia, and I hated upsetting her. She would always pepper me with questions about something I thought was completely irrelevant. She would say it was because she missed me, but I always thought she just liked keeping tabs on me. I'd never given her a reason to worry, but I always felt like I was lying to her even when I wasn't. The inquisitions were becoming more frequent, too. I put it down to moving stress and her growing anticipation of starting a family. But on this occasion, her instincts were bang on the money, and I couldn't really blame her for wanting to know more. I didn't like lying to her about anything, really. It sounds stereotypically misogynistic, but she did tend to overreact sometimes. I felt like I had everything in hand, and I didn't have the brain capacity to keep up with her constant questioning. It was easier to just trivialise what I was doing.

I drove around the corner and parked up; I nearly ripped the steering wheel straight off the column I was gripping so tightly. I took out my phone and gave Steve a call. He answered, but I could barely hear a word over the rowdy sounds of whatever pub where he was currently drinking himself stupid.

"Ste?" I shouted.

"Harry! You back in Filey?" Steve boomed.

"No, mate. I'm down in Manchester. Are you out?"

"Yeah, friend. We are at the Plow. You should come down!"

"I just said I'm in Manchester. For God's sake, Ste, go outside. You can't hear a word," I shouted. I could hear him making his way outside, and the background noise became tolerable to my ears.

"Right, go on. I'm outside."

"That's better. Listen, I need a borrow, and it's a big ask. But it won't be for long."

"Harry, mate, I'm tapped. Everything I've got I spent on the caravans. I'm sorry."

"No worries, mate. I understand."

"What about your mum?"

"No chance, Ste. If Amelia finds out we took a penny from her, I'll be single within the week."

"Well, there's always the Broadheads, but the interest will be steep."

The Broadheads were two brothers up in Leeds. Broad by name and broad by nature. They were the kind of monsters you didn't want to owe money to, and only the most desperate dared to take on a Broadhead loan. I didn't know if it was true, but I'd heard they threw someone from a fifth-floor balcony because they didn't keep up with payments. I worked as a financial advisor, and I knew the worst possible place to get money from was a loan shark. But I'd exhausted all lines of conventional credit, and I didn't have any options left.

"The Broadheads, Steve? I'll end up with concrete shoes," I joked.

"You won't pal. They're sound. As long as you pay up."

"Can you vouch for me?"

"Sure. Me and Nick go way back. What do you even need it for anyway?"

"The house. It's more expensive than I'd planned."

"You're risking your legs getting broken for a house?"

"I thought you said they were sound?"

"Yeah, but a house? Why?"

"Ames will be upset if we don't get it. It won't even matter once my new salary kicks in."

"Oh god, no one can upset Amelia, right?"

"Things have been going well recently, and I don't want to ruin that."

"Fine, that's your business. When do you need it?"

"As soon as possible. We put the offer in today."

"We can drive up there over the weekend, pal."

"Okay, Ste, thanks, I'll be in touch."

My heart was pounding through my chest just from the thought of it. I hadn't done anything like it, and whatever the outcome, Amelia couldn't know what I'd planned. The pressure on me was enormous. We had a plan: get married, buy a house, and start building a family. But embroiling myself in the criminal underworld was a step in a direction I'd fought all my life to avoid travelling in. It's the kind of thing my dad would have done, and I was adamant not to be the kind of father and husband he was. Dad constantly trod on eggshells around my mother, and I saw first-hand what it did to their marriage. I adopted a rather flippant stance on the situation by telling myself it was a makeshift solution to a temporary problem. I had cash flow issues, that's all.

I trusted Steve. If he had said it was kosher, then it was. He knew more about dodgy dealings than anyone else. If it weren't for people like the Broadheads, he would still be selling stolen cars for scrap. He'd built his little leisure empire in Filey with a cash injection from them and was still walking around with his legs unbroken, so they couldn't be as bad as the stories made out. I actually felt a little excited about our little foray into lawlessness, partly because it was so far removed from how I usually react to these situations. I was excited to see Filey again, too. I'd been away from it for far too long. I wanted to scrape the smog of Manchester out of my lungs. I'd swap the car exhaust fumes for the ocean breeze any day of the week, and even though the context of my trip home was a bit grim, I was excited to see my hometown again. I just needed to find a palatable excuse for Amelia so I could get up there. I'd always loved visiting Manchester when she and I started dating, but once you live here, you take off the rose-tinted glasses. You start seeing the problems. The grime. The constant hustle and bustle of people trying to flee their debt-driven existences.

I'd parked the car in the usual spot next to the block of flats we lived at. Luckily, the lift was working, but it was arduous to walk up the stairs to the 30th floor. It was only temporary whilst we were looking for a house. I wished Amelia and my mother got on well enough for us all to live under the same roof temporarily. It would have saved us a fortune; the rent prices in Manchester were astronomical. Amelia could have easily just got another job in the pharmacy in Filey if it came to it, but she was adamant she wanted us to live in Manchester.

I did miss everyone in Filey, and married life didn't allow for as many visits to your hometown as I would have liked. We always had something we needed to do, which always threw a spanner in my visiting plans. I knew for a fact that Amelia hated going there, too, which didn't make it any easier to plan anything. I had loads of friends back in Filey, and in Manchester I felt terribly isolated from them. Amelia's opinion was that our marriage should suffice, but I'd always been very social in my youth, and she wasn't really like that.

Ater the lift had pinged on the 30th floor, I stepped out and walked over to our flat door. I could hear Amelia sobbing inside. It was an extremely specific cry; I couldn't really explain it, but I knew exactly what she was upset about. It had become a common occurrence, regrettably. We'd been trying for a baby for a few months with no success. We thought we got a positive result a while back, but it turned out to be a faulty test. I really wanted it to happen, and I was as supportive as I could be, but it was becoming tiresome. The number of couples we knew who had managed to conceive on the off chance or even by accident made us feel awful about ourselves, as though there was something wrong with us.

It usually went one of two ways. She was usually either upset and would spend the evening either crying unconsolably or throwing fits of rage as she vented on me. To be honest, I preferred the former. I'd much rather be handing out tissues and consoling her than picking up pieces of broken plates and glassware off the floor. It's shameful, but I waited for a minute or two outside the door before entering. I needed to psych myself up for both eventualities.

"Amelia, are you okay in there?" I asked sheepishly through the bathroom door. There were a few seconds of silence before she responded.

"No," she whispered hoarsely through the bathroom door.

"Can I come in?"

"Yes," she responded.

I inched my way into the bathroom, and the floor was filled with packaging from what looked like a full box of pregnancy tests. She was clutching one of them tightly and sat on the closed toilet seat, sobbing like the whole world had ended.

"It's going to happen eventually, Ames. We just need to stay positive and keep trying."

"What if it's not possible, Harry? What if there's something wrong with me?"

"There isn't. It just takes time."

"How long?" she shouted, hurling the negative test against the wall, "we've been trying for months and nothing is happening."

"Maybe we should book in at that fertility clinic. It might make us feel better."

"Why does everyone else get to have children, and we can't?"

Truthfully, I didn't know how to answer that question. The only response I could muster was this bizarre, solemn shrug. I caught a glimpse of it in the bathroom mirror, and it wouldn't have made me feel any better either. Essentially, we were both going through the same thing, and as long as we stayed strong, it would happen eventually, right? For some reason, life had just thrown everything at us, one thing after another. We needed to remain positive; we were going to get the house of our dreams and start building a family, just like we'd dreamt of.

"I don't know, Ames. But it will happen for us."

"I'm sorry, Harry. I know I didn't want a family at first, but I do now. So badly."

"Me too. Come on, I'll make you a cuppa."

I could see her heart splintering in front of me, but mine was breaking, too. It's so hard to comfort someone when you feel the exact same as them. I would have thought it would bring us closer together, but it didn't. If anything, it was starting to create a rift between us. To be clear, not because I blamed her; we didn't know why we couldn't conceive. It was just the constant pressure of reassurance I needed to provide that was getting to me. I made her a cup of tea, and she barely touched it.

I had to get my head in the game. It was Saturday morning, and I needed to go back to Filey to meet the Broadheads. More difficult than that, I had to come up with a plausible explanation for going up to Filey without Amelia. She was still in a delicate state after last night's bad news, so I had to tread carefully. She was still asleep; I don't think she got a wink of sleep during the night.

I started frying up some eggs and bacon for breakfast. A mixture of the smell and the noise would normally rouse Amelia from her deep slumber. It was also my pathetic way of trying to make her feel better before I announced I was abandoning Amelia to her grief for the weekend. As soon as the bacon started sizzling on the skillet, I heard the floorboards creaking as Amelia left the bed.

"Morning, love," I said warmly, "breakfast?"

"Morning. Not hungry," she replied, still half asleep.

"You have to eat something, Ames."

"Honestly, I'm fine. I'll get something later."

"Fine."

I pushed the bacon around the pan with the spatula, and I could feel Amelia's gaze burning a hole in the back of my head. She knew I was about to announce something. Half the time she was able to read my own thoughts before I could even express them.

"Listen, I need to run up to Filey today, but I'm not staying over. Steve needs some help with something."

"Help with what?"

"Something to do with his books. They are a mess, apparently. His accountant doesn't do weekends, and he needs to get them sent off before Monday."

"That's late notice, isn't it?"

"Well, you know what Steve's like."

"I'll miss you, though."

"I'll miss you, but he's my oldest friend, and needs some help. I'll be back before you know it."

"Okay. I was planning to look at that clinic today. We clearly need some help, and you are right. It will make me feel better."

More expense, I thought.

"That's a great idea. Definitely the right thing to do."
"I love you, Harry."
"Love you, too."
Amelia finally conceded she was hungry, and we shared breakfast together and said our goodbyes. I always felt guilty about lying to her, but she couldn't find out what I was about to do. I knew it was wrong, but I didn't think she could handle anything else before she descended into a mental breakdown. Despite my frequent protests, she was already popping those prescription pills like they were sweets. I just needed to get our finances in order, and everything else should fall into place after that.

Once I got out of Manchester, the traffic eased off, and I pretty much had the roads to myself. I wound down the windows on the motorway, and the cool air refreshingly slapped against my face. I liked the long drives back to Filey; I'd never felt at home in Manchester, and the drive was where I got most of my thinking done. I desperately hoped I was making the right decision.

I pulled into Steve's holiday park. It was right next to Filey Brigg, and the salted sea air danced playfully on my tongue. Steve lived in a detached house on the same property, and it was a total mess. Because he was single and didn't mind living like a pig, he didn't have much inspiration to fix the place. I parked on the gravel driveway leading up to the house. Half of the windows had been boarded up, but it was just out of view from the caravans, so I guess it didn't bother him. He was all about business now.

I knocked on the door, and there were no signs of life. I checked my watch; I'd arrived on the wrong side of midday for Steve; he was likely hungover. I fumbled around to try and find my phone to give him a call, but he opened the door before I got to it. When he emerged in the doorway, he was wearing a floor-length silk dressing gown, and I nearly collapsed in laughter.

"What the hell are you wearing?" I laughed.

"Have a little respect, young Harry. This is a traditional silk kimono," Steve announced with a twirl.

"You aren't going to the Broadheads like that."

"They are men of culture, Harry; they will respect it."

"The loan sharks, right," I smirked, "well, at least they won't break my legs. They will be too busy laughing."

"We are meeting at one of their warehouses in two hours."

"Right, well, you better get dressed; we need to get moving."

"Righto."

Steve turned around to go up the stairs. I took a few steps into his house, but I dared not go any further. My feet stuck to the tacky floor in his hallway. I dreaded to think what the substance was. He'd really let this place go to wreck and ruin; it was a state when he first got the place, but he'd only made it worse. Even the wallpaper was trying to flee this place. It was peeling off almost in full sheets. Cans of lager and cider littered the floor, interspersed with half-eaten packets of crisp and wrappers. I was tempted to take a picture, and the next time Amelia accused me of being undomesticated, I could have shown her. Steve was furiously running around upstairs, getting ready. He was only gone a few minutes before he came bounding down the stairs in a shirt and jeans.

"This any better?" He asked.

"Better. But no shower? Classy."

"Just had one."

"I'll keep the windows open in the car."

We both got in my car and began the journey to Leeds. I was bricking it, but Steve had a way of calming me down. He was so laid-back about everything, even casual in the face of lending a huge sum of money from a bunch of notorious criminals. He directed me into the car park of a warehouse in a grim-looking industrial estate.

"Park up here," he instructed.

"What's the plan?" I asked.

"Well, you aren't walking into a bank here, mate. They are going to want collateral."

"Collateral? I don't have anything, Steve. That's why I'm here."

"You must have something."

"Nothing. Apart from our savings, but we are using that on the house."

"Come on, we will have a chat with them."

Steve got out of my car and made his way through the entrance. I followed him a few paces behind; he was clearly not fazed at all by any of this. It was quite a small warehouse, and there was a group of men standing by a makeshift table made from an upturned cable reel. I could feel my heart pounding through my chest as they looked at us on our approach. Steve outstretched his arms in welcome, laughing heartily as he walked over.

"All right, lads?" Steve boomed.

I'm sure I recognised Nick Broadhead from the paper. When he saw Steve, this huge grin spanned his face, exposing his golden teeth. He walked over to Steve, his hand reached out in a handshake, as his entourage followed. I remained at a slight distance. He barely even looked at me.

Nick's hand closed into a fist.

He swung at Steve's head, hitting him square in the nose. It instantly burst, and blood exploded down his white shirt. I stepped forward impulsively, and one of Nick's entourage raised a single finger to signal me to stop. I did.

"What did you think was going to happen?" Nick shouted, stamping on Steve's defenceless body in time with every syllable.

I stood there, like a spare part, watching my oldest friend get beaten to death. I hated violence. I always did. I know that isn't exactly a rare trait, but even seeing it always made me feel vulnerable. Instead of running away or trying to stop it, I'd just want to curl up into a ball in the corner. When Steve stopped resisting and became entirely motionless, Nick's attention moved to me.

"Who the fuck are you?" He asked.

VI

THE TOWER

AMELIA

I couldn't stand people who weren't on time. It was almost a quarter past the hour, and there was still no sign of her. I should have just left without her. When I'd agreed to it, I was in a fragile state, but after I'd had the time to think it through, I'd have preferred to go on my own. Just as I was about to leave, I was scared half to death by banging on the car window. It was Kim, looking fresh as a daisy, clearly excited for our little road trip. I rolled my eyes at her as I wound the window down.

"You're late," I chastised.

"Sorry. I had a doctor's appointment, and it overran," Kim said, climbing into the passenger side as I hesitantly unlocked the door.

"Everything okay?" I asked.

"Yeah, fine. Just routine. Shall we get going?"

"Yes."

I started indicating and merged into traffic. It was busier than usual; I couldn't help thinking the 15 minutes I'd waited would have given us a chance to miss the traffic. Kim was being her usual quiet self, pensively looking out of the passenger side window into the fields and fidgeting. I was expecting a barrage of questions about my behaviour the day before, but she didn't seem to care. Good, I thought. We weren't friends; we were barely acquaintances. Our goals were temporarily aligned; that was it.

"What are we going to ask Steve?" Kim asked.

"What he knows," I responded.

"What if he's somehow responsible?" Kim quivered.

"He isn't. He is one of Harry's oldest friends."

"I hope you're right."

"I am. I'm not even convinced the whole thing wasn't just an accident."

The closer we got to Filey, the more Kim's whole demeanour improved. She was almost chirpy. I couldn't stand that place, and everyone who grew up here had this bizarre affinity to it. I think she spotted my dirty looks, and her mood came back down. We pulled into Steve's caravan park. I hadn't been here in a while. Every plot housed a caravan, and there were barely any available for hire; he must be doing well for himself. We drove through the seemingly endless lines of caravans to Steve's house, which overlooked the Brigg.

If only he showed the same care and attention to his house as the caravans. It was more like a squat or a depraved squalid wreckage, blighting the landscape with its boarded-up windows. It seriously should have been condemned in the name of health and safety; half the render was falling off the walls and lying in piles around the perimeter. We drove up the gravel path, and I parked the car a few metres away from the front door to avoid any further falling debris. There would have been a time that you couldn't drag me into that house by my ankles, but needs must. I could see Kim wasn't excited to go in there either. But if we wanted answers, we would have to brave it.

Kim got to the door first and tapped on it lightly. It wasn't the time for a light touch. With a further eye roll, I bashed the door heavily with my closed fist. Steve emerged a few seconds later.

"Ladies! What can I do for you?" Steve boomed.

"It's not a social call, Steve," I answered.

"Oh? What's happened?"

"I'm hoping you can tell us. Can we come in?"

"Sure."

Steve led us into his home, if you could call it that. Before I could process my other senses, the first thing that hit me was the overpowering stench. The air was thickened by a mouldy cocktail of damp and rotting food. It didn't help that the entire house was almost entirely in darkness. In lieu of curtains, Steve had hung various sheets and scrap pieces of fabric against the windows. Not to block out the light; it was only there to obscure the view of the plywood that replaced the glass. The only remaining light came from the gaps in Steve's haphazard window-boarding, which allowed bright streams of light into the room. The beams of light only highlighted the sheer amount of unknown particles hanging in the air, and I coughed instinctively. There was barely a scrap of floor not occupied by something revolting. We tiptoed through the debris and dodged the humongous cobwebs as he led us into the sitting room. The sofa looked older than me and appeared as if something could be living in it, given the gnaw marks. Steve outstretched his hand to offer me a seat. I politely declined.

"Quite the place you have here," I remarked.

"Thanks," Steve replied, unperturbed by my obvious sarcasm.

"Kim and I just want to talk to you about the night of Harry's death. What happened?"

"Well, he stepped off the Brigg pissed up, didn't he?"

"He wasn't drinking, Ste," Kim interjected abruptly, almost being overcome by her gag reflex.

"Well, he's a clumsy oaf then because he fell either way," Steve shrugged.

"There is talk that his death was suspicious, and I'm starting to believe it. Kim said he was trying to call someone just before, and there was talk about him owing money to some brothers from Leeds."

Steve stared at Kim disapprovingly. "You weren't meant to hear anything about that," Steve turned to me, "The Broadheads."

"Did they kill Harry?" I asked.

"God, no. They lent him some money."

"How much money?"

"A hundred grand," Steve confessed dryly.

"What for?"

"That house you are living in now."

"But that doesn't make any sense. We had the money."

"Yeah. Broadhead money."

I felt like such a fool. Everyone knew about the money issues, except for me. Harry was making secret backroom deals with these criminals, and I was meant to be blissfully unaware, living in the house that they'd paid for. Steve had no reason to lie, and Kim had overheard it directly from Harry's mouth, so the evidence was mounting. It was deeply embarrassing. I should have known every single detail about Harry, but everyone knew what he was up to, and they looked at me like I didn't have a clue.

"Who was he trying to call then? These scumbag brothers?" I asked.

"No, but listen, I can't talk right now," Steve said, looking at Kim and then back at me, "I've got a prior engagement. Come back tonight alone, and I'll tell you everything I know."

"You'll tell us now!" I demanded.

"Amelia, come on, let's just come back later," Kim suggested with a dry cough.

"Fine. But no more lies, okay?" I pointed.

"No more fibs," Steve conceded.

Kim and I both left Steve's dilapidated residence, and I felt like the air there had left a film of grime on my skin. I desperately rooted around in the glove compartment for a stray bottle of hand sanitiser or anything containing soap. Kim didn't look too pleased either, and she was racing to get to the safety of my car. I felt like there were insects crawling all over me. I batted at my arms just to be sure. We both got inside, and I sighed audibly.

"That call couldn't have existed. The police checked his phone records, and there wasn't a call," I said.

"Maybe he didn't have a signal?" Kim mustered.

"We are surrounded by nothing but caravans, Kim. I've got five bars right now; what about you?"

"Five bars. It doesn't necessarily mean Harry had a signal, though."

"I'm more interested in why he wants me to come back alone. Don't tell me Steve is an ex-boyfriend of yours too?" I joked.

"Absolutely not," Kim said with disgust, "I don't think he likes me. He tried it on with me a while ago, and I knocked him back."

"I don't think you're alone in that club. Thankfully, I'm not a member."

"Where do we go from here?" Kim asked with a shrug.

"I'll drop you off in the town. I've got to go and see someone on my own."

We drove through it; Kim wanted to be dropped off at one of the cafés near Filey Beach. As much as I didn't really like her, it was probably useful to keep her around to balance me out whilst we were investigating. I was more of a blunt instrument, and Kim was more diplomatic. She was likely to get more out of people. I still refused to trust her, though, not even a little bit. Her little quip about Steve trying it on with her didn't fool me; she knew the exact reason Steve didn't want her there, and she was concealing it from me. Regardless, all would become clear that evening: I just had to be patient. I dropped her off at the curb next to the café, and she got out of the car.

"Keep me updated, yeah?" She asked.

"I will."

"Just take what Steve has to say with a pinch of salt. He was almost blackout drunk that night."

"I'll text you if I hear anything."

I watched Kim walk into one of the cafés at the seafront and took out my phone to send a text message to James. I wanted his insight into what the meeting with Steve could hold.

> *Why would Steve not want Kim at the meeting?*

> *I sense that Steve feels his tale should only be heard by you.*

> *Are you sure Kim can be trusted?*

> *I see Kim takes great pride in her trustworthiness, and she will steer you in the right direction.*

I started the car again and began driving down the promenade. As much as I didn't want to, I needed to see Yvonne. She might be able to fill in some of the gaps. Yvonne lived just outside of Filey in a renovated farmhouse, which was Harry's childhood home. She married John not long after Harry and I started dating, and John moved in. I thought it was a little quick, but each to their own. Just beyond Yvonne's house was a sign that described Filey as a 'treasure to discover.' I'd never found any treasure here, only misery. The only thing I wanted to discover was the truth about Harry, and then I could leave this miserable place.

I drove down the crushed stone driveway, and I could see plumes of smoke emanating from the back of the house. Yvonne never liked to smoke inside because of misplaced pride but was happy to light one up in my kitchen whenever she visited us in Manchester. I didn't bother with the front door. I just walked around the side of the house and found her furiously chain-smoking. I remained at a distance to avoid inhaling the cancerous fumes expelled by her lungs. I took a deep breath of fresh air before I turned the corner and prepared to be annoyed.

"Amelia? What are you doing here?" She coughed.

"Sorry to bother you, Yvonne. I'm back in Filey to talk to Steve. He knows something about Harry's death," I replied.

"Oh, love," she started, crushing her cigarette on a fence post, "you need to try and move on. That's what I did after Harry's dad passed."

"I know. But people weren't saying Harry's dad's death was suspicious."

"Suspicious?"

"Someone from the funeral told me he wasn't even drinking that night. He was sober when he fell."

"That can't be right, and he had alcohol in his blood. It was in the toxicology report."

"Yeah, but you know what Harry was like. He could drink anybody under the table. He was on non-alcoholic beer."

"So, how did he fall?"

"That's why I'm here. Apparently, he was trying to make a call just before he died, but I don't remember anything on the police report of his phone. Did you see it?"

"I don't remember. But I've got his last bill inside. He never changed his address."

"Can I take a look?" I asked.

Yvonne led me inside through the kitchen doors and started rooting through a drawer in the kitchen island. She was idly flicking through envelopes and letters idly until she found what she was looking for. She placed it on the counter in front of me.

"There. No calls on the night he fell," Yvonne said with a shrug.

"But Kim and Steve both saw him trying to make a call."

"I don't know what to tell you, love. Are you sure it was from that phone?"

"What do you mean, that phone?"

"Maybe he had more than one."

"What are you trying to say?"

"Nothing. Just some men have more than one phone. A phone that their wives don't know about?"

It dawned on me. If Yvonne could see it, it must have been obvious: a second mobile phone. When a married woman finds out her husband has a second phone, there's usually only one explanation. But I'd learned about Harry's deceitful side. There could be a multitude of reasons why he would have another phone other than an affair. Was it for his dodgy dealings with the criminal underworld? Or was it indeed just garden-variety infidelity? I stared at the ceiling and gritted my teeth, feeling embarrassed I hadn't arrived at the same conclusion sooner. A lump appeared in my throat as I tried desperately to stifle the inevitable tears that would ensue. I didn't want to be vulnerable in front of this woman, but I could barely hold it in any longer.

"Was another phone recovered by the police?" I asked, trying to choke back the tears.

"Not that I know of," Yvonne shrugged.

"Are you sure? No mention of it anywhere?"

"I think I'd remember that, Amelia."

The lump in my throat bloated and grew until I could almost taste the disappointment. I felt the blood rush to my cheeks, and they prickled lightly with the change in temperature. I could feel the tears building on my eyelids. Even the slightest provocation would have sent me into a full meltdown. Yvonne could sense it, and I didn't want her to see that side of me. The weak one. I'd always projected an image of strength and maturity, but in truth, I felt like I was behaving like an anxious and paranoid little girl.

"Do you think he was cheating on me?" I uttered pitifully.

Yvonne didn't respond verbally at first. It was more of a look of pity, and I could feel myself losing control, which instantly turned the waterworks on. She left the room to get me some tissues, but the supply was rapidly outstripped by demand, and I pretty much used the whole packet within minutes. I loved Harry, and I thought he loved me. My initial response should have been disbelief, but the disturbing evidence that I was digging up was mounting and leading me to believe that Harry wasn't the man I fell in love with. I just wanted to look him in the eye, grab him, and force him to explain himself. Knowing I wouldn't ever be able to do that was a gut-wrenching reality I had to content myself with.

"Amelia, you can't think like that," Yvonne said softly, "you never gave him a reason to play away, did you?"

"Of course not!" I shouted.

"He loved you; I know he did. He wouldn't have uprooted his life and moved to Manchester with you if he hadn't."

"Do you know something that you aren't telling me?"

"No. Do you?"

"No."

"Well," she sighed, "he was a man, after all."

Yvonne walked to the fridge, leaving me in blubbering pieces on the kitchen island, only to return with a bottle of wine and two glasses. She brimmed them both and drank deeply. I hesitated at first; I could almost hear Harry protesting, but in his absence, I quickly followed suit. Yvonne and I didn't speak for what seemed like hours and silently polished off the whole bottle. Yvonne stood to get another, but I put my hand on her arm to dissuade her. I knew I shouldn't be drinking, and even in his absence, I didn't want to disappoint him like that.

"No, thank you," I mumbled, "I've got somewhere I need to be."

"Where?"

"Steve's place. He promised me he would tell me what he knew about Harry tonight."

"Don't listen to a word that pathetic man has to say. He's nothing but trouble, that lad. He never did a thing for anyone but himself."

"I know, but he knows things about Harry, and he promised me he would tell me everything."

"Well, I wouldn't trust him as far as I could throw him, and let me tell you, it wouldn't be very far. Let me come with you."

I understood why she was so aggressive in her discrediting of Steve, and I agreed with her, to be honest. Besides, I wasn't sure if Yvonne was holding something back. He was repulsive, but that was as far as I'd go. He always seemed to be there for Harry when he needed him. Steve and Harry were friends in school, and they were always getting into trouble. It was not real trouble; it was more like hijinks, but when they got a bit older, Steve obviously progressed to criminality. Yvonne was a fellow blunt instrument, and I couldn't risk her ruining the chance of getting more information from Steve.

"No, it's fine. Kim is coming with me," I lied.

"Kim? Who is this Kim you keep talking about?"

"The girl from the funeral. I just need to use the bathroom before I head out."

I stood up from the table and made a beeline for the bathroom on the first floor. Everything in this house was pristine, which I thought was unusual given Yvonne's lack of sobriety. As soon as I had walked into the bathroom, I took two of the Alprazolam that I kept in my bag. I needed to get back into a routine of taking them as prescribed. I knew the early signs of a panic attack very well, and my hands had already started shaking slightly. The advice was to not take them with alcohol, nonetheless, I would descend into a full panic attack without them. I hated relying on these pills just to feel normal, but I'd taken them on and off for years. I had suffered from panic attacks and anxiety ever since childhood.

I stared into the bathroom mirror. I didn't know whether it was the medication or the alcohol, but I could almost see Harry gazing right back at me. Inappropriately, he had that signature cheeky grin on his face. I wanted him to comfort and reassure me and tell me it was all a lie, but he didn't; he remained silent. I splashed cold water on my face, and he was gone again. By the time I'd returned downstairs, I was feeling a little woozy. Maybe it wasn't a good idea to drink on these tablets. Yvonne was at the back door again, on the continuing task of smoking every cigarette within a ten-mile radius.

"Are you leaving now, dear?" Yvonne asked.

"Yes, can I leave my car here? I don't think I should be driving."

"Of course. You can always stay here tonight if you'd like?"

"I'll think about it. I'll let you know once I've spoken to Steve."

I'd already made up my mind about it, and I'd rather sleep underneath a bus stop shelter than stay at her house. In fairness to Yvonne, she had largely been very supportive and almost nice to me since Harry's passing, but that just made me uneasy, if anything. She always seemed to have an angle she was working, and I knew her sudden personality change wouldn't be without a hidden motive.

I started walking towards Steve's caravan park. It was only a twenty-five-minute walk, and the exercise would give me a chance to clear my head and hopefully work some of the alcohol out of my system. Every step I took on the pavement had to be carefully calculated because I felt like I was going to topple or keel over without warning. I regretted drinking at such a pivotal moment in my search for the truth, but I couldn't resist myself. I found myself thinking about getting soused a lot more since Harry died because it was the most effective coping mechanism I had, unfortunately. I heard my phone ping and clumsily took it out of my bag to read the incoming message. It was from James.

> *Amelia. You need to hurry. I can sense you don't have much time.*

> *What are you talking about? What does that mean?*

He didn't reply, but I set about walking as fast as my inebriated legs could transport me. I was making my way drunkenly through the high street when all of a sudden I noticed the plumes of smoke rising into the sky. It was coming from Steve's caravan park.

In spite of sharing half a bottle of wine and the two tablets, I was instantaneously seized by the feeling of panic that broke through and rushed over me like wildfire. I broke out into a jog towards the source, almost breaking an ankle every other step. That was my only opportunity to find out what Steve knew about Harry's death, and it was quite literally going up in smoke. The adrenaline I felt pushed the alcohol and chemicals out of my pores in the form of sweat, and I could feel my faculties returning slowly. I was almost in full sprint when I reached the entrance to Steve's caravan park. A large group of holidayers stood at the gate, watching the inferno from afar, filming it with their phones.

I pushed through them at speed and continued running down the gravel path towards the blaze. The closer I got to Steve's house, the blacker the sky became. His once-decaying abode was turned into a towering beacon of light in the darkness, throwing a million red-hot embers into the sky. Before I got halfway down the path, the roof had already started to collapse, leaving only the ignited framework behind. Emergency services were already working at the scene, trying to make a futile attempt to quell the fierce blaze engulfing Steve's abode. They dodged and dived the huge burning chunks of the roof as they exploded into the ground.

I didn't know what my plan was: whether I should be running into the building helplessly or stand by and watch the flames engulf my opportunity to know the truth. The choice was stripped from me when I was tackled and restrained by some firemen before I could find out what my intentions were. There was only one thing I knew for certain. If Steve was still in that blazing building, he wasn't alive, and anything he knew about Harry would die with him.

VII

THE SUN

AMELIA

The sun was now completely blacked out and replaced entirely by the smoke and ash falling from the sky. The debris of the house lightly steamed against the mist of the fire hoses. The inferno was finally extinguished, along with my last hope of finding anything new about my late husband. I stared into the rubble of Steve's house at a distance, and it was no more than a smouldering wreckage. Almost the entire town of Filey had made their way down to the caravan park to witness the fire out of morbid curiosity. Kim had seen the smoke from the café and came to see it too. She looked a lot more shaken up than I did while she stood beside me gripping my hand tightly for comfort. It seemed too much of an odd coincidence for it to happen just before Steve was about to give me the full lowdown on what happened to the love of my life. I didn't know, nonetheless, who it would benefit for him to remain silent.

The fire was intentional, according to the fire investigation team. It had started at multiple points and spread quickly throughout the whole building. They still didn't know if Steve was in the house at the time, and it would take them a while before they could say for certain. Kim tried phoning him a few times, but the calls went unanswered. Most probably, any secrets that Steve held about Harry perished in that fire with him. On the one hand, I was mortified that I'd missed an opportunity to find out what had happened, but on the other, I don't think I could take much more. I never thought I'd be in this position; the desire to get in my car and return home was almost overwhelming.

I could taste the ash on my tongue; it coated the inside of my nose and throat, making it difficult for me to breathe properly. I started coughing violently, and Kim, as she lead me to her borrowed car, guided me through the table of onlookers now crowding around the ashes. I leaned on the bonnet with my hands on my knees, and we were far enough away from the fire to be able to breathe again. Kim looked genuinely upset about what could have happened to Steve, but I was more dismayed about being unable to discover what he actually knew. I couldn't banish the filthy feeling that Harry was cheating on me, and I would have found out with whom if it wasn't for the fire. Kim looked at me with tears in her eyes either from misplaced emotions or just the sheer amount of carbon in the air. I wanted to cry, too. Yvonne was probably right, and I should just let it go. I didn't know why I was even here anymore. Every day I spent investigating, the worse I felt. I didn't know if it would be better to just leave it and preserve the perception I had of him. I should have gone to the police there and then and told them everything, but I couldn't.

"Do you think it was those brothers?" Kim asked.

"The Broadheads?" I replied.

"Maybe Steve owed them some money, too."

"Well, by the looks of it, he won't be paying them back anytime soon."

"I didn't like Steve, but he didn't deserve that," Kim uttered.

My phone vibrated and beeped in my pocket, and Kim looked at me expectantly, waiting for me to look at it. I took it out, and it was a text message from James.

> *Your quest is plagued with unfortunate timing.*

> *Who was responsible?*

> *You must seek out the brothers.*
> *They will know where to go next.*

I looked up from my phone, and Kim seemed very curious as to who I was texting. Maybe it was a small facial expression or the way I'd gazed at my phone, but I could tell that she knew something strange was going on. I wasn't ready to involve her in that part just yet, so keeping her in the dark about James for the time being was the best thing I could do.

"Anything important?" Kim asked.

"No. Just a friend," I responded.

"Where do we go from here?"

"We need to track these brothers down."

"Are you serious? They are dangerous. What if they did this?"

"I need to find out what they know."

"But is it worth your life?"

"I don't have a life anymore."

I could see Yvonne threading her way through the crowd towards us, unbelievably contributing to the smog with the usual half-burned cigarette permanently lodged in her hand. She came over and stood in between us, and Kim overtly backed away to avoid the second-hand smoke.

"What happened?" Yvonne asked.

"Your guess is as good as mine. But apparently, Steve was in the house when it went up," I replied.

"Poor Steve," Yvonne whispered.

"You were slagging him off an hour ago."

"Yeah, but no one deserves to die like that."

"Can we get out of here?" Kim asked, "This smoke can't be good for us."

"Come back to mine. We can have a drink," Yvonne suggested.

We all got in the car, and Kim drove us out of the smog through Filey town centre in the direction of Yvonne's house. James was right. I needed to track these brothers down, as they were the only remaining lead. I knew they didn't physically kill Harry and had the gut feeling that someone would have seen something up on Filey Brigg. I had convinced myself that the pressure that the two brothers were putting on him might have contributed to his death, in some way or another. Kim was right; they were dangerous, and I had no idea how to locate them. As soon as we got inside, Yvonne produced yet another bottle of wine, which Kim and I both refused. It didn't put her off, though; she filled her glass and started drinking greedily.

"So, how do we find these brothers?" Kim asked.

I shot Kim a look to tell her to shut up, but Yvonne had already clocked onto it.

"What brothers?" Yvonne asked bemusedly.

"The Broadhead brothers," I explained, "Steve introduced Harry to them, and Harry borrowed some money from them."

"Do you think they were responsible for the fire?" Yvonne asked.

"Maybe. It would definitely make sense if Steve had borrowed money from them in the past," I explained.

"Well, let's go and see them," Yvonne shrugged.

"No, Kim and I have got this. You don't need to be involved, Yvonne. We don't even know how to contact them."

"John will. He's from Leeds, and everyone knows the Broadheads up there."

It came to confirm what I had suspected for years. I'd always thought John was at least a bit dodgy. I'd barely spoken to John, and he had little interest in getting to know me. That feeling was reciprocated. Harry didn't think much of him either because Yvonne shacked up with him very quickly after Harry's dad passed. John was a man of few words, which suited Yvonne down to the ground, largely because she was the exact opposite of him. He was a typical Yorkshire bloke with fading tattoos up and down his arms. Rough around the edges would have been putting it politely. Yet, if he could lead us to the Broadheads, then what other option would we have?

"Stay the night," Yvonne started, "I'll speak to John, and we can head up there in the morning."

"I don't know how I feel about this," I said.

"Me either," Kim added.

"You don't have to come, Kim. I don't even know why you are here, to be honest," Yvonne said plainly.

"I'm just trying to help," Kim mumbled.

"We can take this from here, right, Amelia?" Yvonne asked.

"She could have phrased it a bit more politely, but I do agree, Kim. There is no use in putting our lives in danger," I said.

"Let's just get some sleep. John can take us in the morning," Yvonne suggested.

"I'll be going, then," Kim said abruptly.

"Kim, don't be like that. Thank you for your help. I promise I'll let you know of any developments," I sympathised.

Kim gave me an awkward hug and left through the kitchen door. Yvonne was still chugging her glass of wine. Part of me still wanted to just drive back to Manchester and put all this behind me, even more so now that Yvonne and John were involved. The resolve I felt in finding the truth only an hour earlier was waning already. But I still needed to know what happened to Harry that night and what he was up to behind my back in the weeks prior. I wouldn't be able to rest until I got to the truth, and deep down, I knew that. It would be dangerous, and if these men had no qualms about doing that to Steve's house, they were capable of anything. I just had to be careful and trust my instincts.

Much to my irritation, the only spare bedroom with an actual bed was Harry's old room. Yvonne had almost turned it into a mausoleum, not after his death, but when he left home. Not a single item in there had been touched since he flew the nest, save the odd occasion that Harry had come to stay. Initially, it was almost unbearable being in there, but after a few minutes, I grew to like it. I felt closer to Harry, and I could almost smell traces of his aftershave that had been absorbed by the sheets. The walls were filled with posters and a large corkboard decorated with pinned pictures from his youth. My attention is drawn to one photo; it was only a few weeks after we'd met. We'd driven up to the lake district for the weekend, we went for a walk, and Harry's wellington boots had got stuck in the mud. I'd never laughed so hard in my life; I would do anything to go back there and be stuck in the mud with him. The memory is powerful enough to make me visibly smile, perhaps for the first time since he had gone. It was nice to remember Harry for the man he was.

I didn't expect to get any rest that night, but it turned out to be the best night's sleep I had in a while. Just enough of Harry was left in that room to be of some comfort to me. I opened the curtains and saw the view over Filey. I felt guilty for badmouthing it so much in the past, and I could see why Harry had held it in such high esteem. The sun was rising over the hills, the sea breeze delicately rattling the window. I pulled out my phone and decided to send James a text message.

> *Harry would have enjoyed the view. Will I find out more today?*

> *Be patient. Answers will be received, but you must seek them out.*
> *The journey you have started is a demanding one.*

I got straight into the shower. The soot in my hair circled the drain and blackened the water. I could hear Yvonne shouting across the house to John, even over the cascade of water above my head. I really didn't want her involved in any of this, but I didn't see another option. If John was taking us, and he knew them, it would be at least another layer of protection if things went pear-shaped. I quickly got dressed and made my way downstairs, my hair still wet from the shower. I barely made any conscious effort in my appearance those days. I didn't see the point. Most of the day for me was about survival into the next.

"Ey up, coffee, love?" John asked.

It was too early for the Yorkshire-isms.

"Please," I smiled.

"John says he knows these brothers. They operate out of an industrial estate in Leeds," Yvonne said.

"And how do you know the Broadheads, John?" I enquired.

"Oh, you know. Just out and about in Leeds. When I worked the doors."

Harry told me that John had worked in security in Leeds for most of his life. I say security; he used to stand outside the pubs and clubs judging people's footwear choices. He eventually started his own security business and made quite a name for himself in Leeds. All roads seemed to lead back to the Broadheads, and I wondered if they somehow paid for this fancy house I'd just stayed in, too.

"Do you think they would be responsible for the fire at Steve's place?" I asked.

"I wouldn't put anything past the Broadheads. They've got a lot of fingers in a lot of pies, those lads. But I've known them since they were little. You'll be safe with me."

"What's the plan, then?" I asked.

"No plan, love. We'll just go and speak to them."

"Listen to him, Amelia. You can trust John," Yvonne added.

I didn't trust him. Not one bit. But it was either get in the car with John and hopefully find out more about Harry or go home. I gulped my instant coffee; most of the granules hadn't dissolved yet and stuck to my teeth.

"We can go up when you've finished your coffee," John suggested.

"I think I've had enough, actually. Are you ready now?" I replied.

"Ready when you are."

John gave Yvonne a kiss on the cheek as he brushed past her, and we both walked to his car. He had one of those old 4x4s you find rusting to dust on a farm, but it felt like stepping into a tank. The smell of burning diesel defiled the virgin Filey air as John chugged down the road towards Leeds. John and I barely had a thing in common, so I just sat in the passenger seat in silence, staring out of the window at the endless fields and greenery. After the ninety-minute journey to Leeds, John pulled into a decaying industrial estate filled with shuttered businesses and run-down units. We slowly drove through the estate, finally stopping at the end unit. I hadn't noticed until we had stopped because I'd barely looked at John the entire journey, but he was sweating profusely.

"Are you okay, John?" I asked.

"Listen, love. You've got two choices here. You can either walk in there, and you probably won't walk back out again. Or, the option I'd prefer is we turn back, and you forget all about this," John explained coldly.

I started sweating, too. He had assured me that I would be safe if I came here, but then I started thinking that he was involved in it all to some extent. John continued to look at me menacingly, waiting for my response. I tried the door handle, but the doors were already locked.

"Why did you even take me here?" I asked.

"I couldn't have Yvonne thinking I had anything to do with the fire, could I?" John asked.

"And you did?"

John started to look increasingly more agitated by my line of questioning and turned his head to look at the warehouse with a sharp huff. He turned back to me, and the menacing expression on his face was even more intense. He stepped out of the car and walked calmly over to the passenger door, threw it open and pulled me outside by my arm.

"Looks like you've made your decision," he said.

I desperately tried to wriggle free, but his grip was unwavering. He dragged me like a rag doll through the doors of the warehouse and pushed me forward to the floor. When I raised my head, I saw two men standing over me. John remained behind me, preventing my escape.

"This her?" One of the men said.

"Yes," John replied.

"I'm Nick. This is Damien," Nick said, leaning in.

"We hear you've been looking for us," Damien whispered, "you've found us."

I attempted to stand, but Nick tutted loudly and put his hand on my shoulder, keeping me on my knees. I desperately looked around for some kind of escape route, but nothing was immediately apparent. I could almost feel my heart pumping through my throat, and I was way out of my comfort zone. John had assured me I would be safe; it was the only reason I decided to come here in the first place. I could just try and stand up and run, but I had no idea where I would go or how many men were lurking in this warehouse. The floor was disgusting, covered in debris and dust, with the occasional ominously red stain soaked into the concrete. The debris had already started to cut into my knees, and they began to burn in pain. Nick whistled and clicked his fingers violently to get my attention back.

"Come on then. Spit it out. Why the hell are you here?" Nick shouted, so close to my face I could feel the heat in his breath.

"I'm here about my husband," I fretted.

Both brothers burst out laughing uproariously, but John remained a silent observer.

"He's dead, love," Damien retorted.

"I know. Did you kill him?" I asked.

The laughter stopped.

"Why would we kill Harry? You can't collect a debt from a dead man," Nick said.

"So, he still owed you money?" I replied.

"Yes. And a lot of it. That's why we had to go and cook up Steve's little caravan park. He was the guarantor of sorts. Your man John here lit the match."

I turned to look at John, and he nodded slightly, letting me know it was true. John had a much more intimate relationship with the Broadheads than he'd initially expressed. He was clearly working with them, and now,

I had no one to turn to for help. Damien reached into a large toolbox, producing a tyre wrench, clasping it with both hands. He gave a knowing nod to Nick who then turned back to me.

"Now, we can't have you running around asking questions, so we'll have to put a stop to that," Nick said menacingly.

Damien started walking over to me, almost in slow motion, delicately patting his free hand with the large piece of steel he was holding in the other. I knew exactly what was coming. He was going to take it and crack my skull open with it. My heart had stopped beating entirely, and I was in free fall, waiting for the inevitable impact. Just as he entered striking distance, my self-preservation instinct kicked in.

"Stop!" I screamed, "I'm pregnant."

Damien had stopped in his tracks, staring at Nick for some direction. I could hear John pacing around behind me. All three men were just looking at one another, not knowing what to do next.

The funniest bit about it was that it was true.

What a cruel joke. I'd finally given Harry what he so desperately wanted, and he wasn't around to see it. As planned, I went to the clinic appointment the morning of Harry's death, and it was there that I was given the news. Even though the pregnancy was very much planned at the time, it still filled me with dread. Harry wasn't at the appointment, of course, and I tried desperately to get hold of him on the phone, though the calls never went through. When I found out he'd died, it sounded crazy, but I'd convinced myself I wasn't pregnant. I couldn't cope with that on top of everything else. I cradled my stomach lightly and rose to my feet.

"You don't have to do this. I don't care about you or anything illegal you've been doing. I just want to know what you know about Harry. That's all."

"I'm not killing a pregnant woman, Nick," Damien uttered.

"John is going to take you back now. You keep our names out of your mouth, you hear? Or we'll find you," Nick warned.

"You still haven't told me about Harry," I said sternly.

"Are you taking the piss?" Nick stormed closer, his forehead almost touching mine, "We let you walk out of here unharmed, and you ask more questions?"

"Come on, love," John said, delicately gripping my arm, "we need to leave."

John led me out of the warehouse, the way we came, and to his car. He opened the passenger door to usher me inside. I'd risked my life and that of my unborn child, and for what? A few crumbs of information that I already knew. John got back in the car, and I remained staring into space.

"Are you actually pregnant?" John asked.

"Yes," I replied.

"Why haven't you told anyone?"

"It never came up."

"You should have said earlier. I wouldn't have let you go in there if I knew."

"Well, you know now."

"Is it Harry's?"

"Of course. It's Harry's," I snapped.

"I'll drive you back. We're going to have to tell Yvonne, you know."

Throughout the journey back I felt sick to my bones. I hadn't even accepted it truly myself. I'd just blurted it out in the heat of the moment to save my own skin without so much as thinking about the repercussions of Yvonne knowing. She would now feel some kind of claim on my body, there mere thought of which made me wince. John started the car, and we began the journey back to Filey. We hadn't exchanged words with each other for about thirty minutes. John looked as if it was business as usual, although my heart rate was still going through the roof.

Harry wasn't the kind of person who would go to them for money. He was a financial adviser for a start, and he'd never had a fight in his life. We should have been able to tell each other anything, but for some unknown reason, he was withholding all these financial secrets that he was involved in from his wife. Just meeting the Broadheads was enough to make me terrified of ever returning, but he actually did take money from them. I couldn't fathom what was going through his head when he agreed to that or why he did it in the first place.

"You must know more about Harry," I said.

"Listen, love. You need to let it go. The Broadheads had nothing to do with it."

"Fine. So, tell me what happened."

John stopped the car abruptly next to a farmer's field and turned the engine off. He turned to me with a sigh, obviously weighing up the pros and cons of what he was about to say. I waited patiently.

"Not a word of any of this to Yvonne, deal?" He said.

"Deal."

"Any of it. The meeting went fine, I'm not involved, and they didn't have anything to do with it. No leads."

"Fine."

John sighed and leaned back in the seat slightly, returning eye contact intermittently. I could see he was obviously wrestling with the idea of letting me in on something that he might know.

"Yvonne is going to kill me if I tell you," John reasoned.

"John. Seriously, spit it out," I said.

"Harry had a son."

VIII

THE EMPEROR

HARRY - BEFORE

Steve's face was utterly unrecognisable after the beating he had received from the Broadheads. He barely looked human anymore, and his face was swelled to the point he was struggling to see or breathe. He was producing a wet wheezing sound punctuated by the occasional bloody cough. It took every ounce of my strength to drag him back to the car and get him inside. When I asked the Broadheads for help, they almost turned their knuckles to me. I'd literally never seen anything like it, simply because I'd barely even had a fistfight when I was a kid. Steve seemed bizarrely unperturbed by the whole thing, and he was lying back in the seat like a corpse, only being able to breathe through one nostril. My hands were shaking so much that I could barely get the key in the ignition.

"I'm taking you to the hospital, Steve," I said frantically.

"No, you aren't. Just take me home. I've had worse."

"Steve, you might be in serious trouble here. You need to get seen by someone."

"Take me home," Steve groaned painfully.

I finally managed to get the key in the ignition, and the car started. I immediately peeled out of the warehouse car park like we were running for dear life. We'd got what we came for. After Steve got beaten half to death, the Broadheads and I did a deal, whereby I had all the money I needed. Obviously, after what I'd just witnessed, I would rather have left empty-handed, but I didn't have a choice. I came there to loan some money, and I was either leaving with a bag of cash or leaving in a plastic one with my toes turned up. As bad as Steve's condition was, he didn't seem bothered by it; he was fumbling around in his pockets only to produce a pack of cigarettes and light one. He coughed violently when he took the first drag on it.

"Why did they do that to you?" I asked.

"Fell behind on payments."

"Christ."

"Like I said, I've had worse."

"Why the hell did you suggest we go to them then?"

"I thought bringing them a new customer might have afforded me a bit of flexibility. I was right."

"That was flexibility?"

"Yes. If I hadn't brought you, they'd have finished the job."

Every corner I drove around, Steve wailed like a wounded animal. He must have had some broken ribs, to say the least, but he refused to go to the hospital despite my constant protests. We'd finally arrived at the caravan park, and I helped him inside. He collapsed on the couch on a pile of takeaway food containers. I couldn't believe the sordid life Steve was leading and how little he had told me of it. We used to be best mates growing up, but I'd moved on with my life, and Steve never really did. I felt sorry for him; he was obviously in a bad way and needed help, but I wasn't in any position to give it to him.

"Do you need me to stay?" I asked.

"No mate, you get off. And it goes without saying, make sure you pay them back. And quick."

"I will."

I felt bad leaving Steve alone in such condition, but he was adamant he didn't need any help and could fend for himself. I couldn't help but wonder what I had just got myself into. It started off innocent enough, I suppose. I just wanted to please my wife. But now, I owed a significant amount of money to some unbelievably bad people, and to make anyone's blood run cold, I'd also just gained first-hand experience on what happens when payments aren't kept up with. I took the bag out of Steve's car and placed it in mine. I tried to focus on the few positives and entirely ignore the overwhelming negatives of what I'd just got involved in. I took out my phone before I set off and sent Amelia a text.

> *Setting off back now. Steve sorted. I love you. H*

> *Hurry! I miss you. X*

I missed Amelia, too, but I seeing her now was out of the question. I looked at myself in the rear-view mirror, and all the colour had drained from my face, apart from the occasional splatter of Steve's blood. I franticly rummaged around in my car for something to wipe the blood away with and stumbled upon a cloth. The bag from the Broadheads was sitting in my back seat, almost bulging at the seams from the amount of cash that had been stuffed into it. Part of me wanted to take it back and put an end to this whole nightmare, but there was a chance I would emerge from this whole situation physically and financially unscathed, so I decided to throw caution to the wind and take the calculated risk.

I made a pit stop at my mother's house on my way home. I just couldn't go back to the flat carrying my ill-gotten gains, which is why I'd have to stash it elsewhere. I just hoped against hope that my mother wasn't in or was already too plastered to notice I'd walked in. Unfortunately, I could see the familiar haze of tobacco smoke drifting from the back door as I pulled into the driveway.

"All right?" I asked.

"What're you doing here?" She replied.

"Just need to leave something here. Birthday present for Ames. John in?"

"No, he's at work."

"Fine."

"I've been meaning to speak with you, actually," she said.

Here it comes, I thought.

She had developed an annoying habit of cornering me when I was on my own. It was usually when she wanted to say something negative about Amelia or give me unsolicited advice. I tilted my head slightly and blanked my expression, waiting for the inevitable. She never liked my wife, and I made the regrettable decision of letting my mother in on a few disputes we'd had in the past. Nothing major. Ever since I made those admissions to her, she had been nagging me to leave Amelia by voicing an outright critique of my choice of women or bombarding me with irritating questions about our woes on conceiving a child.

"Are you sure it's a good idea for you to be moving to Manchester?" She asked.

"Yes. My wife and I are moving to Manchester. We're going to start a family. I've gone over this."

"No news on the family front, then?"

"Not yet."

"Well, there's still time to reconsider the move then. It'll help to have family close when the baby comes."

"I think it's the opposite," I whispered wittily.

"Sorry?"

"Nothing. Listen, I can't stay, but I'll be nipping back up in a few weeks anyway."

"Fine. Make sure you get your mail redirected. There is a pile of it on the kitchen counter," Mother said, flicking her finished cigarette aimlessly into the garden.

Ever since Dad died, that had been the extent of our relationship, which limited itself to a few passing comments on my way home from Filey. Truthfully, I didn't know how I felt about it. I definitely wasn't sad; we'd never been close, and the only person keeping our dysfunctional family together was Dad. After he was gone, I tried to keep contact to a bare minimum. It was best for everybody that way.

I went inside the house and walked upstairs into my old room. It was perfectly preserved in its adolescent state, almost hermetically sealed once I'd left for Manchester. I took out some of the drawers to find my old stashing place and carefully piled the cash into the cavity underneath. I crept back downstairs, not eager to be confronted with another forced conversation with

Mother, and noticed the pile of letters waiting for me on the counter. I swiped them all up and made my way back to the car.

There were a few phone bills. I really needed to get that switched over. The rest was all just junk mail, but the final envelope was missing a stamp, which made me realise it had been delivered by hand. It simply had my name written on the front. I opened it, and inside, there was a selection of photographs of people I didn't know, with the exception of the final photograph, which was of me and some random woman, taken about a decade earlier. 'Becky and Harry, Manchester' was written in pencil on the reverse. I checked the envelope again, and a single piece of lined paper fell out of it. It was a letter, which was addressed to me.

Harry,

You won't remember me, but we met on a night out in Manchester ten years ago. I only knew your first name and where you were from. I found you, but I was too scared to get in touch. I've enclosed some photographs of Joshua. He's your son.

I know this come as a shock to you, but he's started asking questions about his dad and wants you to be a part of his life. I'm sorry I didn't get in touch sooner; I just didn't know what to say. I never expected anything from you, so I thought I'd spare myself the disappointment.

We live in Manchester; I've written my address on the back of this letter.

Becky.

My hand was trembling, and truthfully, I didn't know how to feel. It was somewhere in between wanting to hand out cigars and running for the hills. A son, though. He would be about ten years old. I'd spent so long wanting children, only to find out that I already had one in this world was mind-blowing. Shamefully, I didn't have a clue who Becky was, and the enclosed photograph didn't help jog my memory either. I had no idea how many women I'd slept with during university, and to be honest, I'd always thought I was lucky not to have received news like this sooner. I leafed through the photographs aimlessly. I needed to meet this woman and my son. I had to, didn't I? The letter wasn't exactly forceful; it was more of an invitation than a demand. I couldn't make sense of my own emotions, flitting between excitement and joy to abject terror and dread. But I had to act on the news. There was no debate there.

The sheer magnitude of the news made me forget about Amelia for a few minutes. This news would certainly devastate her. Not because I was unfaithful; this happened way before we'd met. However, I knew how she would see it. She was always so paranoid about me cheating on her, and in one way or another, she would manage to find a way to see red about this. Considering how much we were struggling to have children of our own, the fact that I had a son would only come to add insult to injury. I could conjure up images of the rage on her face if I told her, and I just couldn't do it. I hated lying to Amelia, but I had to keep it under wraps for the time being, knowing that I'd have to confess it all eventually. There wasn't a suitable time to tell her the truth, but hopefully, it would be more palatable once we were expecting a child of our own.

I started the journey back home, but the letter was obviously preying heavily on my mind. I decided to make a detour and I put Becky's address into the sat-nav. I didn't have any specific motives, all I wanted was to see where they were living. It was the strangest drive I'd ever taken. It was as if I'd clicked my fingers, and *voilà*, I was a father all of a sudden. I promised myself I'd just take a quick look and then go straight home to Amelia.

I arrived in Manchester. Becky lived on a council estate just outside of the city centre, and it seemed a little rough. I locked my doors and parked further down the street from the address. I had no idea what the plan was; I just sat there, waiting for some sign of life. I leafed through the photographs again, hoping to spot anyone featured in them. My phone started ringing, it was Amelia.

"Hi, love," I answered.

"Harry, where are you?" Amelia asked abruptly

"Yeah, sorry, I hit some traffic on the motorway. I needed fuel, so I just went to the service station."

"Well, hurry up! I miss you," Amelia joked.

"I'll get there as soon as I can. Do you need any—"

I am interrupted by a loud tapping on the driver's window. Because of the angle, I couldn't see who was outside, but it looked like a woman.

"Sorry, Ames, I've got to go. I think I'm blocking someone in. I love you," I fibbed.

"Drive safe! I love—" Amelia was interrupted as I hung up on her hastily.

I stepped out of the car, and the woman from the photographs, Becky, stood sheepishly a few metres away from the car. I was still clutching the photographs, and she stood there staring at me, clearly feeling very uneasy. She looked different to the pictures I'd seen; she was older, and she had her blonde hair scraped back in a ponytail. She was wearing an ill-fitting grey hoodie and jeans, covered in stains and marks. I had no idea what to say to this woman, but she seemed even more nervous than I was.

"Becky?" I asked.

"Yes. Sorry, I was walking past, and I thought I recognised you," she replied.

"It's okay. I'm sorry, I've never been in this situation before. I don't really know what to say."

"You don't have to apologise. It's my fault for not trying to find you sooner. I was starting to think you had ignored the letter, though."

"No, I don't live in Filey anymore. You actually sent the letter to my mother's house."

"Where are you living now?"

"Here, well, in the city centre."

"Fancy. Good job?"

"Reasonably," I shrugged.

"Married?"

"A few months ago."

"Kids?"

"Not yet," I smiled.

"Listen, do you want to come in for a cup of tea or something? Joshua isn't here. He's at his friend's house."

This was all moving way too fast; I was comfortable observing from a distance, but actually going in the house felt like a step too far. What would Amelia think if she knew I was here? My instant reaction was to just say no and leave, but I felt sorry for her. She was clearly struggling for money whilst raising a child on her own. My child. And even though, up until a few hours ago, I was unaware of his existence; I felt like I owed her an explanation and some kind of apology.

"Sure," I smiled.

We walked towards Becky's house through the front garden where she unlocked the door and led us inside. The house itself was a bit of a mess, with toys strewn across the floor and clothes desperately trying to dry on the cold radiators. She walked straight into the kitchen, and I followed her, sitting at the small dining table. She put the kettle on, turned around and leant on the kitchen counter.

"How old's Joshua?" I asked.

"He's ten in February," she smiled.

"Wow. Ten years old. Sorry, this is all shockingly new to me."

"It's fine, honestly."

The kettle had boiled, but Becky didn't take any further steps to produce a cup of tea. She simply continued staring at me with a weak smile.

"What is it?" I asked.

"You've just changed so much. Did you remember me?" She smirked.

"Of course," I lied.

"That's a fancy car you are driving. What do you do for a living?"

"I'm a financial adviser. But I'm moving into investments soon."

"I always knew you would do well for yourself."

"Thank you," I replied awkwardly.

It's the most bizarre feeling when someone knows who you are, but you don't have a clue who they are. I wished I could remember a single detail about her life so I could ask her, but I was unable to. I felt so guilty; I'd been living my life carefree, and she'd clearly been struggling for a while. She seemed very happy to see me, though, so I must have made a good impression all those years ago.

"So," I smiled, "Joshua."

"He doesn't want much. He just wants to know who his dad is, that's all."

"I understand that."

"Can I take your phone number? Just so we can arrange a time to meet. If you want to, of course."

"Of course, I want to meet him."

I impulsively got my phone out and slid it across the table towards Becky, and she put my phone number on her phone. She returned it to me with a smile, and it buzzed on the table as she sent me a text message, so I had her number, too. It immediately felt like a mistake. She could contact me whenever she wanted once she had my number. The only thing worse than me telling Amelia about this would be her finding out by accident.

"This is a little awkward," I started, "but my wife, Amelia, doesn't know about Joshua yet, so could you keep contact to a minimum until I've told her?"

"Of course. I totally understand."

"I think the news will upset her, so I just need to find the right way of telling her."

"Why would she be upset?" Becky asked, stepping forward from the kitchen counter with her arms folded.

"Well, to be honest with you, we have been trying to conceive, but haven't had much luck. I just don't want her to have another setback."

"Setback? Did you just describe Joshua as a setback?" Becky said venomously.

"No, I didn't mean it like that. We've just been struggling so much with everything."

"Well, if that's what you think of him, you can just forget the whole thing."

"Becky, honestly, I didn't mean it like that. When the time is right, I will tell her. But not right now. I can't."

"Get out," she pointed.

"I'm sorry," I said, standing from my chair, "I'll be in touch, I promise."

"Out!" She shouted.

I walked out of the front door, and I heard Becky slam it behind me. I regretted what I'd said, and I tried to say it as delicately as possible, but it was what it was: the truth. This would break Amelia, and she would see it as if I'd been lying to her when, in reality, I was completely unaware, too. If Amelia's paranoia took hold, there would be no telling what she would do. She was already at breaking point, and I just wanted to spare us the heartache. I didn't know Becky, and to be honest, deep down, I didn't think I owed her anything. I felt bad for Joshua, but I meant what I said: once things had settled down between Amelia and me, I would be in touch. I got back in the car and made my way home, and Amelia was waiting for me in the flat.

"Bad traffic?" Amelia shouted from the kitchen.

"Nightmare," I replied.

"We didn't have much in for dinner, and I found a lasagne in the freezer."

"Fine," I shouted back.

My phone vibrated in my pocket; I unlocked it. It was a text message from an unsaved number.

> £10k. Or Joshua and I will pay Amelia a visit. Bring it by the house tomorrow by 12 pm.

I reread the text message multiple times before it even started to sink in. In the space of an hour, I'd gone from being a new father to being blackmailed. Things had taken a very sinister turn. Maybe she never intended for Joshua and me to have a relationship, and this was the entire plan all along. She saw my car, asked her questions, and decided she could get some money from me. Becky was clearly struggling financially, and if she had just explained her situation and asked, I would probably have granted her request. She had been raising my child for years with no help from me, after all.

It did occur to me that I didn't even know whether Joshua was mine or not, but in reality, it didn't matter. Even if Amelia found out there was a hint of me having an illegitimate child, all hell would break loose. I panicked at first, but then when I realised that she barely knew who I was, she only had my first name, mother's address, and my phone number, there wasn't much damage she could do with that. I just had to contain this for at least a couple of months until I'd paid back the Broadheads. I heard Amelia making her way into the sitting room, and I quickly placed my phone back in my pocket. I felt it vibrate again as she started plating up the lasagne at the dining table. I went over to join her, brandishing the most realistic smile I could muster.

"I made an appointment at the clinic, by the way," she said.

"Oh, that's great news. When?"

"The initial consultation is Tuesday, then we go from there."

"Do you have any idea how much it costs?"

"No, I didn't ask. We can find out on Tuesday. Is there a problem?"

"No problem," I lied, "just asking, that's all."

"I'm so nervous about it," she said as I could feel my phone vibrating constantly in my pocket.

"Sorry, Ames, I just need to visit the little boy's room," I announced, standing from my seat.

I went into the bathroom and locked the door. Becky had left me three missed calls and sent two picture messages; one was a screenshot of our address she had found online using my phone number, and the second was a screenshot from Amelia's social media account. I had no other choice but to concede, and I hoped this was the first and last time she would try this.

> *You will get your money.*
> *Please, don't contact her.*

IX

TEMPERANCE

AMELIA

Take me back to the Broadheads, I thought. I'd hand him the tyre wrench myself. I felt like I'd been punched in the throat. It was closing up further every second I continued to process what I'd just heard: Harry had a secret son.

John, looking uncharacteristically uneasy, waited for my response. I didn't give him one. I repeatedly and aggressively tugged at the passenger door handle until John finally unlocked it. I left the car and started stumbling clumsily in a straight line into the field he'd parked up next to. I dropped to my knees in the dirt and muck, digging my fingernails into the loose soil as deeply as I could. I screamed at the top of my lungs and started to beat the ground with my fists. The unanswered questions spread in me like a virus, multiplying exponentially until my head was almost at bursting point. I started this journey because I wanted to find out what had happened to Harry that night, and I'd been blindsided at every turn. The man I had married, the man I loved, was a question mark, an unsolvable, cruel riddle leaving me a breadcrumb trail of sadness and shame from beyond the grave.

It all felt like a savage wind-up. Harry had been all supportive when I couldn't have children naturally, but the entire time, he was concealing the existence of an illegitimate son from me. I was still screaming; I just couldn't understand what I'd done in my life to deserve to be treated this way. As pieces of information go, it was cataclysmic, but I didn't understand what it had to do with his death. Did Harry find out about his son and then intend to take his own life out of guilt? Out of shame? I knew I wouldn't have reacted well, but he could have found a way of telling me.

I never expected to be here in this field, probably covered in horse manure, ploughing the ground with my bare hands. I found myself starting to curse Harry for putting me in this position. I didn't have a clue who he was anymore, and I couldn't decide if I wanted to find out anything else. Every small piece of information I revealed came with hundreds more questions attached, and I couldn't bear it any longer.

I could feel that my heart rate had increased, and I'd started sweating. As soon as I became aware of it, a single thought popped into my head that it could very well be the start of a panic attack. The suggestion alone was enough to induce it, and I started scouring my bag for the pills before it took hold. My hands had already started going numb which didn't make it easier, as they were transferring the filth I'd been touching to my bag. I had to rapidly inhale and exhale to keep the oxygen flowing, and I could feel the dizziness coming on. I found the tablets and shakily threw them down my throat with my soiled hands.

I'd just caught it in time, and once the attack started to recede, I'd noticed that John had left the car too and was standing behind me, waiting for me to get back up. When I turned to look at him, I could see the concern and the regret he felt for telling me anything. He was awkwardly rubbing his hands together, waiting for me to speak.

"Who was she?" I asked.

"A lass named Becky. She lives in Manchester. The lad is called Joshua, and he's about ten years old. Yvonne knows more than I do," he explained.

"Why didn't Yvonne tell me? Why did Harry keep me in the dark about it?"

"He only found out shortly before he died. We only found out by accident. She'd sent a letter to the house."

"What was he planning to do? Leave me for this, Becky?"

"Honestly, love, I've no idea. Come on, let's go back, and you can speak to Yvonne."

John was once again leading me to the car by my arm, but much more delicately this time. I couldn't believe Harry had kept me ignorant of his secret parenthood. I didn't know if I was misremembering it, but I thought we had the kind of marriage where we could tell each other anything. If he hadn't been unfaithful like I initially thought, and his son was ten years old, it happened way before we met. It didn't make me feel any differently, though. If he felt the need to conceal it, I needed to know why. I couldn't help but think he was planning to leave me for this woman when we started struggling to conceive.

And John and Yvonne knew they had no intention of ever telling me. John only told me so I would stop pursuing the Broadheads and save his own skin. I didn't speak a word to John during the entire journey back; he didn't deserve to be entertained with my civility. I was done. Done with this entire family. I didn't want or need their help or their sympathy. All I ever wanted was to finally find out what kind of a man Harry was and what had happened to him. Was that too much to ask? We pulled up outside Yvonne's house, and John cut the engine and turned to look at me again with a huff. I could tell he was almost nervous about us going inside.

"Remember the deal. Not a word of the Broadheads or what I've been up to. Yvonne needs to stay in the dark about all that."

"I remember John," I insisted.

We walked inside together, and Yvonne looked eager to find out what had happened on our little field trip.

"Well? How did it go? Did you find anything out?" Yvonne asked.

"So," I started, sitting down at the kitchen island, "when were you going to tell me about Harry's son?"

All the colour had drained from Yvonne's face, and she turned to John, who was awkwardly looking in another direction. She knew that she had been exposed. She had ample opportunity to tell me about this before and after Harry died, but she chose not to.

"How did you find out?" She murmured.

"John," I said.

"John?" Yvonne shouted.

"She was upset; the Broadheads were a dead end, and it explains why he did what he did, doesn't it?" John replied.

"Explains why he did what?" I asked sternly.

"Stepped off the Brigg," John said matter-of-factly.

"He didn't kill himself! Is that what you think, Yvonne?" I shouted.

"I don't know what to think," she mumbled solemnly.

I ran upstairs to collect my things. I wasn't about to stay in that house a moment longer than I needed to; it was filled with liars and snakes. I walked into Harry's old room, and I wanted to smash the place up. The walls were littered with pictures of him and his achievements, and the very smile I fell in love with was featured in every single photo. I wanted to rip them all off the walls and tear everything down. I collapsed on the bed, sobbing until I heard my phone beep.

> *Amelia, I sense you are getting closer to the truth. Seek out the woman. She can point you in the right direction.*

> *If you are so psychic, why didn't you tell me about this? Why can't you just put me out of my misery?*

> *The path makes itself clear, one step at a time. I only see the direction, not the destination.*

> *Did he love her?*

> *It was a fleeting encounter long before you met. Put your energy into finding this woman. She will point you further.*

James' message was actually quite comforting. As annoying as his style of writing was, he did have a knack for saying exactly what I needed to hear. I started to feel like I could rely on someone for the first time since Harry had died. It did feel slightly pathetic that it was a clairvoyant man I'd never met, but beggars can't be choosers. My sobbing ceased, and I continued packing my things away. James' words didn't change anything, and I still needed to get out of that house.

Yvonne entered the room, and I couldn't even make eye contact with her without clenching my jaw. I started to aggressively pack my things away, totally ignoring her presence. She remained standing in the room, waiting for me to speak, but I was far more stubborn than her.

"John has just told me. You're pregnant?" Yvonne asked.

"Yes. And if you think you are having anything to do with it, you are mistaken," I warned.

"It's my grandchild, Amelia."

"Not your first grandchild, though, is it?"

"I was going to tell you," Yvonne began, sitting on the end of Harry's bed, "I just didn't know how. I hadn't even spoken to Harry about it. I found out by accident."

"Who was she?"

"They met on a night out at university. It was just a one-night thing. She got pregnant and didn't know how to get in touch with him."

"Is that why he had a second mobile phone? For his other family?"

"I don't know, love. But he didn't cheat on you, and Joshua was an accident from ten years ago."

The whole thing made my skin crawl. When I was losing my mind because we couldn't conceive a child, he was speaking to some tart he met at university about their son. Even though I didn't want to, I kept picturing them together as a family, living the life I wanted. I knew I was getting carried away with myself, but if I wanted the truth, I'd have to find her and ask her myself.

"One more thing, love," Yvonne started, "about the drinking, are you going to stop now?"

The brass-necked, unbelievable cheek of it.

"Are you for real?" I laughed.

"It's bad for the baby."

"I've just lost my husband. And you are the last person I would accept a lecture from about drink."

"I'm just saying, that's all."

It couldn't have been more obvious if Yvonne was holding a little flag ready to plant directly into my stomach. She was already making a claim on my body and my child, just like I knew she would. But I meant what I said. If I had my way, that woman would never even meet this child. Part of me thought that Harry would also actually approve of that course of action. She had already messed her own kids up, and she wasn't going to be involved with mine.

"Did this Becky leave an address with the letter?" I asked.

"Not that I saw," she replied.

"Harry must have kept it somewhere."

"Amelia," Yvonne said, putting her hand on my knee, "just leave this alone. You need to relax. You don't want to put too much stress on the baby."

"I need to know what was going on."

"I know, but this will only end badly."

I zipped up my packed bag and left Yvonne sitting on the edge of Harry's bed, staring into space. I didn't care about Yvonne's opinion on the matter. I lost Harry at the height of our love, and I deserved answers. Being pregnant didn't affect that. John gave me a nod as I walked through the kitchen. I wished I'd dropped him in it with Yvonne as a parting gift, but I didn't have the energy.

I drove straight home; there must have been something in that house with Becky's address on it. I doubt he would have kept the letter that was sent, but he must have scribbled it down somewhere. Harry was the most organised person I'd ever met, and he kept diligent notes about everything; it was engrained in him from his work. I cradled my stomach protectively as I sped down the motorway towards home. As much as Yvonne's words didn't matter to me, I couldn't help but dwell on what she'd said. Who knew what damage I'd already done to the baby with the drink and the anti-depressants I was taking? I had been waiting for these fabled parental instincts to kick in, but I must have been born without them. I'd only found out I was pregnant after Harry had died, and to be honest, I was so numb about the whole thing that I didn't believe it myself. We'd gone through so many failed attempts and early miscarriages that I didn't think I'd get to full term this time either.

I felt like the entire world was against me. The list of people I could trust was growing shorter by the day. I always knew I couldn't trust Yvonne and John, but I never thought they would keep something so important from me; they knew how it would affect me. Steve probably also knew about Harry's son, and it's what he was going to tell me the night he died, along with the Broadhead ballad. It was my own fault, really. I'd never had time for anybody else; I was just so wrapped up in our marriage. And with Harry gone, I was quite literally alone.

I finally got home; it wasn't the first time that I had destroyed the entire house looking for something. But I must have missed it, a clue, a tiny scrap of paper that looked irrelevant at the time but now would hold significant value. I emptied every single drawer onto the floor, and I even looked between each book in the bookcase. Nothing. I sat on the kitchen floor, surrounded by the sheer carnage I'd just inflicted on the house, and none of it could help me. As a final attempt at finding it, I decided to text James.

> *I can't find her address.*
> *Is it here, somewhere?*

> *Remember, you are walking a path once travelled by Harry.*

As cryptic as James' message was, I knew exactly what he was getting at. Harry had an awful sense of direction and always used his sat-nav religiously. The police gave it back along with all the belongings from his car once they'd catalogued everything. They sat underneath the stairs in a clear bag that I hadn't had the courage to go through yet. I opened the cupboard door, and I could already see it through the plastic. I quickly ripped it out of the bag and turned it on. I recognised most of the addresses on there, but one stood out.

Once I was only a few minutes out, it became apparent how rough the area was. I locked the doors instinctively; youths littered the street corners with their hoods up, smoking and drinking with no regard for the people who lived there. I pulled up outside the address, and it was an unremarkable house, the same as the other fifty houses on either side of it. There was a child's bike left there to rust in the garden. I didn't feel safe here, but it couldn't have been worse than coming face-to-face with the Broadheads. I made my way up the garden path, and I saw the curtains twitching. She knew I was there. I knocked on the door politely at first, but when no one came for a few minutes, my knock got progressively louder. I just needed to gain entry, and I'd decide later how I was going to deal with this based on her answers to my questions.

"I know you are in there; I saw the curtains moving," I shouted through the letterbox.

The door remained locked. I pounded on the door as hard as I could.

"Becky, I just want to talk. Please," I said through the letterbox, "Harry's dead. And I just want to know what kind of man he was. I don't blame you," I shouted.

All at once, the emotions of the day and the constant banging on the door got to me, and I slumped down with the door against my back. I was so tired of it, sick of not getting anywhere. I started sobbing and banging my head against the door. I heard the door unlocking slowly behind me, and I stood up to greet whoever was behind.

A woman answered the door, but she wasn't what I had expected. She had greasy blonde hair scraped back in a ponytail, and she was wearing pyjamas and slippers. In her right hand, she was clutching a rolling pin, brandishing it as some kind of weapon. It was incredibly shallow of me, but I instantly felt better. There was no way Harry would have left me for her.

"You aren't going to need that, Becky. I just want to talk," I said softly.

"Harry's dead?" She asked.

"Yes. Three weeks ago. He fell off Filey Brigg."

"Did he tell you about Joshua?"

"No. But I've found out since. Can I come in?"

Becky beckoned me inside. I walked in cautiously, and she placed the rolling pin on the table beside the front door, which put me at ease slightly. Toys and clothes were absolutely everywhere, but there was a narrow walkway through the hall into the kitchen, clearly made by Becky sweeping the objects littering the floor to one side. Maybe my parental instincts were kicking in because I felt sorry for her instead of turning my nose up at her. She sat down at the dining table in the kitchen, and I sat facing her; she was fidgeting with a small toy soldier she had picked up, choosing to look down rather than in my eyes.

"So, what was going on with you and my husband?" I asked.

"Nothing. It wasn't like that," she replied.

"So, why was he here?"

"I told him Joshua wanted to meet his dad."

"Did he meet him?"

"No."

"Why not?"

"Because he didn't want you finding out. He said you were trying to conceive, and it would upset you."

"He wasn't wrong. But he could have told me."

Becky stood up and started pacing the kitchen. She started breathing rapidly and out of nowhere. I instantly recognised the signs; she was a few steps away from a full-blown panic attack.

"I would have never got involved if I knew it was going to end like that. I just needed the money, that's all.

I'm sick of the threats, and the phone calls, and I just want her to leave me alone."

"Who?"

"Yvonne."

"What's Yvonne got to do with this?"

"She's the one who put me up to it. To get in touch with Harry."

"She encouraged you to find Joshua's father?"

"No, you don't understand. Harry isn't Joshua's father."

"What do you mean, Joshua isn't Harry's son?"

"Yvonne paid me to tell him he was."

"What? Why would she do that?"

"I don't know. But I was desperate."

"How did you even meet her?"

"I did meet Harry at university on a night out. She found the photograph of us both and tracked me down on social media."

The admission gave me an almost instant headache, and I could feel the table creak and crack under the sheer pressure I was putting on it with my hands. My instant impulse was to pick it up and throw it at her, but she looked terrified, dragged into this mess by my spiteful mother-in-law. If Harry had chosen to step off the Brigg, this could have been one of the contributing factors, and I couldn't take it. Tears started to form in my eyes, not of sadness, but of pure, unadulterated rage that Becky had somehow slinked her way into my family and was poisoning it from within. Becky must have been telling the truth, though. There was no way she would start lying when she was clearly so terrified of me.

Yvonne was as much to blame. She always hated me, but I never thought she would go this far. I never put her down as the scheming type, more the sniping from the gutters type. Becky had been trapped in Yvonne's web as much as I had, and as furious as I was, she was a victim in this, too.

"I'm not going to hurt you, Becky. Just calm down," I began softly, "when was the last time you had contact with her?"

"An hour ago."

"I assume she was warning you I might be coming here?"

"Yes. She offered me more money to keep quiet, but I can't take the lies anymore."

"Good. When I've gone, you are going to ring her back and tell her you've thrown me off the scent. Take the money if you want to."

"Amelia, I really don't want to be involved—"

"Well, you are involved," I reviled, raising my voice, "and if you don't want the police involved with you, I suggest you do what I say."

Becky broke down immediately, sobbing into her hands. I did feel a sting of guilt as I walked through the front door, but she knew she was playing with fire when she accepted Yvonne's assignment. I just needed to be a step ahead of Yvonne; she was clearly gunning for me.

I had to take a leaf out of her book. Smile to her face, but hold a knife to her back.

X

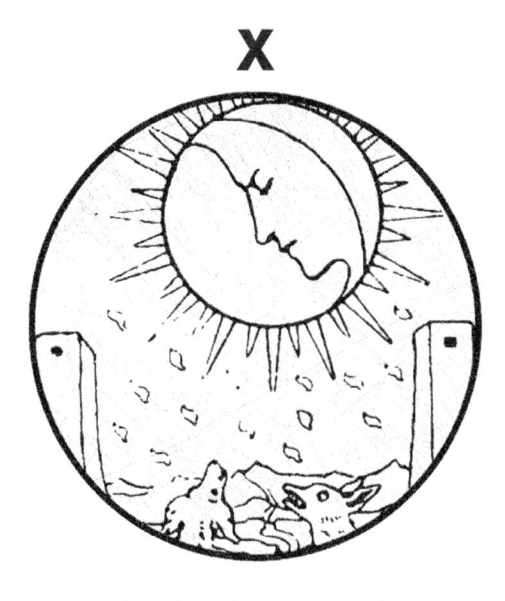

THE MOON

AMELIA

For the first time, probably ever, I was actually excited to go back to Filey. Because I had Yvonne exactly where I wanted her. She was bang to rights. I had evidence that she was manipulating everything from the shadows, and she'd been doing it long before Harry died. I needed to speak to Poppy; she had first-hand experience dealing with Yvonne's manipulation. I felt like I was finally ahead of the game, and I was making progress. I was still disappointed in

Harry for not coming to me himself with the truth, but I understood why he didn't. I did tend to fly off the handle, sometimes at the slightest thing, and this would have been as good a reason as any. I was disappointed that I clearly wasn't the kind of wife that her husband could tell absolutely anything to, and I'd always thought Harry was an open book, but that was just what he wanted me to believe. And I did, for the longest time.

I hated how Harry had been tricked by Becky; he died thinking he was concealing a dark secret from me, and my heart broke for him. His mother could have spared him the pain, but she chose not to, just so she could play her little games. I didn't understand why she would go to such lengths to try and split us up; as far as I was concerned, I hadn't done anything to her. She made the decision a long time ago that she didn't like me and viciously held onto that opinion for the rest of our relationship. Part of me was of the opinion that she thought I was some kind of rival. She seemed to always fight for Harry's attention with me, and from what Harry had said, Yvonne always seemed to prefer him to Poppy. But because Harry was so distant from her, she felt more of a need to seek constant reassurance from him that she wasn't a terrible mother.

I was torn between driving straight to Yvonne's house to confront her head-on or getting Poppy on my side before I did. Josephine, Poppy's wife, never seemed to have any trouble with her mother-in-law. Yvonne just accepted they were in love and left them to it, or so it seemed to me. I frequently racked my brain to try and work out why Yvonne hated me, but I could never understand why. Harry would just laugh whenever I asked him and said it was just what she was like.

Poppy and Josephine lived in a newly built housing estate in the neighbouring town of Gristhorpe. Even though it was only a few minutes away from Filey, I always thought it was just enough space to keep Yvonne from intervening in their lives. Then again, it didn't stop her from getting involved in my marriage, and we lived three hours away. In the previous few months, I'd felt more of an affinity for Poppy; they were trying to conceive, too, and had gone through all the same process we did. From what Harry had said, they were also struggling with it all and had exhausted their funded IVF attempts. Neither of them had a great job, so they had to save up for months for every attempt. Poppy worked from home, selling jewellery online.

Even before Harry's death, I envied their life slightly; it just seemed so simple and easy-going. They never seemed to argue or have disagreements. It was not that Harry and I were locking horns with each other every night; they just always seemed so calm and content with their lives. Harry and I always seemed to be striving for something or planning ahead, but they were happy to just casually live in the moment. They didn't even seem upset about their failed IVF attempts. If I were in their shoes, I would have driven myself insane, and I probably did.

I pulled up to their house, and I could see Poppy diligently crafting in the window. Her face lit up when she saw me, and she waved furiously as I pulled onto the drive. I really liked Poppy, but she was a bit much sometimes. She radiated positivity and mindfulness, which was the complete opposite of how I was feeling. I'd avoided her purposefully since the funeral; I couldn't stand being around someone with such radiant positivity when I felt like I did. I got out of my car and knocked on the door. Within half a second, it was thrown open, and Poppy was standing there with a beaming smile.

"Amelia! Come in!" she said.

"Thank you. How are you?" I asked, walking through the front door.

"Amazing, thank you. Mum has told me the fantastic news: how far along are you?"

"Only about six weeks, I think."

"How are you feeling about it all?"

I knew the answer; I just didn't want to tell her. Mortified was probably the most apt description. If Harry was still here, I would have been ecstatic, but instead, I felt like I was staring down the barrel of a shotgun. I tried not to think about the pregnancy too much. Every time I did, I just felt overwhelming dread. I could barely look after myself, let alone a child. I knew that if I told her all that, it would upset her. So, I decided the easiest thing to do would be to smile, ignore the question entirely, and move the conversation on to why I was there.

"So, I know about Harry's son," I announced.

"Oh. Come in and sit down. I'll put the kettle on," Poppy said.

As I sat down in the living room, I could hear the kettle whistling in the kitchen. The room was filled with photographs of Poppy and Josephine; in every single one, they had beaming smiles on their faces. You could tell just by glancing at them that they were undeniably happy. In the corner there was a pile of boxes that looked like baby supplies, boxes of wipes and nappies. I didn't understand how they could remain so positive after suffering as much heartache as we had. I used to turn the TV channel over if there was an advert even vaguely related to babies or pregnancy. Nevertheless, they were content with it, just staring at them in the face. Poppy returned with the tea and sat down on the couch opposite.

"So, Joshua," Poppy began, taking a sip of her tea, "how did you find out?"

"John told me," I said.

"I hope you don't think we were keeping it from you. It just seemed cruel to bring it up after Harry had passed."

"I understand, I do."

"I don't even think Harry had managed to meet Joshua. They were building up to a first meeting."

I knew it. I couldn't hold back the smile. Yvonne had kept this to herself, and she hadn't even told Poppy. At least Poppy wasn't involved in the scheme to try and split us up. If Yvonne had been hiding this from me, there was no telling what else she was keeping from me. I had Yvonne exactly where I wanted her; I just needed to get Poppy on my side so I could unravel this mess. From what Harry had said, I didn't think Poppy would take much convincing either. I felt like this whole thing was a distraction from the actual task at hand, but Yvonne deserved to face the consequences for what she'd done. If Harry did take his own life, then this mess would have been a very plausible explanation as to why. And I'd take great pleasure in telling Yvonne that if it were proven true.

"Joshua isn't Harry's son. Yvonne made it up," I announced.

"What?" Poppy gasped, leaning forward on the couch.

"It was some elaborate plot to try and split us up. Yvonne tracked down this woman from Harry's past and paid her to say Joshua was his son."

"She wouldn't go that far, surely?" Poppy responded.

"Yeah, she would. And she did. I've spoken to Joshua's mother."

Poppy sat back on the couch with a sigh, "I never thought she was capable of something like that."

"Me either," I lied.

"What about all the money Harry gave to her?"

"What money?"

"That Becky was asking for. Harry gave her some money for Joshua."

"How much?"

"I'm not sure, but it was a lot. He was really stressed about it because you were buying the house at the same time."

Well, Becky had never mentioned that. She must have seen Harry as a pay day. Not only was she taking Yvonne's money for agreeing to do it in the first place, but she was also making some on the side from Harry. I regretted not putting her head through that kitchen table. To think I actually felt sorry for her. My list of enemies was rapidly growing by the day, but I'd deal with her later.

"So, is that why everyone is saying his death was suspicious?" I asked.

"Suspicious? How so?" Poppy said, looking confused.

"Everyone I've spoken to seems to think he jumped off the Brigg."

"Do you think he jumped?" she asked.

I didn't know what to think. If Harry did step off the Brigg, they were to blame. All of them. He was being blackmailed by Becky, hounded by loan sharks, and even his own mother was trying to manipulate him. Harry was always sensitive; it was one of the reasons that attracted me to him in the first place. I'd realised how much pressure was actually being thrust upon his shoulders. Everybody that I'd spoken to ended up confessing they thought Harry killed himself. Aside from me, Poppy was the person closest to Harry; if she thought Harry did away with himself, then I'd start believing it.

"I don't know. Do you?" I asked.

All the colour drained from Poppy's face, and she took a sharp inhale. She didn't even have to respond to my question. Her eyes said it all. "Yes," she said.

"But why would he do that? We had everything going for us," I asked.

"I can't imagine the pressure he was under. None of us can."

"Why couldn't he just speak to me about it though?"

"I don't know, Amelia," Poppy said sullenly.

We sat in silence for a few moments in quiet reflection. The thought of Harry choosing to end his life filled me with bitter fury. I'd chosen to believe that his death was an unfortunate accident, but the more I spoke to the people in his life and the more evidence I uncovered, the more it felt like he might have actually jumped. Poppy started to look awkward and kept giving me pitying looks whenever we made eye contact. My phone beeped and vibrated in my pocket. It was a text from James.

> *Remember the man Harry was. It will lead you to the truth.*

I scrunched up my face when I received the text, and Poppy looked at me eagerly, waiting for me to explain it.

"Sorry, Poppy. James has just texted me," I said.

"Oh, are you still in contact?"

"Yes, he's been helping me get to the truth about Harry."

"James is so gifted. You won't go far wrong following his advice."

"It's not advice, as such. It's mostly riddles. I can barely understand what he's trying to say most of the time. Have you actually met him in person?"

I asked the question innocently enough, but Poppy looked almost embarrassed by it. It hadn't occurred to me that people could get addicted to this kind of thing, and Poppy was definitely the kind of person who would. It's so easy not to make any decisions for yourself when you have your own personal psychic a few taps away. James' motivation to help me wasn't clear either because no money had changed hands between us. I'd always wondered why he was so interested in helping me. It was definitely a macabre hobby.

"Yes, I've met him," Poppy said, "a few times, actually."

"What's he like?" I asked.

"Do you mean does he look psychic?" Poppy joked.

"No, just what is he like as a person."

"He's kind. And he loves helping people. He's helped Josephine and me many times."

"James has never asked me for payment or anything. He just seems content with helping me."

"He's like that. I think he'd charge you for an in-person meeting."

"I'd like to meet him. When all this is over."

"He's incredibly busy. You have to book well in advance."

Poppy picked up her cup of tea, and I did the same. It had gone cold whilst we were talking. I placed it back on the table in front of me and sighed. I couldn't tell whether it was the constant stress I was under or the advancing pregnancy, but I was so tired. I couldn't remember the last time I'd sat down and just had a cup of tea without it ending in tears or screaming. Poppy was in a very calming mood that day; she would usually be constantly at a hundred miles an hour. I think she could sense just how fatigued I was about the whole thing.

"I better get going. I'm off to see the mother-in-law," I announced.

"Do you want me to come with you?"

"It's up to you. It might get ugly."

"Well, I can stop that from happening."

"I might not want you to."

"Amelia, my mother is troubled. I'm not condoning what she has done, but just speak to her before you get angry."

"Fine. You'd better come with me and keep the peace then."

I had one more sip of tepid tea and arose from the couch; we both exited the house and got in my car. On the ten-minute drive to Yvonne's house, Poppy shared even more stories where James was right about something. He seemed to have genuine psychic abilities, and the stories she told me rang true to my own. From what Poppy had described, James just loved helping people, and he had definitely been of assistance to me. I felt a need to thank him properly; if it hadn't been for him, I would have never gone down this road and would have lived the rest of my life in blissful ignorance.

We arrived at Yvonne's house, and for once, the back door was shut. Poppy raced ahead of me on the driveway and tapped on the front door. Yvonne answered, looking as though she had just woken up despite it being midday. I was feeling a mixture of excitement and worry. I wanted to finally unmask Yvonne as the horrible and spiteful woman that she was, but I had no idea how she would react.

"Mum, you look awful!" Poppy jabbed.

"Thanks, love," Yvonne croaked to Poppy. "Hi, Amelia," she said to me through a thin veneer of politeness.

"Good afternoon," I said sarcastically.

"I suppose you all better come in."

I was stunned. The house looked like it had been ransacked. There were smashed glasses and plates thrown all over the floor. We all watched our steps carefully as we made our way through the hallway and into the living room; it seemed to be the least affected by whatever had happened there. Yvonne had dispensed of her no smoking in the house rule and openly lit a cigarette up as she sunk into the sofa.

"What's happened, mum?" Poppy asked.

"John and I had a disagreement, and he didn't come home last night," Yvonne responded.

I didn't give a damn about their petty disputes.

"Anything to do with lies, manipulation, or perhaps blackmail?" I asked wryly.

"So, you visited Becky. Come on then, out with it. Do your worst," Yvonne goaded.

"Why would you do all that to me?" I asked.

"Because, sweetheart, you are a grotesque, vapid woman, and you were never good enough for him."

"All I ever did was love your son. That was my only crime. And you've hated me from the start."

"Not from the very start. But I saw the change in Harry, and I knew it was because of how you treated him. That's when I started hating you.

"She's pathetic," I said to Poppy in a desperate bid to garner some support.

"I'm pathetic? The only way you could keep hold of a man was by isolating him from his friends and his family," Yvonne shouted, pointing in my face.

"Isolating him? What on earth are you talking about?"

"It did feel like that, sometimes," Poppy added.

"So, you agree with her?" I barked.

"Harry and I used to talk almost every day, but as soon as he met you, I barely heard from him," Poppy admitted.

"What has that got to do with me?"

"I don't know, and forgive me if I'm wrong, but it did look as if you were trying to keep him away from his family and friends. We'd always been as close as siblings can be, but as soon as he moved in with you, that changed," Poppy said as diplomatically as she could.

Harry and I were in love. No one could understand how powerful it was. Yvonne and Poppy were making me out to be some kind of monster, keeping Harry locked away in Manchester. They were wrong, and it wasn't like that at all. I'd always treated him with the utmost respect and rightfully expected he would reciprocate. I didn't isolate him at all; I just liked spending time with him, and Manchester was a better place to do so. Not to mention that Harry came to Manchester willingly; it was even where we first met. How dare she throw these accusations around, especially when Harry wasn't here to back me up.

"I loved Harry!" I shouted.

"I'm not saying you didn't," Poppy started, holding her hands up, "but some of the stories he told us—"

"What stories?" I asked.

"The arguments. The horrible things you said to him. And the violence," Yvonne maliciously interjected.

"What violence?"

"He told me about the pills, the alcohol, and the fights, too, Amelia. I just always thought it would resolve itself," Poppy shot from the hip with venom.

"Oh, so now I have a problem with drink and drugs?" I yelled.

"We aren't saying that. He just told me when you'd had a drink, sometimes you got aggressive," Poppy explained.

I'd show them aggressive, I thought. Poppy was lying outright to hurt me or, at the very least, misconstruing whatever Harry had told her. Yes, we had our moments, but all couples do. I definitely didn't have a problem with drink and drugs either, but after everything I'd been through, could I be blamed? Our arguments rarely got physical. There might have been the odd smashed plate or impulsive slap across the face from me over the years, but that was normal, wasn't it? We were in a passionate, committed relationship, and when feelings that strong are involved, those kinds of arguments are inevitable. They were making it sound so one-sided, but Harry gave as good as he got. But I wouldn't tell them that because I didn't want to tarnish his memory with them. All of the details aside, my relationship and marriage to Harry were none of their business.

"So now I am some kind of abuser? Anything else?" I screamed mockingly.

"Amelia, calm down. I'm just repeating what I've been told," Poppy said, backing away from me slightly.

"I will not calm down. I've done nothing but love and honour Harry. How would you feel if someone accused you of that?" I shouted.

"Disgusted. Absolutely disgusted in myself," Yvonne answered.

"Well, it isn't true. You don't know what happened behind closed doors," I said.

"Agreed," Yvonne said, looking increasingly more agitated the longer the conversation dragged on, "I think you should leave."

"Oh, I'm leaving. I don't have to put up with this," I reviled.

I got up, burst through the front door, and slammed it as hard as I could on my exit. I strode back to my car and screamed into the steering wheel as loudly as I could. Everything they'd said was gratuitously over-exaggerated and twisted. I fully admit to having arguments, but show me a marriage that doesn't have disputes. I never set out to isolate Harry from his loved ones, and I would never do that to him. I hated them all, all of his family and friends. I wanted to line them up and scream the truth in each of their faces.

The comment about alcohol was really grating at me. When you looked at Harry's mother, I was teetotal in comparison. The most I'd admit to was liking an occasional drink. Did it turn me into a domestic abuser as soon as I'd had a drop? No. And in the months leading up to Harry's death, I'd barely touched it. Was I misremembering our marriage, and I really was abusive? If Harry did decide to jump off Filey Brigg, did I contribute to that decision? I found myself carefully going back through every single argument and counting each time it got physical.

I stopped when I ran out of fingers.

XI

STRENGTH

HARRY - BEFORE

Drowning described it best. Every time I got my head just even slightly above the water, I was dragged back to the brink of bankruptcy by something else. Our offer on the house had been accepted, and we had a few weeks until completion day. I was almost back in the same position as I started, and the Broadhead bag grew emptier by the day. It was meant to be a one-time thing with Becky, but every few days, I'd receive a text asking for more. The amounts were insignificant at first, but it was starting to mount up. I still hadn't met Joshua, and I started to question if he even existed. It got to the point where she didn't even want me to come into the house anymore; she would instruct me to post it through the letterbox.

I endured the constant barrage in survival mode, putting out financial fires where I found them, and continued to conceal the whole thing from Amelia. The weight on my shoulders was massive. I was desperate to tell her what was going on just to get it off my chest, but I knew it would only make matters worse. The first Broadhead repayment was due soon, and I'd be paying it back with the money I loaned from them in the first place. I was so anxious and nervous all the time that I even toyed with the idea of taking a few of Amelia's pills to take the edge off.

We'd completed the first round of IVF, and Amelia was excited that this would be the time we would finally become parents. I should have been excited, too, but I wasn't. I was in a state of perpetual terror. Scared stiff by every knock at the door or incoming phone call. Each time Amelia had a notification on her phone, I found myself checking it, just in case Becky had decided to come clean to her. Everything was just hanging in the balance, and I waited for the day that it would all come crashing down. I could tell that Amelia knew something was wrong, too. The way she started looking at me whenever my phone made a noise, or if I took it into the bathroom with me. She'd always been so paranoid that I might be cheating on her, but I wasn't sure the truth would be any less upsetting. I did the only thing I thought I could, and I carried on lying about everything in a drastic attempt to keep the peace. I dreamt of threading the needle and somehow making everything right before I was exposed, but it was starting to seem impossible.

I was still working as a financial adviser, albeit over the phone from Manchester. Geoff, the owner, was really understanding about it all and continued to let me work remotely. The clients didn't mind either; I'd actually built up a really good relationship with some of them, and I'm sure they would actually miss me when I left.

I'd given up stashing the Broadhead money at my mother's house, and it sat in the compartment underneath the boot mat in my car. The fortune seemed to dwindle by the day. I stopped planning for the future. I could barely plan twenty-four hours in advance. I just dealt with each day as it came, waiting for the inevitable landslide. I should have felt hopeless, but I actually didn't. I was so wrapped up in frantically trying to hold everything together with my bare hands that I didn't stop to process just how dire my situation was.

Thud. Another five hundred pounds was posted through Becky's letterbox. I didn't even know how much I'd given her at this point or what she was spending it on. Every text request came with its own excuse, each more fantastical than the last. I'd be more content with just a pounds and pence figure from now on; I started to feel ridiculous that she thought I believed her lies. I had only seen Becky a few times since I'd first met her, and at first, I thought I was almost doing a good thing, but it quickly became evident I was being taken advantage of. During the previous few deliveries, I could tell from outside that Becky couldn't even be bothered to get up off the sofa. I dutifully continued the cash drops without hesitation because I would have done anything to keep Amelia from knowing about it.

I got back in the car and started to drive back home. Just as Becky's excuses were becoming implausible, so were mine to Amelia. I kept saying I needed to nip into the office of my new job to complete some paperwork or meet someone. But the reasons I was giving were becoming increasingly thin. It was probably my paranoia talking, but I was convinced she knew exactly what I was doing, and she was just waiting for me to admit it.

When I returned home, Amelia was crashing around in the kitchen. She had been getting increasingly agitated with the time it was taking for the house to complete, but I was grateful for every day it got delayed. Every day was another day to try and magic up some funds. I had no idea where to get the rest of the money from; I was just hoping there would be some kind of miracle, and the whole thing fell through.

"Amelia?" I shouted whilst kicking off my shoes.

She responded, but I couldn't make out what she was saying from the kitchen. I came in and found she had emptied every cupboard and set of drawers onto the floor. The kitchen looked like it had been looted by a pack of monkeys. Amelia was violently swaying from side to side, and she was clearly drunk. I was standing there open-mouthed, waiting for some kind of explanation.

"We are dry!" she slurred, shaking an empty glass in her hand.

"Dry?" I asked.

"No more booze left, duh!" she responded.

"Amelia, you said you were going to stop drinking. It makes it harder to conceive, remember?" I explained.

"Oh, calm down, killjoy. I did a test, negative, again."

"I'm sorry, Amelia. But you shouldn't get like this regardless."

"Well, what else am I supposed to do whilst you are out, doing god knows what?"

"I had to nip out to the office. I can't help that," I said.

Amelia came over to me, aggressively pulled my face closer to hers with my cheeks, and smiled.

"The office, right," she slurred.

I pulled away. "It's the truth, Ames," I argued dishonestly.

Amelia seemed to be satisfied by my response for a few seconds and started almost dancing around the kitchen, smiling. But all of a sudden, the smile slipped from her face sinisterly, and she gave me this really maddened look. She stopped dancing and ran into me, gripping me by my throat and pinning me ferociously against the fridge. It rocked violently, knocking over all the contents inside when I impacted it. I could barely breathe under her grasp; her grip increased the pressure as her disturbing smile widened.

"Bullshit," she laughed, her grip still strengthening, "who is she, Harry?"

I tried to pull away from her, but the more I flailed, the more her hold around my neck tightened. I started to struggle even more, and I accidentally stood on a discarded wine glass on the floor. It smashed, slicing into the bottom of my foot. The noise distracted Amelia enough for her to temporarily lose her grip, and I managed to escape, dropping to my knees and breathing desperately.

"What the fuck, Amelia?" I gasped.

She looked alarmed at what she had done at first. The blood had already soaked through my sock and began pooling on the kitchen floor. I saw the expression on her face change as if she'd decided I deserved what had just happened to me. She casually threw a tea towel by my feet for me to soak up the blood. I obediently picked it up and wrapped it around my bleeding sole. The wound wasn't nearly as bad as the amount of blood suggested, but the pain was staggering.

"There isn't anybody else, okay? I honestly just nipped into the office," I protested.

"So, it's some slut from the office, then?" She asked.

"No. I just had to drop off some more paperwork."

"No. You are lying," Amelia accused, nodding knowingly.

"Believe what you want. I'm done trying to convince you," I said, hobbling out of the kitchen and through the front door.

I intended to leave immediately, but in my haste to escape Amelia, I'd forgotten to put my shoes back on. I walked a few feet away from our flat door, and the blood from my foot was producing a grim smear across the usually white floor tiles. I sat on the cold floor, and I could still hear Amelia smashing up things in the flat whilst I was in the safety of the corridor.

I had no idea what the statistics were in regard to how common this is within a relationship, but I definitely felt like I was in the minority. Don't get me wrong, she didn't get like this often, but it was becoming more frequent. Drink was almost always involved. Amelia wasn't an alcoholic, and I'm not sure there was a word invented for what she was. She didn't need to drink, but when she did, it just changed her into a different person. I tried to ease her off the drink by telling her it hurt the chances of conceiving, which was true, but as a matter of fact I just wanted her to be sober for my own sake. The booze didn't agree with her at all. In my head, I had this idea that having a child would fix everything in our marriage, and I was just hanging on until it finally happened. I tried giving her everything that she ever wanted, but it seemed to only make matters worse.

It started off small, wanting to know every last detail whenever I'd been away from home. Later came the accusations. Before I knew it, I found myself not going out with my friends anymore. It just wasn't worth the resulting inquisition. Everything had to be prearranged, with notice, and approved by her. Every time Poppy called, and Amelia got to my phone first, she would cancel the call or answer it herself. It took me a while to notice what was going on, and by the time I did, I felt like I was already too isolated to see a way out.

Then she started putting me down in public. I was known for constantly making jokes by everyone who knew me. Instead of laughing at them, she would give me a disgusted look, like I had no right to speak. Every time it happened, I felt myself receding further into myself, and the jokes became less and less frequent. She would often talk to a complete stranger and then tell them intimate details about my life, which seemed insignificant at first, but as time went on, the stories became even more inappropriate.

The time that stuck in my head the most was when she begged me to drive her to the supermarket to get more drinks. She got chatting with the woman serving us, making the odd joke about me being boring or a wet blanket. That's what she did to people; she used to start small, gauge their reaction, and, if it was positive, say something even more tactless. Within a few minutes, Amelia was laughing her head off, telling this poor woman how terrible I was in bed and how I'd never managed to give her an orgasm. At first, I used to defend myself, but I quickly found out that it only made matters worse. So I kept silent as Amelia cackled with the awkward-looking retail assistant, who gave me the occasional look of pity.

Instead of backing away from her and potentially ending the relationship, I started blaming myself and doing everything I could to fix it. I was desperate for our marriage not to be like my parents' marriage. I felt myself transforming into my father, silently taking it all and not saying a single thing in response. I didn't feel like a man anymore. It made me feel pathetic and weak. She'd covertly chipped away at my dignity until there was almost nothing left but debris and dust. Just when I thought I was at my lowest moment, she stepped it up.

She started getting physical.

That started small, too, a harder than playful tap on the back of the head or an overly efforted shove when I said something she didn't like. It was always in private and in the house, but if I said something she didn't like in public, it would come to haunt me later. She did this thing where she would grab my hand and dig her fingernails into it, and I knew I'd be on the receiving end of worse after it. Some days, I'd have marks or even bruises from it for days. It got to the point that every time she had a drink,

I'd receive a slap from her for something. Or, more often than not, for nothing. I didn't know what her rules were, and it seemed to be random most of the time. Once she started closing her fist, that's when I noticed the intensification.

The choking was new, and every time there was an escalation, it still caught me off guard. I loved her so much, and I thought she loved me back. I just didn't understand why she was doing it to me. The day after an altercation, we wouldn't even talk about it. I didn't dare bring it up for fear of it happening again. We just continued like nothing had happened. It was as if as soon as a drop of alcohol touched her lips, she transformed into this monster that was lurking inside her.

The worst part of it all was that no one knew.

I hadn't told a soul what she was doing to me. I think it was due to a mixture of shame and disbelief. I felt like telling someone would be self-emasculating, like I couldn't handle myself. I just kept imagining me telling Steve he would have laughed me out of the house. I just bottled it up, let her continue destroying everything good about me, and hoped one day she would see who she was becoming and go and get help.

That day was different, though, because it was the first step I'd actually taken to regain my independence back and fix the mess I had slipped into. I didn't realise I had a line, but she had unquestionably crossed it. I could still feel Amelia's grip around my throat when I made the call, and she was still screaming as if she was being tortured in our flat.

"Hi! Harry!" Poppy answered.

"Hi, Poppy," I croaked.

"Are you okay, Harry? You sound weird."

"Can I come and speak to you? Amelia and I have had an argument."

"Of course you can. You know that you don't have to ask permission."

"Thank you. I'll be there in a few hours."

I stood at the closed flat door; I could still hear her crashing around inside. I took a deep breath and inched back inside. She flounced out of the kitchen to face me. Judging by the state of her face, she had clearly been crying and screaming the entire time I was outside.

"I'm going to stay at Poppy's house tonight," I announced.

"Harry, I'm sorry. Please stay. I didn't mean it," Amelia pleaded.

"No, I need to go and clear my head. You should do the same."

Amelia's monster took over again. I saw it snarling at me from behind her eyes.

"Going to your sisters, sure. You mean staying with your whore?" she bellowed.

"No. I'll be at my sister's house. When I get back, we need to talk about this for a long time. I can't take it anymore."

"Take what? You're a coward."

"I am not a coward. I just can't talk to you when you get like this. You could have killed me."

"Now you are overreacting. It was in the heat of the moment because I love you so much."

"People who love each other don't do that."

"You provoked me, and I responded. I can't be blamed for that."

"If you believe that, you need help," I said directly.

Amelia stormed towards me, holding an empty wine glass in her hand. My initial thought was that she was going to smash it over my head, but she dropped it at the last minute and slapped me across the face instead. I had become so twisted that I actually felt grateful she elected to just slap me when she could have done so much more damage. She continued shouting and bawling at me, but something inside of me had snapped, and I was no longer willing to keep enduring the continuous torrent of abuse. I calmly moved through the flat, almost ignoring her existence, collecting the things I'd need for an overnight trip. I packed a bag and left through the flat door without exchanging further words.

The farther I drove away from Amelia, the more freedom I felt. I almost felt guilty leaving her in that state, and I had to keep reminding myself it was the right thing to do. I know I was technically in the wrong for lying to her, but when she reacted like that to something seemingly insignificant, how would she react if she found out what I'd really been up to? I felt like my decision to conceal the truth from her was vindicated. If I'd told her the real reasons I'd been so distant, I probably wouldn't have been breathing.

I arrived at Poppy's, and she came out to meet me in the driveway with a big hug. I hadn't realised it, but Amelia had left bruises on my neck in the shape of her hands, and even after the long drive, I had an alarming red handprint across the left side of my face. Poppy led me inside, and her wife, Josephine, ran up to me and hugged me too.

I told them *everything*.

Every disgusting and foul detail. It was only when I said it out loud that I realised how bad it had gotten. If I had done this months ago, I would probably have put a stop to it, but for some reason, I was terrified of doing this. I felt like I was trapped in the marriage, and I couldn't make a single decision for myself. Every time I tried to move the relationship in a different direction, Amelia would immediately correct me with a biting insult or a slap. Confiding to my sister and her partner the hell that Amelia was putting me through made me feel so much better. We all cried for hours as I slowly made my way through each aspect of the torture my wife was increasingly subjecting me to. I had never cried as much in my life, and the release made me start to almost feel like my old self again.

"You have to go to the police," Poppy demanded, "she is unhinged."

"No. I can fix this. She just needs help," I argued.

"What if she doesn't let go when she starts choking you next?"

"I won't let it happen again."

"It will happen again," Poppy insisted.

"It won't. I promise."

"She sounds like she just needs help," Josephine interjected.

"Jo, she is physically beating him and trying to choke him to death," Poppy responded.

"I know, but some couples lose their way."

"It's not about that anymore! She could end up killing him!"

"They haven't even tried counselling yet or anything. They can at least try to make it work."

"Look at his neck, Jo! You can literally see each of her fingerprints bruised into it."

Their argument faded out of my consciousness. They were still arguing, weighing up the pros and cons of me leaving her or ringing the police. Although, neither of them had actually asked me what I wanted to do. It was the most bizarre feeling I had ever experienced; I simultaneously loved and loathed Amelia. When we were good, our marriage was amazing. But the lows were horrific; I fully agreed with that. I also felt like I had committed far too much time and energy into our relationship to just let it go. I wanted to get back to the good times. The happy times. We were amazing together, but I thought Josephine had a point; we had just lost our way.

"Oh my god. Just stop it!" I shouted.

Both Poppy and Josephine were startled by my outburst and ceased their debate immediately.

"I appreciate you both giving me your points of view, but I didn't come here for that. I just needed to talk to someone. To be honest, I haven't decided yet what I am going to do," I explained.

"I'm sorry, Harry. I just hate seeing my big brother like this," Poppy said softly.

"You don't need to be sorry. I'd be the exact same way. Can I stay here tonight?"

"Of course you can," Josephine said.

"I just need time to think," I muttered.

We all hugged again, and they finally let me go upstairs by myself. I loved my sister; she had always been there for me since we were kids. Growing up with our parents was difficult, and if I were an only child, I don't think I'd be the same man I was that day. Josephine was perfect for Poppy, and I envied their relationship. They were so supportive of each other and of each other's families. They were even facing the same trials as us, but they had reacted to them entirely differently.

I went into the bathroom and turned the shower on. Amelia's handprints on my neck had already started going a ripe purple colour. It was sore, too, and it still felt like she had her hands around my neck. I couldn't place where it all went wrong for us. I found myself endlessly listing possible reasons for how we got there, and I realised that every single one of them was my fault. Or was that what I was meant to think? I didn't know whether the thoughts I had were my own or they had been forcibly implanted in my head by Amelia.

Any sane person would have walked away from her. I knew that, but I was in love with her. It complicated things. I'd devoted my life to making her happy, and to use a financial term, I was hoping to see the return on that investment. I just wanted to wind back the clock a few years before all this started and try again. My wife, the love of my life, might still be underneath this beast she was becoming. I sat on the edge of the bath with my phone in my hand, searching for couples' therapists or counsellors who could help. There were plenty of alcoholic groups we could go to that would help her with the drink. I started to feel hopeful until I realised I would have to pitch these to Amelia before she would actually go. That in itself felt like a monumental task.

I hadn't slept that well for a while. I didn't know whether it was because Amelia wasn't beside me or because I'd finally got the abuse off my chest. Nothing had been sorted out officially yet; it just felt good that I was making positive steps in the right direction. Poppy knew now, at least, and I felt so much better unburdening myself of it all. My strength had returned, and I started feeling like I could take on the world again.

It might have been a mistake, but I decided that I would stick it out and at least try to fix the issues. I owed the marriage that, right? Maybe with a bit of external help, we could get back on track and be in the relationship that we always wanted. I didn't know how I would approach it with Amelia, but I'd have to make her understand that if we didn't go down that road, the marriage would be over. If it was going to work, I had to take the strength I'd found in Filey back home with me.

I just hoped I wasn't kidding myself.

XII

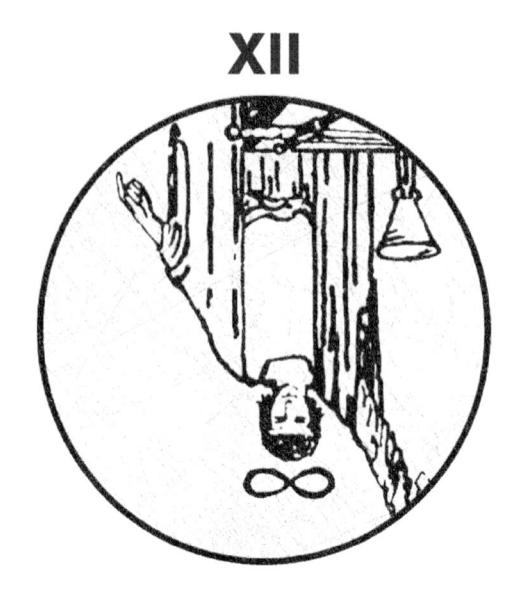

THE MAGICIAN

AMELIA

Was I really the person they were describing? I didn't feel like it. In the heat of the moment, it felt like they were describing someone else. The suggestion that I was a domestic abuser or drunkard made me feel grimy. I methodically went through our relationship from the start until the end, and I began to remember things I'd said and the violence I'd inflicted. Whatever Harry had told them must have been blown out of proportion, and he was no longer around to correct them. If they had this perception of me ever since we met, why wouldn't they have intervened sooner?

I wouldn't stand back and be lectured by Yvonne about drink and drugs. She chain-smoked an entire tobacco harvest each day and drank enough to kill herself ten times over. I could take or leave the drink, truthfully. I wasn't addicted to it like Yvonne was. The tablets I was on were taking were prescribed to me by an actual doctor, and I didn't take them often enough if anything. I'm sorry that I couldn't be a saint like my darling sister-in-law Penelope in her perfect home and marriage, and I needed something extra just to feel normal. I resented what they'd said about it making me aggressive, and if Harry was there, he would have defended me. The more I mulled it over, the more I thought they were just trying to hurt me for no apparent reason.

I fully admit that we were going through a rough patch ever since we'd started trying for a baby. What with the house move and Harry changing jobs, we'd taken too much on at once. Nevertheless, I didn't think the episodes of violence between us were regular enough to be considered a problem. Why would he want to have children with me if he was so scared of me? Harry always championed our relationship and fought for it, but that didn't fit the image his family had of our marriage.

Poppy and Yvonne were standing in the bay window, staring at me in the car. I decided to start driving. I couldn't stand to be in their gaze. I didn't intend it, but instinctively, I'd started driving towards where Harry was buried. I suppose subconsciously, I needed to feel close to him, and I hadn't visited the cemetery since the funeral. I parked the car and started the long walk to his grave. I took out my phone and sent James a text as I walked.

> *Did Harry hate me for all the arguments we had?*

> *Harry yearned to solve the disputes between you. I can see he loved you very much.*

James' message confirmed to me what I thought. Either I was misremembering our entire marriage, or they were lying. I reached the grave; the flowers that had been left there had already started to rot after being constantly attacked by the Filey sea air. I removed the unsightly ones and tidied the grave up the best I could. I should have brought something with me.

"Harry," I whispered, "if you felt like I was ever abusive to you, I'm sorry. I just loved you so much."

Harry remained silent.

"Whatever you told your mother and sister, it's fine. I'm just so sorry for everything that happened," I said.

I was interrupted by the sound of a vehicle pulling into the car park in the distance, and a figure alighted from it and started walking towards me. As they got closer, I realised it was Kim, holding a bunch of flowers. She paused briefly once she'd recognised me but then continued the walk.

"Do you mind if I join you?" she asked.

"I could do with some company, actually," I said, pointing at the flowers, "are those for Harry?"

"Yes, I thought I'd freshen them up while I was here."

"That's kind of you."

We both stood at the grave in silent reflection for a minute or two after Kim placed the bouquet on the ground. I felt myself starting to cry, and I turned to Kim, who must have been crying the entire time.

"Did Harry ever tell you about any arguments between us?" I asked.

"No. Like what?" Kim responded.

"Poppy and Yvonne have been spreading around that he'd told them I used to get drunk and hit him."

Kim looked shocked when I mentioned it and started shaking her head. "No, he said nothing of the sort to me," she said.

"I'm starting to think Harry wasn't the man I thought he was," I confessed.

"How so?"

"It turned out he did loan a huge amount of money from the Broadheads. Oh, and he thought he had a son from a one-night stand a decade ago. That ended up being a lie, though. He was actually being blackmailed and kept it all a secret from me."

"Oh my god," Kim gasped.

"I just can't help but think if he was lying about that, what else was he lying about?"

"What do you mean?" Kim asked.

Years of jealousy and paranoia broke through the defensive line of antidepressants I'd built up in my system. My quiet tears of reflection quickly turned to outright sobbing. Kim looked increasingly concerned and confused. She touched my arm to console me, but I batted it away impulsively. For all I knew, she was one of the secrets he had kept.

"He was cheating on me. The entire time," I confessed.

"Oh god, who with?" Kim asked.

"I don't know. But I could just feel it. I'd felt it ever since we moved to Manchester."

"Harry wouldn't do that."

It was innocent enough what Kim had said, and if the roles were reversed, I would probably mustered up the same lame response. Yet, she didn't know Harry like I did. She didn't hear the constant excuses to get out of the flat and the times he would just leave me alone in it for hours. I knew that there was someone else. It was the only thing that made sense. I just didn't know who. It could have been a string of women, for all I knew. I despised people speaking for Harry, and I was the only one who truly knew and loved him. Everyone else needed to stay in their lane. I thought Kim could help me get to the truth, but she was starting to become a nuisance. I just wanted to be alone in my grief, but like magic, she appeared whenever I was at my lowest moments.

"Oh, piss off, Kim," I said matter-of-factly.

"Excuse me?" Kim gasped.

"You didn't know him. You had a short relationship with him a lifetime ago. Keep your opinions to yourself," I said scathingly.

"You know what? I'm off. I thought about turning around as soon as I spotted you at his grave, but somehow I felt sorry for you."

"Sorry for me?"

"Yes."

"I don't need someone like you taking pity on me. You aren't welcome here, anyway."

"Fine. And for the record, Harry didn't need to tell me about you hitting him. I saw the bruises with my own eyes," Kim said with her finger pointed at my face. She turned around dramatically and thundered back down the path to the car park.

Everyone thought it, apart from me, it seemed. I'd convinced myself that Yvonne and Poppy were just being cruel and making things up, but Kim shared the same notion. My hands and feet started trembling erratically, the pins and needles moving up my limbs to the back of my neck. I hadn't taken the tablets that day, and I could feel the panic attack setting in. I hastily rifled through my bag, looking for the pills, but I struggled to find them. I emptied the bag out on the grass next to Harry's grave and saw the tablets. I frantically took two and lay on the grass, waiting for the panic attack to subdue.

But it didn't go away.

Usually, two tablets and a few minutes on my back would do the trick, but it wasn't working. I couldn't stop my mind racing. Every single argument I'd ever had with Harry flashed in my mind like a gruesome slideshow. It featured every time I screamed in his face. Or each instance that I'd put my hands around his neck. I remembered the injuries. I heard every vicious put-down and all of the wicked cruelty I'd subjected him to. I recalled every single time I'd falsely convinced him it was all his fault or he was to blame for my actions. I tried to ignore it, but the panic-induced horror coursing through my system forced me to look at it head-on. Everything they had said to me was true.

I started feeling faint and dizzy; the clouds in the sky started to swirl and blur. A sharp pain shot from my left shoulder to the right, and I clutched my chest in agony. The extreme nausea hit, and I took another two tablets. Followed by more; I had lost count. The tablets weren't working, and I could feel my heart slamming against my rib cage as the panic attack grew stronger and stronger. That was it; I was going to die at Harry's grave. And at that moment, I thought I deserved it. Just when I thought the panic attack was at its peak, it kicked up into another gear. I'd never had a panic attack so strong in my life, and I was convinced this was the end. Just the thought of that made it even worse; I could barely feel my arms and legs at that point as I thrashed intensely on the floor.

I didn't know whether it was the copious amounts of drugs in my system or if I was actually having a heart attack, but I started to sweat profusely. I was wheezing and struggling to take every breath. I was still on my hands and knees in the dirt, too dizzy to even think about standing up. The delicate sway of the grass and trees in the graveyard slowed until they were perfectly still. Every bird and creature fell totally silent and stared at me alarmingly. Even the breeze had ceased. I felt like I was trapped in a place devoid of time itself.

Was this it? Was this the end?

I felt terrified of what was coming, and I couldn't help but think this was how Harry felt in his final moments.

"Amelia," a familiar voice said to me.

I'd recognise *his* voice anywhere.

"Harry?" I asked.

"What are you doing on the floor, Ames?" Harry asked sarcastically.

I was able to lift my head just enough to see Harry standing above me. I could barely recognise him; it was as if he was made of fine dust that was constantly eroding in the breeze. His hair was darker than I remembered, and his skin much paler. His eyes were the most off-putting part; they were almost entirely black. He reached out to offer his hand to help me stand, but when I reached for it, my hand went through it like I'd tried gasping fog.

"Tough luck, Ames. Looks like you are on your own," Harry jested with a smile.

"What are you doing here?" I gasped.

"Well, I'm not really here, am I? I'm where you put me. About three feet to your left and six feet under."

"Harry, I'm so sorry for how I treated you."

"No, you aren't," Harry said, pacing around his own grave.

"I loved you!" I shouted," Of course I'm sorry."

"Then why did you do it? You tortured me for almost the entire time we were married."

"That's not true."

"You left bruises, Amelia. You broke bones. But worse, you made me feel like I was nothing. Less than nothing, even."

"I didn't mean to. I had a problem."

"Had? You *have* a problem. It's taken you this long to even face it yourself. All this time, I thought I was the pathetic one, but that was you. You had to control me just to feel better about yourself."

"No, that's—"

"Every single time you called me a nasty name or you told a stranger something embarrassing about me, you put me in that hole over there."

"I'm sorry!" I screamed.

"I was planning to leave you, you know? Everybody knew. My mother, my sister, everybody. They were even helping me do it."

"You are just trying to hurt me."

"Yes, I am trying to, just like you hurt me. But I'm not lying. I'd found someone else, and I was going to leave you. A few more days, and I'd have been gone."

"You cheated on me?"

"All the time, Ames. At every opportunity I had. That was the only thing you were actually right about. If anything, I did it just to get away from you for a little while."

I mustered what little energy and coordination I had left and took a swipe at the apparition before me with a scream. My hand travelled straight through Harry, and the dust reconstituted itself back into his ghastly form as soon as my hand made it through.

"Even now, you can't help but take a swing at me, can you?" Harry laughed ironically.

"This isn't real. This isn't real," I repeated to myself.

"That's it, Ames, keep telling yourself that. Keep justifying and hiding your vile actions, even to yourself."

"You gave me as good as you got."

"You really believe that?"

"It's true."

"Anything I did, I did to protect myself from you. Stop kidding yourself."

"Why are you doing this to me?" I whispered.

"Oh, Ames. I don't know what to tell you. I could tell you it was because of the way you treated me, but that's only half true."

"What is it then?"

"I was going to leave you because you weren't even capable of giving me a child. And because you are a venomous, barren monster who doesn't deserve a second of happiness. The only thing I regret is wasting so much time with you."

"I am carrying your child!"

"Whatever you are carrying, that is not my child. A child is made from love and happiness, not hatred and violence. You will lose it. Just like you've lost everything."

"Don't you say that!"

"In fact, I hope you lose it. For their sake. You wouldn't be able to look after it anyway."

"Just leave me alone! Please."

I tried to crawl away from Harry's shadow, but he followed me everywhere as I tried to move. It was as if he was all around me, and I couldn't escape him. Harry started to smile sinisterly, and he backed away from me as I remained on my hands and knees at the grave. Pleased that he had sufficiently broken me, the particles that made up his image started to corrode and disappear. I watched him slowly fade into nothing as what was left of him scattered into the air. I plunged my face into the dirt, screaming and sobbing into it. My heart was beating faster and faster, and I prayed each thump would be its last. I wished the ground would open up and swallow me whole.

The sky began turning black, and what little light that was making it through the clouds shrivelled into nothingness. Every tree in the cemetery shed its leaves in synchronisation, and the grass underfoot me turned to ash. The very ground disappeared underneath me, and I was granted my wish. I started falling at speed down a huge shaft made from soil and earth. I fell for what felt like miles, gathering speed as I continued down the passage in freefall. I extended my arms, and my fingernails started to drag in the dirt walls of the mud chute to try to slow my fall. I could just make out the bottom of it, and there lay a single coffin. Just before I made an impact with it, everything turned completely black, and I was left unconscious.

XIII

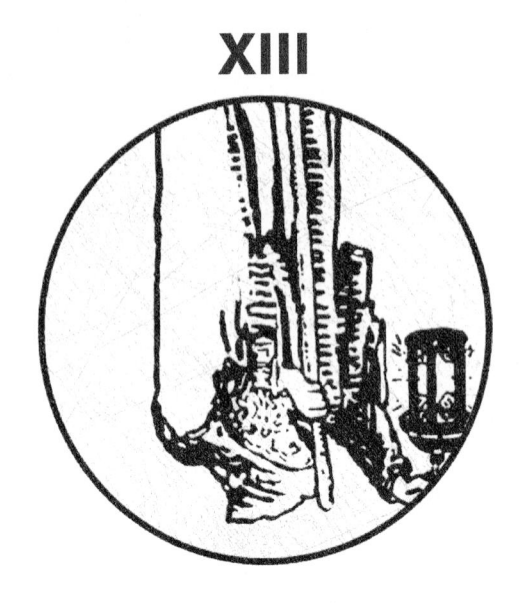

THE HERMIT

AMELIA

The first thing I noticed when I woke up was the flickering fluorescent light above me and the brown-stained ceiling tiles surrounding it. The light popped with every flicker, each time making my skull-splitting headache even worse. I had no idea where I was, but I barely had enough energy to turn my head. A doctor came into my field of vision, but I could barely focus on him because he was that blurred. He shined a small torch in my eyes, and I closed my eyes in response.

"Do you know where you are? Amelia?" The doctor asked.

"No. What happened?" I asked wearily.

"You are in Bridlington Hospital. You were found unresponsive next to some tablets; we think you overdosed. I have to ask, were you intending to harm yourself?"

"No, I had a panic attack. The tablets are prescribed to me."

"How many did you take?"

"About six. Maybe more. I'm not sure."

"That is very dangerous, Amelia. We've checked your records, and they say you are pregnant, too?" the doctor asked, looking vexed.

"Is the baby okay?" I said.

"The baby will be fine, and so will you. You just need to rest now," the doctor explained calmly.

For the first time since I found out I was pregnant, I actually felt the sting of parental instinct. My child was innocent and hadn't even been born yet, but I'd threatened its life. Even though I knew it was a paranoid manifestation of my overdosed state, Harry was right, and I felt repulsive about it. His words had cut into me deeply, and at that moment, I would have given anything to undo all the damage that I'd caused him. The only part of him that still existed was nestled safely in my womb, and I had a renewed urge to protect it at all costs. Maybe all the mistakes I'd made would be somehow forgiven if

I managed to keep it safe. That was the only thing Harry was wrong about. I was going to keep the baby.

"We had to give you Flumazenil, which counteracts the Alprazolam in your system. You might have some mild side effects like dizziness or a headache, but it should be all out of your system quickly," the doctor explained.

"Thank you, doctor," I replied.

"Are you experiencing any chest pains or shortness of breath?"

"Not anymore, I just feel rough," I said with my hand on my head, "can those pills I took cause hallucinations?"

"Those drugs in the right quantity can be very dangerous. There have been reports of extreme paranoia and hallucinations given the right circumstances. Did you experience some hallucinations?"

"I think so."

"Usually, it's a delusion of whatever you are struggling with to begin with. Alprazolam is a very strong drug, which is why it isn't usually prescribed in the UK. May I ask where you got the tablets from?"

"I have a private prescription."

"I see. I'd recommend seeing the doctor and changing to something more appropriate. You should continue taking it in the prescribed dose until then. It can be quite addictive."

"Thank you, doctor. I will."

"You have a visitor outside. We were unable to get in touch with your next of kin. Would you like to see them?"

"Sure."

The doctor returned my chart to the end of the bed and continued making his rounds. I'd never felt so nauseated in my life. When I was remembering the hallucination, it felt entirely real. It was the same kind of feeling as when you have an argument with someone in a dream, and you wake up still angry. Harry had never spoken to me like that, ever. Every single insecurity I'd held over the years was repeated back at me with malice. I kept telling myself that it was just an illusion and it was my own paranoia talking, but I knew that everything he said about me was true. I started this journey to discover more about Harry, and I had to accept it meant looking at some hard truths about myself, too.

The door opened, and Kim sheepishly walked in with a punnet of grapes. For the first time ever, I didn't roll my eyes at her. I felt guilty for speaking to her the way I did; she was only trying to put my mind at ease. If someone had spoken to me like that, there was no way I would be coming to their bedside bearing gifts. I needed to put aside my own obsessions and paranoia and accept that she was just trying to help. In a way, she was the only friend I had left.

"How did you know I was here?" I asked.

"I came back to apologise when they were putting you in the ambulance. How are you feeling?" she asked.

"Rotten. You?"

"Guilty."

"Why?"

"I shouldn't have left you there like that. I could see you were struggling. I should have been kinder. I'm sorry."

"You are fine, honestly. I'm sorry for how I spoke to you."

Kim sat down on the chair beside the bed and offered me a grape, which I refused. She took one herself and entered a reflective state. I could see her building up to say something in her usual way, and I turned my head to make eye contact with her keenly.

"The doctor mentioned it. You never said you were pregnant," Kim said softly.

"It never came up," I uttered.

"How are you feeling about it?"

"About what?"

"Having a baby."

Kim was leaning in, expecting an insightful response, but I didn't have one to give her. More than anything, it just didn't feel real. I wasn't even far enough along to have a scan. I'd been told by plenty of medical professionals that I was pregnant, but I didn't believe it. I'd built up a curious defence mechanism from the constant failures when we had tried to conceive, and it was a hangover from that.

"It's scary," I mustered awkwardly.

"Yeah. I bet it is," Kim replied.

"Listen, don't feel like you need to hang around here until I am back on my feet. I think I am just going to head back to Manchester and forget about all this."

"No, you can't go! We need to find out what really happened!" Kim exclaimed.

I already knew what really happened. I'd finally accepted it; Harry had taken control of his situation and killed himself. And I was the one to blame. Everything else that happened to him might have contributed to that, but I was the one who pushed him over the edge. As galling as that admission may have been, there was a level of satisfaction in finally knowing the truth.

"I don't think I can take anymore. I just want to go home."

"I didn't want to bring it up, but I have a lead."

"A lead?"

"I got speaking to an old dear at the café. Apparently, there were some irregularities with some of Harry's customer accounts."

"What kind of irregularities?"

"Missing money, from the sounds of it."

I was sick of it. The constant secrets and malfeasance Harry had kept under wraps all those years were being unearthed one piece at a time. My journey was born of curiosity more than anything else. But since then, I'd found out things about Harry that I wish I hadn't. I found out things about myself that I'd rather forget, too.

Because of the way I'd treated him, I didn't even feel like I had the right to care anymore.

"I'm sorry, Kim. I'm going home," I said insistently.

"Okay, well, if I find out anything, I'll let you know," Kim said defeatedly.

"Thank you."

Kim left my bedside and walked out of the room, leaving the punnet of grapes behind. I plucked one from the top and bit into it. As time went by, I started to regret my decision. I had convinced myself that if I continued to look into Harry's secret past, maybe I would find a reason that would absolve me. I'd felt like we had barely scratched the surface, and maybe I didn't have to feel guilty for the rest of my life after all. I felt so twisted and warped by the accusations and the drugs that I didn't know what the truth was anymore. In the absence of clarity, I decided to consult James for some guidance.

> *I feel like giving up. I just want to go home. Is it the right decision?*

> *The story hasn't concluded yet. You must remain strong if you want to discover the truth.*

As ambiguous as the message was, it was just enough to change my mind. I called Kim and told her I'd meet her when I got discharged from the hospital. James was right. I needed to discover the truth.

It took a few days to track down Harry's old boss, Geoff. It wasn't immediately apparent from the outside, but the financial services company that Harry worked for had been shut down. Apparently, Geoff had moved to Leeds to escape the hordes of people constantly banging on the doors, wanting to know why their pensions had been illicitly tampered with. Word on the street was that Geoff was the main suspect, and there was a fraud case mounting against him and his business. Harry had always spoken very highly of Geoff, and I didn't think he was capable of something like pension fraud. I just hoped, for once, that Harry wasn't involved in any way, and I could just go home. But from what I'd learned about my husband since his death, it bore all the hallmarks of something he would have done. Geoff had been quite slippery once we had made contact, and he was extremely careful not to incriminate himself. He wanted to meet us at a pub in Castleford on the outskirts of Leeds. Kim and I were heading up there in the car when he called Kim's phone.

"Geoff, I've told you a hundred times. We aren't interested in anything illegal you may have done. We just want to talk about Harry's part in this," Kim said on the phone.

"Tell him to make sure he is there," I instructed.

"Please, just meet us. We aren't going to the police. Amelia just wants to find out what happened to her husband," Kim said to Geoff.

"He had better be there when he said he would be. Tell him. Or we'll find him," I threatened.

"No, she isn't threatening you," Kim explained, with a finger on her lip, indicating that I should be quiet. "Please just be there. It will take five minutes of your time, that's all," she said.

Kim pulled away from the phone and sighed. The phone made a beep as the call disconnected.

"Has he hung up on you?" I asked.

"Yes, you should have left it to me. I think you've scared him off."

"He's a coward."

"I agree. Which is why we needed to be gentle with him."

"We are only five minutes away. We might catch him as he's leaving."

I put my foot down, and we pulled into the car park of the pub we'd agreed to meet at. I had no idea what Geoff looked like, but Kim pointed him out as he walked to his car. We started to follow him, and he seemed to be unaware we were a few cars behind him.

"Where is he going?" I asked.

"Home, I guess," Kim responded.

"Fantastic. If he doesn't talk, we'll have leverage. We can always go and have a chat with his wife afterwards, depending on how it goes."

"Amelia, you are scaring me today. What has gotten into you?"

"I'm just tired of this, Kim. Every time we find out something new about Harry, it makes me feel sick."

"He might've not had anything to do with this."

"We'll see."

Geoff had pulled into a housing estate just near Woodlesford Train Station, and we slowed right down so as to not spook him. He stopped at a semi-detached house and pulled onto the driveway. I put my foot down again and blocked the driveway behind him and any hope he had of running. I got out of the car and started charging towards him.

"Geoff?" I asked.

"Oh God. Not here, please," Geoff begged, looking up at the neighbour's windows.

"Amelia, calm down," Kim suggested.

"I will not calm down. My husband is dead, and apparently, Geoff here has information about that, but he's holding it back," I shouted.

"Listen, just come in. I'll tell you everything I know. Please," Geoff conceded, trying to defuse the situation.

I gave Kim a victorious smile, and she rolled her eyes at me for a change. Geoff nervously led us into his house, and it didn't seem like anybody else was home. We were shown to the sitting room; it was incredibly old-fashioned. Decorative plates were hung on every free space on the walls, dotted with family photographs and the occasional clock. Kim and I sat down on one of the plastic-covered couches, and Geoff sat on the one across from us. This place didn't look like he had money to burn; it already felt like this could have been Harry's fault. Geoff's hands were shaking violently.

"Calm down, Geoff. We just want to talk about Harry," Kim said softly.

"I know you aren't meant to speak ill of the dead, but that lad has left me up shit creek," Geoff announced.

"What do you mean?" I asked.

"He was a fiddler! He had his hand in the till!"

"Geoff, honestly. Just breathe and keep it simple. What are you talking about?"

"Fraud. He was taking money out of our client's accounts and putting it in his own. Is that simple enough?"

I didn't need to ask for evidence. I believed him. It was probably the only way that Harry thought of, and would allow him to pay the Broadheads back and pay off the supposed mother of his long-lost child. Not to mention all the bills from the IVF clinic and the new house. The sheer pressure he must have been under just to keep our heads above water must have been astounding. I wish he'd just come to me and told me about it; maybe we could have worked it out together. But I made that impossible for him, didn't I? He was terrified that any misstep would end in me beating him up or trying to strangle him. I'd stopped seeing this as Harry's mess, and instead, it was a mess of my own making. If I hadn't treated him so poorly, he might have been comfortable enough to come and speak to me about all these issues. Instead, he buried them and continued the lie until it was too big to even look at.

"Why haven't you gone to the police?" I asked.

"Are you kidding?" Geoff laughed, "Like they are going to believe me. It was my business; all the transactions were approved by me."

"Why did you approve them if they were dodgy?" Kim asked.

"Because I trusted him," Geoff said bitterly.

"Where was he sending the money?" I asked.

"A string of accounts. I tracked most of them down to a small bank in Leeds called Sterling and Fishwick."

Because Harry never had a will, and I had to apply for probate, it's sometimes difficult to find all the accounts that someone holds. I'd never seen an account registered to that bank on any of the paperwork. He must have been keeping it secret. I let out a huge sigh. Secret phones and bank accounts, I wasn't even shocked anymore. The farther I went down this path, the more it just felt never-ending.

"Do you have an account number or something?" I asked.

"Yes. But you didn't get this from me."

"Fine."

Geoff copied some numbers from a piece of paper and handed it to me. I put the scrap paper in my handbag and stood up, and Kim followed me up a second later.

"Unless there is anything else, we'll leave you to it," I said.

"No, nothing else," Geoff said anxiously.

"Wasn't that bad, was it?" I said sarcastically.

Kim and I both headed out of Geoff's house and got back in the car. I started searching for 'Sterling and Fishwick' and found their closest branch. I started the navigation on my phone and pulled away.

"Are they just going to give you access to the account?" Kim asked.

"I have the probate documents on my phone. They legally have to if it was in Harry's name," I said.

"How much do you think he has in there?"

"I'm not sure. I wouldn't put anything past him, to be honest."

We were only in the car for a few minutes before we arrived. It was a tiny little bank that I'd not even heard of before, and there were only two counters inside. I walked over to the counter, and the cashier greeted me with a smile.

"Welcome to Sterling and Fishwick. How can I help?" she smiled.

"Hi," I gulped, "so I've just been made aware my husband had an account here. Regrettably, he's no longer with us, and I'd like access to it."

"I'm so sorry to hear that. Unfortunately, we require some identification, and we will need to see your grant of probate."

"I have it right here," I said, and showed the cashier the documents on my phone.

"Please bear with me for one minute; I just need to speak to my supervisor."

The cashier disappeared through a door behind the counter for a few minutes, taking my phone and identification with her. She returned with a man in an immaculate, well-fitting suit and it was him who was now holding the documents with an awkward smile.

"Hi, Amelia. Firstly, I'm so sorry for your loss," he said.

"Thanks," I uttered.

"Your husband had a few accounts with us, with a not insubstantial amount spread across them. He also had a deposit box with us at this branch," he explained.

"A deposit box?" I asked.

"Yes, ma'am. And given the circumstances, I will be able to open it for you. If you would like to follow me."

The man walked around the counter and led me through a series of doors into a fairly large room; each of the four walls was made entirely of little steel doors. He unlocked one of them with two keys from his jacket pocket, removed the box inside, and placed it on a large table in the centre of the room.

"I'll give you some privacy," he said as he left the room.

I took a deep breath before I'd even touched the box on the table, and I placed the anti-anxiety pills from my bag next to it in preparation. I was terrified of what I would find inside. The box wasn't very heavy, so I shook it lightly, and the contents rattled inside. I slowly lifted the handle to open the box, and to be honest, it was a bit of an anti-climax. The vast majority of it was paperwork. Endless printouts and handwritten logs of every fraudulent transaction Harry had made. I removed the stack of papers, and I leafed through them aimlessly, barely understanding a single line. The scale of it was far worse than I'd imagined, though. Some of the transactions dated before we even got married.

I sat on the floor and tried to concentrate on piecing together what I was looking at. It looked like a ledger, showing the ins and outs of Harry's illegal dealings. He started small, at first, a few thousand here or there, and he was returning the money before it had been missed. As the ledger continued, the amounts got larger and more frequent, and it was impossible to track if he ever returned it or not. It told a story, the approximate dates I could correlate to events in our lives. The first withdrawals started just before our wedding and then again when we were looking for a flat. When we started IVF, he had stolen the exact amount from someone's pension to pay for it. Then it became a mess, and the numbers were almost frantically scratched into the paper rather than written.

Harry had made his last entry a few days before his death, and he wasn't even meant to be in Leeds at the time, but at his new job in Manchester. I couldn't help but think I'd forced him into this. Every time I moaned about not going out often enough or every unreasonable request I made for our wedding, he happily obliged. Even the house, when he wrote down the offer number, I nearly had a heart attack, but he seemed so sure. I decided to return the papers where I had found them and leave them buried for now. I had too much going on in my life, and unduly worrying about the repercussions of his creative accounting wasn't high on my list of priorities.

When I stood back up to return the ledger, I noticed there was a small envelope taped to the bottom of the deposit box. I unpicked the tape and opened the envelope. Inside there were two matching yet non-descript keys, which just looked like any regular ones, but there was no writing on them or any distinguishing features of any kind. I turned the envelope over and a hastily written phone number in Harry's handwriting was scrawled on the front.

I took out my phone, entered the digits carefully, and clicked call. The number was already saved in my contacts list, and the digits were replaced by the name I had set for it.

"Calling Psychic James," it read.

XIV

THE CHARIOT

HARRY - BEFORE

*C*lick. My finger continued pressing the button on the mouse, and the edge of my fingernail went white with the sheer force I was inflicting on it. I released it, and after a short loading animation on the laptop screen, confirmation of the completed transfer popped up on it. I had dabbled in this before, but in relatively tiny amounts, and I'd always transferred the money back before it was missed. However, that transfer was altogether different, mainly because of the number of zeroes in the figure. With one simple click of a button, I now had the funds to repay the Broadheads in full, enough money for the house, and enough change to give Becky a final payment in exchange for leaving me alone.

I never wanted to have to do that, but I always knew it was the nuclear option if everything else went awry. I was operating under the assumption that if I kept the amounts low, the withdrawals irregular, and I replaced the money quickly, I would go undetected. I'd also borrow little amounts from various accounts just to try and cover my tracks, but none of my clients had enough money in their accounts to cover what I needed that day, apart from one. Just before I got married, a retired doctor had walked into the office, wanting to redistribute his finances to get the most out of his retirement. He said he had sizeable savings, but I didn't believe the figure when I saw it. I made a note of his account details and kept it safe just in case I ever needed it.

Part of me must have thought I'd need those details someday, but I never wanted to use them. However, I didn't see any other option. It wasn't long before the Broadheads would be knocking on my door, trying to collect the debt. It had been a few weeks since I had the argument with Amelia, and I was due to start my new job on the following Monday. I just needed to keep the plates spinning for a few months, and I'd be able to start replacing all the money I'd taken without anyone noticing.

I felt like my marriage was strained, but Amelia hadn't mentioned the incident. I tried bringing it up, but she refused to believe that it even happened. She would change the subject right away. Something must have got through, though, because she hadn't laid a finger on me since. I had plans of staging a big intervention and telling her exactly how I felt about it all, but I always chickened out at the last minute. Without the help she needed, I was worried that she would backslide into the same pattern of abuse, though I was trying to remain positive. I hadn't seen her touch a drop of alcohol ever since, and I was careful not to bring any back to the house. She continued to take her prescribed tablets, and I stopped opposing them. I didn't think they were doing her any good, but whatever she needed to do to remain calm, I was fine with it. I just desperately needed to hold everything together for a few more weeks. Besides, the new house was due to be completed on the following Monday, so it was going to be a big week for us both. I thought the change in scenery and job would have a beneficial and calming effect on us, as it would at least pave the way for our marriage to become healthy again.

Even though I had just committed some pretty heavy fraud, a weight felt like it had been lifted off my shoulders. All the financial mistakes I'd made in the previous weeks had been corrected, and I'd definitely learned my lesson. I shut my laptop with a congratulatory smile, and Amelia was standing behind it with her arms crossed. She suggested we go out and celebrate with lunch. I accepted because I thought it would be an air-clearing opportunity that could hopefully help us get back to normal.

"Are you ready now?" she asked.

"Yeah, all done. Where do you want to go?" I asked.

"I thought we could go somewhere for a spot of lunch."

"Sounds good!" I enthused.

We walked down to the bar near the park, and during the rare times we visited, I'd always loved going there. Places like that could never exist in Filey; they were all little quirky pubs that hadn't seen a paintbrush in decades. It was a fashionable and happening place, full of twenty-somethings and Mancunian executives enjoying their lunchtimes. I'd be joining their ranks shortly once I started my new job. I'd spent the last few weeks dreading the start of every day, but I had so much to be grateful for, really. Maybe Amelia was right, and a celebration was long overdue.

I sat across from Amelia and stared at her as she perused the menu. She was beautiful. And I loved her. Maybe the last few months were just a blip, and there was finally some light at the end of the tunnel. Once we had a little family of our own, and our money troubles were a thing of the past, perhaps everything would be okay.

"What can I get you?" the waiter asked.

"I'll just have the chicken burger, please, and a glass of coke," I responded, "Amelia?"

"I'll have the same," Amelia replied, closing her menu. The waiter scribbled our order down and walked away with a courteous smile.

"I love you, Amelia," I said.

"I love you, too," she smiled.

"Listen, about everything that happened a few weeks ago, I don't want to bring it up, but I can see you are making an effort."

"An effort?"

"Yeah, and I just want to thank you."

Amelia didn't really respond; she just exhaled through her nose and smiled awkwardly. I was discomfited by her reaction, but we were good at that moment, and I didn't want to ruin it. I didn't need her to admit what she had been doing. I just needed her to change for the better. The waiter arrived with our cokes and placed them on the table. Amelia lifted hers in cheers, and I followed suit.

"To us," Amelia announced.

"To us," I repeated.

We actually had a really nice lunch. It felt like the old times when we didn't have anything to worry about or anything hanging over our heads. I started feeling like everything was going to be okay and our marriage could be saved. It was premature, but it felt like Amelia and I against the world again. It would have been nice to celebrate Amelia's pregnancy at the same time, but we still didn't have the news we were both hoping for. I remained focused on the positives. It was a clean slate and a chance to repair all the damage that had been done.

The weekend continued as happily as it started. We mostly spent it packing our possessions into boxes ready to move. We went through everything, all the photographs and memories that we had made together. On balance, we'd enjoyed a very happy marriage, and we had the photographs to prove it. It was nice going through everything to remind us why we were married in the first place.

The big day arrived, and I set off for my first day at my new job a little earlier than I needed to. I had an errand to run first. I withdrew £2,000 from my account and placed it in an envelope. This was the last money Becky would ever see from me. I was done being taken advantage of. I'd already decided I was never going to see Joshua, and she was just using me for money. She had already had thousands of pounds from me, and I needed to let her know that it wasn't an endless supply. If Joshua was proven to be mine, there would be a day that I would step up and take responsibility, but on my terms, not hers.

I did plan on visiting the Broadheads over the weekend, but Steve kindly offered to drop the money off in my absence, so I'd never have to see them again. I started looking forward to the future again, and it felt amazing. I was excited about what the next days and weeks would bring.

I arrived at Becky's house, and I didn't use the letterbox; instead, I bashed the door with my fist. I saw the curtains moving and heard a commotion behind the door. Becky opened the door, still in her dressing gown, looking quite angry that I'd had the bottle to actually knock on.

"Here," I said, throwing the envelope through the open door, "make it last. That's the last money you will see from me."

"I don't think so," Becky said, laughing.

"I've decided. Tell her I don't care. But I won't be blackmailed any longer."

I didn't wait for her reply. I walked down the garden path and slammed the gate behind me. I didn't turn around to look at her as I did, but I felt like I'd been forceful enough for it to stop. I got back in my car, and she was still standing at the front door holding the envelope. I started the engine, turned in the road, and had no intention of ever returning.

The investment firm I'd got a job at was incredible. I felt like I'd entered the big leagues. People I'd never met before inexplicably greeted me by name as I walked through the doors. I felt like a rockstar. I was met by the office manager, and she showed me to my very own office. It was like walking through the financial gates of heaven. My feet were enveloped in the plush white carpet as soon as I walked in, like a warm hug. The Manchester sun beamed through the huge windows and warmed my face as I started to explore. My brand new, polished desk shined in the sunlight, with a huge welcome hamper sitting on top. It even smelled good, like freshly washed cotton sheets or a spring meadow. I walked over to the window and peered outside. The view over Manchester was astounding. I felt like I'd finally made it. As I turned around to look at Susan, the office manager, I realised there was another section I'd completely missed when I walked in.

"Is this all mine?" I asked excitedly.

"Yes!" Susan smiled.

"I can't believe it, it's amazing."

"I'm glad you like it. We are really excited to see what you can do here."

"Me too."

"Your assistant is new and still in training. If you can manage today without her, that would be fantastic. She will be joining you tomorrow."

"An assistant? No way, really?"

"Yes way! We can't have you doing your own stapling, can we? I'll leave you to get settled. Just give me a call if you need anything."

"Thank you, Susan!"

Susan left, and I sat down at my desk. The chair was so comfortable I didn't think that I'd ever be able to stand up again. It had been left in the sun and was warm and cosy. I leaned back and put my feet on the desk, only to instantly remove them through fear of leaving a mark on its sublime surface. I couldn't wait to tell Amelia what was going on, so I got my phone out to text her.

> *Oh my god, Amelia. This place is incredible. I miss you.*

Amazing. I miss you, too.

> *How is the move going? Did the movers turn up on time?*

Everything is going fine. They are loading all the stuff now.

> *I'm sorry I couldn't be there to help.*

Don't worry, I've got this.

> *You won't believe it, but I've actually got an assistant, and she's starting tomorrow.*

What's she like?

> *I've no idea yet. I've not met her. Things are finally going well!*

I waited a few minutes with my phone unlocked for a response, but she didn't reply. Amelia was directing the movers, so I just thought she was busy. I put my phone away and set about exploring every crevice of my new office.

My first day was indescribable. It was the kind of job I'd always dreamed of doing when I started studying finance at university. I'd finally made it. It felt like everything was clicking into place, and the unpleasantness I'd just got through quickly became a distant memory. Everyone in the office was so nice and helpful, and the culture was exactly what I was looking for. I'd even picked up a few new clients on my very first day, which was a record for a new investment specialist, apparently. Once I'd left for the day, I was formidable, and I felt like I could take on anything that was thrown at me. I just wanted to get to my new home and share everything with Amelia.

I parked up in our brand-new driveway and just took a moment to appreciate and take in the new house we had bought together. Although I didn't think it at the time, it was definitely the right decision. It felt like I'd stepped into someone else's life overnight, and the relief I felt was pure ecstasy. I didn't have a key for the front door yet, so I skipped over to it and knocked on, but the door had been left ajar. I was expecting a little welcome to your new home surprise from Amelia if she had time.

From the outside, the house was immaculate. The garden was impossibly groomed and maintained, and every single brick was impossibly aligned and cleaned. The front door was spotlessly clean and so polished that

I could see my own reflection as I sheepishly walked through the front door. However, much like our relationship, the inside was only chaos and detritus. All the moving boxes that we had so diligently packed had been haphazardly emptied everywhere. Broken ceramics and ornaments littered the floor, and they crunched underfoot as I slowly made my way through the house. A large wall-mounted mirror that sat in our flat was leaning against the wall, but something had struck it, and it was shattered and cracked. I could hear sobbing, and I inched closer to the source of it, not knowing what to expect.

Amelia was on the kitchen floor, surrounded by the smashed memories and torn photographs of our lives together, holding a half-drunk bottle of vodka in her left hand. I'd been so quiet on my entry that there were at least a few seconds where I could have simply turned around and walked away, but I was so stunned I missed the opportunity. The sheer contrast between reality and what I expected was impossible to turn away from. Amelia got to her feet, still holding the bottle in her hand, and her deadened eyes told me exactly what was about to happen. The only thing that remained a mystery was why.

"Did you meet the slut, then?" she slurred.

"What are you talking about?" I asked.

"Your 'assistant', the slut."

"Ames, it's work. Nothing is going to happen."

Amelia started rummaging around in the wreckage of the kitchen for something drunkenly until she found her phone amongst the debris. She placed the bottle on the countertop and unlocked her phone. She walked straight over to me and grabbed me by the collar of my shirt, pinning me against the wall.

"I texted you, 'What's she like?' and you responded, 'I've no idea yet.' What did that mean?" she snarled in my face.

"It didn't mean anything," I huffed.

The grip on my collar started to tighten around my neck, barely allowing me to breathe, let alone utter a sound. I recognised the look in her eyes. It was the same crazed look she gave me the last time she put her hands around my throat. I didn't struggle this time; I just went limp, and we both slowly slid down the wall in a pile of limbs on the kitchen floor. She had landed on top of me, not allowing me to move. Then, she removed the hand from my collar and dropped her phone. She forcefully grasped my right hand with both of hers and every attempt I made to wriggle it free, she gripped even harder.

"You are going to leave me for her, aren't you?" she cruelly whispered in my face whilst she bent my little finger back beyond its normal range of motion.

"No! I love you. Please don't do this," I pleaded as she continued to put pressure on the finger; I could feel the bone creaking.

"Just admit it, Harry. And I'll stop," she sinisterly whispered in my ear.

"No," I mouthed silently. My display of meagre defiance is enough to push her over the edge, and she puts all her weight behind my finger, and it pops and snaps out of place. The sudden jolt of pain leads me to jump to my feet sharply, and Amelia is thrown off me, sending her flying towards the corner of the kitchen island. As I whimpered whilst cradling my broken finger, Amelia turned her head to me and was bleeding profusely from her nose.

"Now look what you've done to me!" she screamed.

"I think you've broken my finger," I sobbed.

"You've broken my nose. Look at the state of me."

"Amelia, I'm sorry. I just reacted."

"This is all your fault. If you weren't cheating on me at every opportunity, none of this would have happened."

"Not once have I ever been unfaithful to you, Ames," I yelled.

Amelia grabbed a cloth from near the sink, scrunched it up around her nose, and immediately left the house, slamming the door behind her. I did think about chasing after her, but I thought better of it. I was just glad it was over more than anything else. To be clear, I knew I wasn't in the wrong, and I was only defending myself. But what Amelia said made me feel like I was to blame. That's what she used to do. Whenever she would act up, somehow, I was always the only one who felt guilty afterwards. I knew all about gaslighting, but it just didn't seem to apply here.

There was no ice in the freezer, and I ran my finger underneath the cold tap in desperation. It had already begun to swell and bruise. As I remained standing in front of the sink, watching my finger inflate into a purple mess, I couldn't help but think how stupid I was only hours before. To go from the soaring high of the weekend and my first day at my new job to this crushing low was devastating. It wasn't going to get any better, but I felt trapped. I didn't even feel like I could go to Poppy for help. I'd already assured her it was going to be fine, and I was back in the exact same position. Amelia didn't come home that night, and I barely slept for a few consecutive minutes. At any moment, I expected her to burst through the door in another sustained attack. I strapped my little finger to its neighbour, and just like my marriage, I hoped it would fix itself on its own.

I got to the office in the morning, and it was a completely contrasting experience to the day before. For a start, I looked like I'd just been dug up, and I was already late. I'd bandaged my finger up the best I could, but the empurpled swollen stump protruded from the end of the dressing. The warm greetings I'd received from my new colleagues the previous day before instead looked like concern about my conspicuous injury. I got in the lift and made my way to my personal office. I just wanted to get in there and lock the door. Susan was waiting for me when I got to my floor, and I was running a little late.

"Good morning, Harry," Susan smiled before noticing my finger, "are you okay?"

"I'm fine. Trapped it in a door," I lied.

"Looks nasty. Are you sure you are okay?"

"Honestly, I'm good. I just want to start work."

"Perfect. Well, your new assistant is waiting for you in your office."

"Fine."

I'd forgotten about the first meeting with my assistant. Part of me wanted to turn around and get back in the lift and go home rather than face her. Although I didn't know her, she was part of the reason why I had a broken finger. I felt almost guilty going in and meeting her, and Amelia had been so paranoid about her that I didn't know what to expect when I walked through the door.

I recognised the voice in my head as Amelia's rather than my own, and I decided I was being ridiculous, so I entered the office.

"Good morning, Harry," she said.

"I don't believe it. Kim?" I gasped.

XV

JUSTICE

AMELIA

After the fifth attempt at calling James' number, which was written on the envelope, I gave up. I developed a splitting headache instantly, trying to work out how that phone number got into Harry's deposit box. I checked the numbers about twenty times, and they were the same number. I pocketed the keys and the envelope, and I locked the rest of the papers back in the box. I grew impatient from ringing James time and time again and decided to send him a text instead.

> *How did you know my husband?*

Given the number of times I'd called him unsuccessfully, I wasn't expecting a prompt response. Every single time Poppy had brought up psychics and mediums, Harry always said the same thing: it's a load of nonsense. The fact that he was in possession of James' number didn't make the slightest bit of sense. Could it be that he was somehow consulting with him prior to his death?

> *Harry had contacted me about his sister, Poppy.*

> *And you didn't think to mention that sooner?*

> *We only spoke briefly. It wasn't relevant.*

> *What did he want to talk about?*

> *He was concerned about her. That's all I can say. It would be unethical.*

Unethical? I couldn't believe what I was reading on my phone screen. Even though James had been the only person I could trust through this whole thing, I was beginning to suspect he too may have been lying to me. I abandoned the texting and started calling him again persistently, but he wouldn't pick up. I tried calling Poppy, and not surprisingly, she wouldn't answer either.

If she was somehow behind this, and she'd been tricking me the entire time, I don't know what I'd do to her. The only reason I was put on this path was because of her recommendation to text James in the first place. The more I thought about it, the more enraged I got. It had to have been Poppy this entire time.

I left the bank in a fury without saying a word to the manager, throwing the keys on the counter as I stamped past. I felt like a laughing stock. Was Poppy just trying to manipulate me all along, or was it just a cruel joke? Either way, she would pay for her deceit. I saw Kim waiting on a bench, sipping at a bottle of water, and I didn't even stop to tell her what had happened; I just tapped her on the shoulder.

"Let's go," I ordered.

"What's happening?" Kim asked as she stood up.

"We need to go and see Poppy."

I stormed back to the car with Kim lagging a few steps behind. As soon as the car doors shut, I wasted no time and started driving towards Poppy's house. I could see Kim was getting increasingly scared by the speed I was driving, but I didn't care about her safety. Or mine, for that matter. I just wanted to get there as quickly as possible and find out what had been going on. When we arrived at Poppy's, I could see her standing at the window. I threw the car door open and thundered up the garden path to the front door and bashed it with my clenched fists rapidly. Kim caught up with me and delicately put her hand on my arm.

"Calm down, Amelia. What is going on?" she said.

"It's her," I said through gritted teeth.

"What's her?"

"The person who has been manipulating me the entire time!" I shouted for Poppy's benefit.

"What are you talking about?" Kim asked.

"Here," I said, handing Kim my phone.

Kim read the messages whilst I continued to pound on the door. I could see Poppy in the bay, trying to make a phone call, presumably to the police. Poppy opened a small window to try and talk me down before I took the door off the hinges.

"I don't really understand what's going on, but just stop so we can talk about this," Poppy shouted through the window.

"It's you. It's always been you!" I screamed at her.

"What are you talking about?"

"James! It's been you all along, hasn't it?"

"You need to calm down, Amelia. The police are on their way."

"Good, they can arrest you for torturing a widow."

"I haven't done anything wrong!"

I could hear the sound of distant sirens, and I knew they were coming for me. I only had seconds left to get to Poppy before they arrived, and I decided to abandon my attempts to force the door open. Instead, I picked up a large plant pot from the driveway and threw it at the window. Glass and ceramic exploded in every direction as the pane gave way into a thousand pieces. Poppy dived out of the way, and just as she returned to her feet, the police arrived and began sprinting up the path.

"I'll get you for this, Penelope," I threatened.

"It wasn't me!" she pleaded.

The police arrived behind me and restrained me. I fought back at first, and they decided to use handcuffs. In the commotion, Poppy made her way through the house, opened the front door and stepped outside. Just as they started to put the handcuffs on, I heard my phone make a beep in Kim's hands.

"It's James. He's just sent an address," Kim announced.

I was humiliated. And I'd shown Poppy and Kim the monster that was lurking within me. All because of a scrap of paper I didn't fully understand. Poppy stood shrugging in the doorway, waiting for my immediate apology, but I was too proud to give her one. Instead, I lowered my head and stared at the carnage I'd just created. In one swift motion, Poppy's beautiful home had been destroyed. The glass from the broken window and soil from the pot I'd thrown lay all over the baby supplies they kept inside. I had a real problem with apologising for anything, but it was blatantly obvious that I should. Just as I was about to open my mouth and convey some semblance of remorse, Poppy began speaking.

"Be careful, officers," she started, her eyes locked with mine, "she's violent."

Violent. I detested that word. I wasn't violent, and I wouldn't apologise for feeling passionate about my marriage or my husband. In a way, I felt even more wrath from the single use of the word violent than when I thought she was pretending to be James. I always thought Poppy and I were alike; I certainly thought she was different from Yvonne. But the apple doesn't fall too far from the tree. Poppy was just as manipulative and dangerous as her mother and had me bang to rights. She must have been waiting for this moment for so long to see me in handcuffs. I could almost see her gloating over it, and the thought of her smug expression at me in cuffs boiled my blood.

"I'll show you violence," I hissed through a clenched jaw.

"She's the reason my brother is dead. She's an alcoholic and a domestic abuser," Poppy said, holding back tears.

"If Harry killed himself, it was because of you and your ridiculous family."

"My big brother killed himself because you constantly battered and belittled him for your entire marriage. You have to live with that, not me," Poppy said, pointing in my face.

The police didn't let me have the final word, and they started dragging me away to the van they'd arrived in.

They threw open the doors and pushed me into the cage that resided in the back of it. Whilst I was in there, they hastily read me my rights and slammed the door as I stared at Poppy with venom at a distance.

Whilst I was being transported to the police station, I thought I would have calmed down, but I didn't. As far as I was concerned, Poppy had put me in this cell. Yvonne would know what had happened by now, too, and she was probably on her way to the police station with Poppy to tell them all their wild theories. I started to worry that the police would actually believe them and my name would be dragged through the mud looking for the truth. When the original police enquiry into Harry's death was going on, everybody was under scrutiny. When it was decided his death was accidental, they closed the case, and that was that. But if the police thought there was any merit in what Yvonne and Poppy had to say, they could reopen it.

The indistinguishable tingles started to build on the back of my neck, and I lost all sensation in my hands. I banged my head rhythmically on the cage wall to try and knock the panic attack out of me, but it was coming, and I wouldn't be able to stop it. My feet started to go numb, and the sensation slowly crept up my legs like I was being immersed in ice-cold water. The waterline reached my chest, and I could almost feel my lungs filling with the liquid, so much so that I could barely breathe. Once it arrived at my neck, my throat started to close, and I began to cough erratically.

"Help!" I shouted as loud as I could, kicking the cage.

One of the officers had opened the little hatch from the cabin and looked at me with contempt. He assessed that I wasn't in any immediate danger and closed it again with a huff.

"Help me! I'm having a panic attack," I shouted again.

The officer opened the hatch once again and placed one finger on his lips before shushing me loudly. He then replaced the hatch, and I heard music playing from the cabin. By the time I arrived at the police station, it was the weakest I'd ever felt. I was so sweaty I think I could have slipped out of the handcuffs with ease. They tried to remove me from the cage, but my legs wouldn't hold my weight, and I immediately fell on the tarmac outside the van.

"Ma'am, you need to get up," the officer said.

"I'm pregnant, and I'm getting pains,"

"Jesus. Get help," the other officer said.

In my weakened state, they realised I wasn't much of a threat and placed me in a wheelchair they had from inside the station. They wheeled me in, and I got checked over by their first-aid trained officer. They checked everything they could, and according to them, I was fine. But I was still going through the most intense panic attack since I'd been at Harry's grave. My heart felt like it was beating in my throat, but apparently, all my vitals were normal. The officer actually told me it was 'all in my head', and as soon as he said so, the attack miraculously started to fade.

I was placed into a cell where I was constantly observed to ensure my condition didn't worsen. A female officer was sitting on a foldaway chair in the doorway, watching my every move. My prediction was correct; both Yvonne and Poppy were at the station and agreed not to press charges if I gave a heartfelt apology. If not, I would be looking at a night in the cells and possibly a community service order for criminal damage.

After an hour or so, when I'd calmed down, I was taken to a room, and Yvonne and Poppy were already sat down inside it. Poppy had clearly been crying, and Yvonne had her arm around her, trying to comfort her. A detective joined us, and I recognised her, she was called Angela, the same detective that had looked into Harry's death.

"Okay, Amelia. If you apologise for the damage you've done, Penelope is happy to drop the charges. Is that still the case, Penelope?" Angela said.

"Yes," Poppy whispered.

I began to mouth the words before I could utter them. It took every last ounce of energy just to produce the sound, but I swallowed my pride out came the words.

"I'm sorry," I said as sincerely as I could manage.

"I accept your apology," Poppy uttered.

"So, you aren't behind the texts?" I asked.

"Of course she bloody isn't," Yvonne interrupted.

"If you are happy with that, you two can leave now," Angela said to Yvonne and Poppy, "but I'd like to speak to Amelia if I can."

Poppy stood up, and she could barely make eye contact with me. Whatever courage she felt at her front door an hour before had faded. Yvonne, on the other hand, stared at me intensely and with venom as they left.

"How are you doing, Amelia?" Angela asked.

"What do you think?" I said.

"I think that you are going through a tough time."

"That's putting it mildly."

"You should speak to someone. You can't deal with something like that on your own. It's just not possible."

"With all due respect, Angela, you don't know what I am dealing with.

"True. But I spent some time with you and Harry's family. I know you all loved him very much."

"I did."

"I've heard about the allegations that Poppy made on her doorstep," Angela said, leaning back in her chair, "Is there any truth to them?"

"No."

"She was pretty specific about the types of injuries that Harry allegedly sustained. Would we be able to verify those if we looked at his medical records?"

"No, because it isn't true," I insisted.

"Amelia?" Angela said with a sigh.

"Is the baby Harry's?"

"Of course it's his."

"Well, you need to smooth things over with his family. They are going to want to be involved in the baby's life."

"They aren't getting anywhere near this baby," I said, clasping my stomach.

"Fine, but regardless, you should stay away for a while."

"Did you tell them to stay away from me?"

"I did."

"Good."

"Listen, I'll get your things, and you will be free to leave. But consider this an official warning. If there are any more arguments or plant pots being thrown, charges will be pressed. Do you hear me?"

"I hear you."

Angela led me out of the room and got my things. I had to sign a document explaining that I understood that I'd received a caution and that if I repeated the offence, it could lead to prosecution. I had no intention of going near Harry's awful family ever again. No wonder he was so keen to leave Filey in the first place. They were all insane. I know I apologised to Poppy, but I didn't mean it. Not one bit. I did what I did for the wrong reasons, but she deserved it. They all deserved everything that was coming to them. When I went outside the police station, Kim was waiting for me outside with my phone.

Ironically, she had become the only person I could even remotely trust now.

"That was one hell of a throw," Kim joked.

"I know," I smiled.

"Remind me never to get on your bad side."

"It's not advised."

"Are we checking this address out then, or what? I've driven your car here; I hope you don't mind."

"Let me see my phone."

I unlocked my phone, and several messages were waiting from James.

> *Flat 15, Bayside Court.*
> *Your anger is understandable but is misdirected. Channel it into your journey, and you will uncover the truth.*

As much as I hated the fortune cookie advice, I knew James was absolutely right. I still didn't feel guilty. Poppy was getting in the way of me finding the truth, and if I wanted to get to it, I had to remain determined. I had no idea what was waiting for us at that address, but I was pretty certain that I had the key to the door, found in the envelope in Harry's deposit box. A quick internet search showed that the address was in a block of flats overlooking Filey Beach.

We both got in the car and started the navigation. I could see in my peripheral vision that Kim was itching to say something to me.

"Out with it," I said.

"The psychic guy. Have you been speaking to him for a while?" Kim asked.

"Poppy recommended him to me at the funeral. So ever since then."

"My name was mentioned. How did he know where you would find me?"

"Psychic," I said, waving my hands in the air.

"Spooky. So, you thought Poppy was behind those texts?"

"Yes, I found James' number in Harry's deposit box. Apparently, Harry and James were speaking about Poppy."

"Maybe Harry was getting advice, too."

"About what?" I asked.

"I don't know. But everyone needs someone to talk to, and there's no shame in that," she said.

"He had me."

"I know."

We arrived at the block of flats, and I parked the car. Whatever was inside, it wasn't good news. You wouldn't catch me living here. The façade of the flats looked like an office building rather than a living accommodation. The exterior was entirely pebble-dashed, used as an extra line of defence against the corrosive Filey sea air. Beach towels are hung outside of the open windows in the block, allowing the cigarette smoke to flow into the open air from inside. The interior was no better; the strange, juxtaposed aromas of dampness and dust lingered in the hallways. The carpet was balding and unvacuumed, and the yellowing walls begged for a lick of paint. We began to make our way up the groaning stairs.

We reached flat fifteen, and I knocked on the door slowly. There weren't any signs of immediate life, and I produced the keys that I'd found in the envelope. The key turned, and the door opened with a click. Kim and I leaned our heads around the door, and as it creaked open, it appeared as if we were alone. It was a small, one-bedroom flat with an open-plan living room and kitchenette. A huge pile of unopened letters lay on the countertop, along with the occasional food wrapper or unwashed cup. Kim and I remained together, moving from room to room as quietly as possible, but once we had made an initial first sweep, we began to relax.

I had no idea why James had led me here, but there must have been a reason. He could likely sense that I was getting annoyed with the constant mysteries and riddles, and he was trying to distract me with some actual information. Once we had decided it was safe, instinctively, Kim and I split up and started searching for any clues. I went into the bathroom first, and my eye was drawn to a bottle on the sink. It was aftershave, and I recognised the brand because it was the exact same brand that Harry used. I opened the bottle and sprayed it into the air, and it was definitely his.

"Amelia, come here," Kim shouted from the other room. When I entered the main area of the flat, she was sifting through the letters that had been left on the countertop.

"What is it?" I asked.

"Most of these letters are addressed to Harry," she said, holding a letter to my face.

"They can't be."

I started going through the letters myself, and she was completely correct. The vast majority of them were all addressed to my late husband, apart from the odd piece of junk mail. The more we looked through, the more items we found that looked like they could belong to Harry. The clothing that was there I didn't recognise, but it was all definitely something he would wear. Even down to the obscure medicated shampoo he swore by. He had definitely been living here, or at least stayed here on occasion, but I was totally in the dark about this place. Kim concentrated on the huge pile of letters and started opening them if they looked like they would contain a lead. I heard her gasp, and I turned to see what she had found.

"Jackpot. There's a phone bill here," Kim said excitedly, handing it to me.

"Weird, that isn't his number," I said, studying the bill. There weren't any calls on there, just a standing charge. I recognised the number, and I compared it to the scrap of paper I'd found in Harry's deposit box. The numbers matched. I nearly passed out on the spot and had to brace myself against the counter.

"What is it?" Kim asked.

"The number on this bill matches James' number."

It wasn't possible. That number had been texting me pretty much every single day since the funeral, and if it was Harry's second phone number, there was only one explanation I could think of. Harry was alive. Before Kim could reply, the sound of a key entering the front door lock stopped us. A male figure walked in, holding a carrier bag full of shopping items, and dropped his keys on the table next to the door. It was so dark in that dingy flat I couldn't see him properly, and to make matters worse, he was wearing a hoodie with the hood up.

"Harry?" I shouted, "is that you?"

XVI

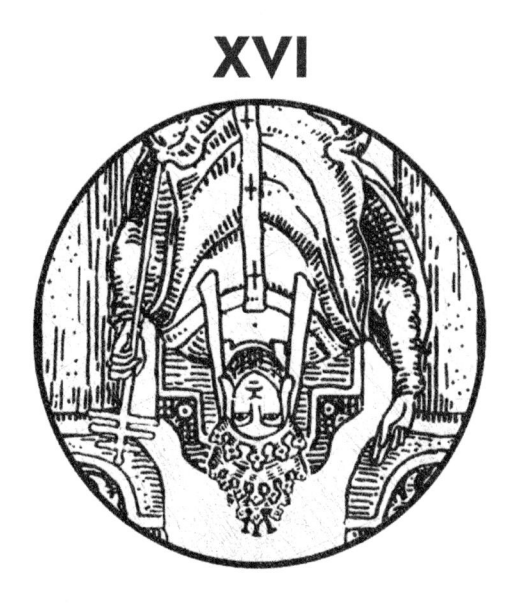

THE HIEROPHANT

HARRY - BEFORE

It was one of the darkest times of my life, and Kim appeared when I probably needed her the most. She almost looked like a mirage; the last time I'd seen her was shortly after my Dad had died.

"What a small world," Kim laughed.

"Honestly, I can't believe it. When did you move to Manchester?" I asked.

"Not long ago. I needed a change from Filey."

"Yeah, me too."

"I saw this job advertised and decided to go for it. I had no idea you worked here, too."

"I literally started yesterday."

"What happened to your hand?" she asked.

I had been so lost in the moment and wondering how to feel that Kim was standing in front of me that I'd forgotten about everything for a minute. Her innocent question brought the whole experience flooding back, and the smile was wiped off my face. Amelia was already paranoid about me having a female assistant. If she found out she was an ex-girlfriend of mine, there was no telling what she would do to me. I still hadn't heard from her since she walked out of the house in the morning. For all I knew, she could be scaling the building to spy on me.

"I trapped it in a door," I said. Kim stood in front of me and delicately cradled my injured hand with the warmth of hers.

"Was it a revolving door?" Kim joked.

"No," I laughed, "a regular one."

Something happened in that moment. I don't know if it was our proximity or the gentle warmth of her soft hands against mine, but I wanted to break down and tell her everything. Every disgusting and vicious detail of what Amelia was doing to me, and yet I couldn't because I was terrified Amelia would somehow find out and hurt Kim. I hastily pushed her hands away from mine, and she looked troubled by my physical response.

"Sorry, Harry. That was a bit unprofessional of me," Kim said.

"Don't be sorry. We should probably start work, though," I replied.

Kim and I barely spoke for the entire day. I wasn't getting any work done. I was just sitting in my office wondering what to do about Amelia. I knew that deep down, she wasn't ever going to stop. I'd enjoyed a few weeks of respite, but since then it had escalated, if anything. I could barely think because of the searing pain from my little finger, and every twinge brought back the violent memory of what had happened.

I came to an obvious realisation: I didn't deserve what happened to me. Or what happened to me for the months before. I didn't deserve any of the ferocious snipes or excessive criticisms she gave to me. Poppy was right, and I needed to get out of this toxic relationship and probably go to the police. In a moment of strength, I decided to send Amelia a text.

> *We need to talk.*

Measly though it was, I'd taken the first step in escaping this brutish woman that was none other than my wife. An outpouring of self-pride suddenly washed over me. I never even thought I'd be brave enough to take this step. I mistakenly thought that everything with Amelia was going to work itself out, but I'd been kidding myself. I wasn't expecting miracles, but her increasing volatility made me finally realise she was never going to change, and, unless I jumped ship before it got sucked into the giant whirlpool, I was bound to wither away and fade into an unrecognisable shadow of my former self. Then, when I would least expect it, she would probably end up killing me in a drunken rage. I needed to remain strong and actually follow through this time.

With every minute that passed without a response, I felt even more anxious. I imagined her tearing the house apart in a fit of unrelenting wrath. She probably knew she was losing control; what if she did something to herself? Something irreversible. The thought entered my head that she could be swallowing the entire packet of those tablets she had been taking, and I'd find her that way when I returned home. I fought every urge to contact her again; she had been playing games like this with me for years, but thankfully I'd finally begun to wise up to them.

Kim popped her head in the door, and I suddenly realised the time. It was almost 6:30 pm, and I could have left an hour before.

"Am I okay to leave now, Harry?" she asked.

"I'm so sorry, I totally lost track of time," I replied.

Kim gave me a look of concern, and instead of leaving, she came into the office and shut the door behind her.

"What's going on?" she asked.

"What do you mean?" I said.

"I know you, Harry. You aren't yourself. You should be ecstatic. You've got this amazing job. You look utterly miserable."

I couldn't bottle it up any longer. Every emotion I'd silently buried fiercely rose to the surface all of a sudden, and I started crying uncontrollably. She didn't waste any time and ran straight over to me and embraced me comfortingly, while and I continued crying inconsolably for what felt to me like hours. I told her every detail of what had happened to me, and Kim wept, too. It could all be traced back to the death of Dad. I wasn't ready for a relationship at the time, but Amelia said and did all the right things. Once she had her claws in me, that's when everything had turned sinister. Kim's opinion was the same as Poppy's, and I should have left her immediately and contacted the police. But they didn't know her like I did. She wasn't going to let me go without a bitter fight.

"Do you want to stay at mine?" Kim asked.

"Thank you, but no, I can't," I responded.

"You can't go home."

"I have to. I have to face her."

"What if she gets aggressive again?"

"Then I'll walk away."

I took my time on the drive home. Truth be told, I had no stomach for yet another one of her episodes. I didn't want to face her, but with Kim's words of encouragement fresh in my mind, I felt like it was the best time. I sat in the car for a while before I even thought about entering.

My finger was still throbbing, and the memory of the night before kept flashing through my mind with every pulse of pain shooting up my arm. I just had to go in and tell her, without pulling any punches, that it was over. If she started getting aggressive again, I'd walk away.

I unlocked the door and opened it slightly. There was soft piano music playing from the dining room. I fearfully put my head around the door, and Amelia was sitting at the table with a full meal prepared and candles lit. She had a white plaster spanning the width of her nose and a slight suggestion of a black eye.

"Hi, husband," she smiled.

"Hi… what's going on here?" I asked.

"It's an apology. Sit down."

Just the mere thought that Amelia was going to apologise was a genuinely new experience for me. She was always in the right, even when she wasn't. For her to own up and take the blame was something I actually found quite shocking. Because at first glance she looked calm, I decided to comply and sat down across from her. She smiled charmingly as I did. Amelia had prepared sirloin steak and peppercorn sauce with a side of roast potatoes.

"Dig in while it's still hot," Amelia suggested.

"I'm not hungry," I said.

"Listen, I'm sorry for what happened," Amelia sighed, putting down her knife and fork, "but you gave as good as you got."

"Excuse me?"

"This," she said, pointing at her face, "I thought you'd broken it."

"I was trying to stop you from breaking my finger."

Amelia stood from the table, walked over to my right-hand side, delicately clasped my injured hand and inspected my finger closely.

"Is it broken?" she asked, with an overly dramatic pitying look across her face.

"I think so. The swelling won't go down. I've not had time to get it looked at."

"You don't need to do that. Stay there, and I'll get you some ice."

Amelia left the dining room for a minute to go and fetch the ice. I did think about getting up and striding out of the house, but her whole demeanour was totally alien to me, and to be honest, I was somewhat curious about what she had to say. She returned with this facial expression, copied directly from a 1960s dutiful housewife, knelt down next to me and tentatively placed the ice on my finger. She moved her attention from my finger and looked up directly into my eyes.

"I went to the clinic today," she announced.

"What for? I didn't think we had an appointment until next week."

"I moved it," she started, standing up above me again and touching her stomach, "they did another implantation. I could be pregnant with your child right now."

If Amelia was pregnant, it wasn't a child in there. It was a hostage. She had felt me slipping away and outmanoeuvred me. At that moment, I knew I was never going to get away from her, not cleanly, anyway. Across her face she had a beaming smile that one would typically find on a woman who was pleased she was pregnant, but I saw it a different way. It was a smile of victory. She knew that I wouldn't leave her if she was pregnant with my child. The only was I was going to get away from this vapid and abusive woman was to plan carefully and play her at her own game.

"That's great news," I smiled deceitfully.

"Oh, Harry. You are going to be a dad this time. I can feel it," Amelia beamed, grabbing both my cheeks and kissing me passionately, "we can put all this unpleasantness behind us and finally enjoy each other."

"I agree."

"And I promise no more alcohol. I can't be drinking if I'm in the family way."

"That's good."

"Now come on, eat up; it took me hours to prepare all this," Amelia said, picking up her knife and fork.

I felt like an actor in a play. Having already lost my appetite, I unwillingly started to eat Amelia the cheesiest grin I could muster. The mask had slipped, and suddenly, everything she did, even something as mundane as eating, seemed sinister. She sawed the steak open with her knife and stabbed the pieces with her fork. Then she drowned the roast potatoes with the peppercorn sauce before she crushed them, like she did to me, prior to eating. Even though I was trapped in this abusive marriage, to say the least, the fact that I could see who Amelia was for the first time was very liberating. I'd do what I always did, strive to give her everything she wanted, but behind her back, I would be covertly planning my long-overdue escape plan.

Amelia chatted about the future and suggested baby names all evening. I laughed at her jokes. I forcedly reciprocated all her poisonous kisses. I stood behind an emotional mirror, reflecting everything she did to me back at her, desperate to just walk out of there and never return. But I didn't. I continued the charade, and as soon as she got tired and went to sleep, I started looking for somewhere to escape.

I couldn't afford anything in Manchester without selling the house or committing even more fraud. It broke my heart, but if I had to give up my dream job to get away from this situation, I would. I found a flat in Filey, right near the seafront. It was a huge step down from where I was living right now, but I wouldn't mind coming down in the world so long as my whereabouts remained unknown to Amelia. I sent the estate agent an email asking for a viewing as soon as possible. It would be like a safe haven from her, at least until I could find something more permanent.

I went upstairs and into the bedroom. Amelia was out for the count, sleeping like a baby with her back to my side of the bed. I crept over and pulled back the covers slowly to get inside. The disturbance was enough to wake her slightly, and she turned to put her arm around me. Just the warmth of her skin was enough to turn my stomach and make me shudder in disgust.

The next morning, I continued the gruelling pantomime until I got in the car for work. Amelia was standing on the porch, waving me off. I played along, smiled, and pulled a silly face as I drove away. Part of me wondered if she knew exactly what I was plotting behind her back, but in truth, I didn't even know that myself. I just had to get out of there and ensure that she wouldn't come looking for me after I did. Once I'd been driving for a few minutes, I stopped the car and pulled up on the curb. I exhaled loudly and started hyperventilating. I'd felt as if I had held my breath the entire time I was in that house with her. I could finally breathe again, and I took out my phone. The estate agent replied that they were happy to allow me to view the property. I called in sick at work, citing my finger as the excuse, and began the long drive to Filey.

The estate agent had arranged to meet me outside the block of flats. They didn't look anything like the photographs online; they were decaying and dingy. I spotted someone who looked like they could be the estate agent, and they waved at me as I parked the car.

"Harry?" she asked.

"Yes, is it Leah?" I replied.

"It is! I'm here to show you around. Have you seen the pictures online?"

"I have, let's get to it, shall we?"

"Follow me!"

As soon as I walked through the entrance, a combination of humidity and grime wafted into my nostrils. Leah didn't seem bothered by the smell. She simply continued smiling brightly and led me up the stairs to flat fifteen. She unlocked the door, and thankfully, the smell hadn't already drifted inside. It was basic, ugly and barely functional. But it was perfect. Even if Amelia found out about this unsightly place, I doubt she would even get past the smell downstairs.

"Gas and electricity are included. So is water. If you want the internet, there is a surcharge. What do you think?" Leah asked.

"I'll take it," I announced.

Within the hour, I'd signed the paperwork, and I had the set of keys for my very own secret flat. I had done it on impulse, but I urgently needed somewhere to escape to. It was imperative that Amelia should never find out about this place. If she broke my finger when she found out that I'd been appointed an assistant; she would then surely kill me if she ever discovered this place. I went out to Filey town and did some shopping. Essentials really, toiletries and some clothes in case I needed to stay here in an emergency. I also got a burner phone on a whim. I had no idea why I would need it, but it seemed like it might be useful if I were planning to vanish into thin air.

I sat on the sofa in my new flat and felt like I could finally see a way out. I just had to play the game for a few weeks. For the first time since we started trying for a child, I prayed that the latest IVF implantation was proven to be unsuccessful. Once we had the sad news, I could finally leave her and be done with our poisonous marriage. If the attempt was successful, it wouldn't bear thinking about. It would undoubtedly compound things further, and I wasn't the kind of man who could leave his child, especially in her care.

Once I was happy that everything was in place, I took the spare key and drove to the bank where I had an account in Leeds. I had a deposit box there. I used to keep a paper ledger with all the money I had 'borrowed' from pension funds. I'd store the spare keys there in case of emergencies. By the time I had arrived back in Manchester, I still had a few hours left to kill before I could go home without arousing suspicion, so I decided to call into work and keep up the pretence.

When I walked out of the lift, Kim looked at me like I was a ghost. I'd forgotten to get in touch with her and tell her where I was that day and, more importantly, that I was okay. God knows what she thought had happened to me, and I felt terrible when I saw the intense concern on her face.

"Harry! I thought—" she started.

"I'm so sorry, Kim. It's been a busy day."

I took Kim into my office and brought her up to speed. She approved of my plan in principle and offered me her help if I needed it. I'd be lying if I said it didn't feel like old times; we never had closure after what had happened, and we kind of just drifted apart. Maybe if I'd accepted Kim's help when Dad died, things would have been different. She was amazing. I hadn't seen her in years, and she was right there for me when I needed her. I'd made a lot of mistakes in my life, but Kim was never one of them.

"Thank you for all your support, Kim," I said.

"You are so welcome," Kim responded.

"I just can't believe after all these years, and how I treated you, you are still willing to help me."

"What happened between us wasn't your fault, Harry. Your dad died."

"I know, but I could have handled it better."

"It was just bad timing, that's all."

I was staring into Kim's eyes, and so she into mine. The mischievous side of me wanted to suggest running away together, but I thought it was a step too far, even for a joke. When I first saw her face again after all those years, it suddenly brought back the feelings I had for her.

In a way, I don't think they ever left. I just buried them deep down, along with all my other feelings, positive or otherwise. I didn't realise just how strong my feelings were back then. Just as I was almost getting lost in the fantasy, Kim's hand slowly crept towards mine and gripped it tightly.

She smiled, and her full lips parted slowly as they made their way towards mine. As soon as our lips touched, the chemistry and attraction of bygone years exploded inside both of us. The passion started to build, and suddenly, I found myself almost frantically undressing Kim as she unclothed me. I paused for a moment to lock the office door, and then I did something I hadn't done for a while. I made love.

I thought I would have felt guilty about it, but I didn't. Not one bit. Emotionally, I had been all over the place in the weeks leading up to that moment, but I was feeling something I barely recognised because it had been that long. Happiness. Kim felt it, too; she giggled and smiled as she got dressed again.

"I'm definitely getting fired. I've not even been here a week, and I've been late, rang in sick, and now this," I joked.

"You're getting sacked? I've just slept with my boss on my second day," Kim laughed.

I felt cheated that the happiness had only lasted a few short minutes before I realised that I had to go home. The smile must have slipped from my face because Kim noticed my mood change, and her smile faded, too.

"Where do we go from here?" Kim asked.

"I don't know. You don't fancy running away together, do you?" I smiled.

"I'm being serious."

"Me too."

"Are you going to tell Amelia?" she asked sullenly.

"I've just got to wait those two weeks. Then I'm leaving her."

Kim came over to me and gave me another kiss and an amorous hug. We stayed like that for what felt like twenty minutes. I looked outside the windows and saw the city plunge into darkness; we had been here for hours. I didn't know what I'd tell Amelia, and for the first time, I didn't care either. Why should I? The next fortnight was about survival, nothing more.

"Do you believe in fate, Harry?" Kim asked.

"If you'd asked me a week ago, I'd have said it was nonsense," I replied.

"And what about now?"

"I believe in fate," I smirked.

XVII

THE STAR

AMELIA

My heart had stopped beating and hadn't produced a single beat since I'd said Harry's name. The shadowy figure of a man remained at the door in total silence as I edged towards him anxiously with my shaking hand outstretched.

"Please, don't freak out," the figure whispered softly.

"Take your hood off," I said.

The man reached to his head, removed the hood slowly and turned to me. He had certainly been resurrected, but it wasn't Harry.

"Steve?" Kim asked.

"Yes. Calm down, ladies, please. I can explain everything," Steve said gently.

For a few moments, I thought it was all a deliberate lie. Even though I'd buried him, I somehow convinced myself that he could have walked through that door. Any feelings of hope or happiness were quickly overridden by bafflement and quiet anger. There was still a chance, though. Maybe he managed to fake the whole thing as a cunning plan to escape the Broadheads. He wouldn't have been able to get in touch with me either. It would have put me in danger. Or maybe this whole thing was a tactical ploy he'd come up with to remove me from his life. It was the only way out for him, and he knew I wouldn't let him go easily.

One thing was for certain: Steve wasn't leaving this room until he had divulged all the secrets he had been harbouring. He had already got away with that once, and I wouldn't let him disappear again until he spilt the beans and confessed every single thing he knew about Harry. If, by some divine miracle, Harry was still breathing, I would force Steve to take me to him.

"We are calm, Steve. What the hell are you doing here?" I said impatiently.

"This is Harry's flat. He gave me a key, so I've been staying here since my house went up in flames."

"Have you seen him?"

"Who?"

"Harry!" I shouted.

"Am I missing something here?" Steve said to Kim in bewilderment.

"We thought Harry might have been living here, but it was obviously you," Kim explained.

"Harry's dead, love," Steve said.

I wasn't sure whether Steve was lying to cover for Harry or it was the actual truth. I knew what a rational person would believe, but I needed to be certain. I marched towards him and pinned him by his throat against the wall. I turned to look at Kim, who seemed absolutely petrified by what she'd just witnessed me doing. For a second, I'd forgotten she was there because of the blind rage I felt. I tightened my grip and leaned into Steve's face forcefully.

"Tell me everything. Right now," I ordered before releasing my grip.

"Jesus, you only had to ask," Steve panted.

"I did. I won't be asking again."

"The Broadheads burned my place down because I couldn't pay them back. So, I've been lying low here," Steve explained.

"The Broadheads told me they came after you because they couldn't collect from Harry. They said you were his guarantor,"

"Harry thought he'd paid up. But I used half of his money to clear some of my own debt. According to them, he still owed them half," Steve confessed.

I was still within reach of Steve, and he deserved to feel some pain for what he'd done. I took the opportunity to deliver a swift kick between his legs. He yelped and crashed to the floor like a sack of rocks. I intended to do some more damage, but Kim managed to stop me before I clocked him again. He was coughing convulsively in a pathetic bundle on the floor, and Kim, looking anxious to diffuse the violence, suggested I sit down. All these people who had wronged Harry behind his back were still pretending to care about what happened to him. I was the only one who really cared. Everyone else was flagrantly using him. If Kim wasn't there, I would have been able to stop myself, but I wasn't ready for her to see my true colours just yet.

"I deserved that, I reckon," Steve said as he stood up and made his way over to the other sofa.

"You deserve more than that," I threatened.

"Can we all just calm down, please," Kim suggested.

"What were you going to tell me on the night of the fire?" I questioned abruptly.

"Are you sure you want to know?"

"Yes, I'm sure."

"Well, considering this place, isn't it obvious?"

"Enlighten me."

"Harry was planning to leave you. He got this little love nest to escape to."

Steve never liked me, and I did just deliver a kick to one of his favourite parts, but I could see in his eyes he was telling the truth. Even though I didn't want to believe it, all my worst insecurities confirmed so. His use of the words 'love nest' is what really irked me. Was Harry bragging to Steve about what he was planning to do, and that's how he ended up having a key? Who was this other woman he intended to live here with? Were they laughing at me behind my back? The questions continued to pelt me, and I could feel my old adversary anxiety bubbling away beneath the surface.

Whoever this other woman was, she couldn't have been classy. You wouldn't catch me dead roughing it in a place like this. He must have been willing to throw away our entire marriage for some common street whore; what does that say about how he felt about me? He wished to start a family with me. He wanted me to be the mother of his children. Was the whole thing just a cruel joke? To what end?

Breathe.

I was starting to get too worked up, and I could feel the inevitable attack coming. I couldn't let Steve see me in that state, and I wasn't done with him.

"Pass me my bag, Kim," I asked.

Kim it over to me. I didn't have to wait for the signs; I knew I was seconds away from another panic attack, and it was better to take them now rather than wait. I swallowed the tablets dry rather than touch a glass of water in this squat. Steve stood transfixed, staring at me while waiting for my response.

"Was there someone else?" I asked.

"Yes. But I don't know who. He never said," Steve replied.

I couldn't tell if Steve was lying. There wasn't much that Harry wouldn't tell Steve, but I didn't know him well enough to make an assessment. I stared at him for an uncomfortably long time, but his resolve remained unwaveringly.

"Are you James?" I asked.

"Who the hell is James?" Steve said with a look of bemusement.

"The person texting me."

"Amelia, I have no idea what you're talking about at this point."

"Well, someone seems to be taking immense pleasure in manipulating me, using a number that Harry registered,"

"It isn't me, sweetheart."

"Don't call me sweetheart."

"One thing I do know is you can't trust her either," Steve said, pointing at Kim.

"Oh, and why is that?" I asked.

"I'll let you find that one out on your own."

Steve started to look increasingly agitated by me by my combative temperament and leaned forward in the chair. I could already tell I wasn't going to like what was about to come out of his mouth next.

"Let's cut the bullshit," Steve started, "it's no surprise to me Harry started playing away after the horrendous way you treated him. I know all about what you were doing to him, and it's fucking disgusting."

"You don't know anything about our relationship."

"I know that if he jumped off Filey Brigg, as everyone says, you may as well have pushed him yourself."

The rage instantly ignited within me, and I leaned over the coffee table to smack Steve right across the face, but he caught my wrist before it could make contact. He then took his free hand and slapped me across mine, knocking me to the floor.

"Harry may not have defended himself against you, but I definitely will," Steve said as he stood up.

"Steve! She's pregnant!" Kim shouted.

"She should have thought about that before she started throwing her hands about," Steve said with a shrug, "get out, the pair of you."

Kim helped me up. I'd bitten my lip hard on the impact, and it was bleeding down my chin. Kim grabbed my bag and escorted me out of the flat, and Steve slammed the door behind us. The tablets had kicked in, and after being hit by Steve, I was feeling very dizzy.

Kim put me in the passenger side of the car, and then got in the driver's side. As soon as the tension of the situation had blown over, I started crying my eyes out.

"Are you okay, Amelia?" she asked.

"He's right. I deserved that," I sobbed.

"No one deserves that."

"You're right. And Harry definitely didn't deserve it."

"No, he didn't."

Kim was wrong. If anyone deserved a slap across the face, it was me. If anything, I deserved far worse. As the blood flowed into my mouth, leaving me with the bitter taste of iron on the back of my throat, I couldn't help thinking this was how Harry had felt. Every time I hurt him, he must have felt this vulnerable and helpless, like I did with Steve towering over me. For a time, I was adamant Harry gave as good as he got, but I knew deep down that he didn't. Steve was right; if Harry had jumped off Filey Brigg, then I might as well have pushed him myself.

With each awful and devious thing I said to him, I doomed him even closer to the precipice. Each time I placed my hands on him in anger or hurt him, he was pushed even further. I'd given him an infinite amount of reasons to leave and barely any to stay, which made his decision an easy one, in the end. He was going to end our marriage and leave, and I could hardly blame him for that. I just wished I could turn the clock back and fix it all, but even if it were possible to go back, our marriage was beyond repair. I'd taken Harry, a bright and joyful soul and trampled him underneath my boot to the point of suffocation.

One thing that kept playing on my mind over and over again was what Steve had said about Kim. I remembered what he had said back at his house, that he didn't want Kim there when he spoke to me. I started to think she was more heavily involved in all this than she had originally let on.

"If you don't mind, I'd like to drive us somewhere," Kim said softly.

"Where?" I asked through the tears.

"You will see when we get there."

Kim started driving excruciatingly slow, and about halfway to our destination, I realised where she was taking me. I'd specifically avoided going there ever since it happened. Kim was taking me to Filey Brigg. I'd only visited once since my husband lost his life there, and it was only because of the police investigation. They had to basically drag me there kicking and screaming, and after that ordeal, I knew I never wanted to go there ever again. We arrived at Steve's caravan site, which had remained closed since the day of the fire. Kim pushed opened the unlocked gates and then returned to the car to drive through them. We made our way down the gravel road to where Steve's house once stood. The rubble was still there, and it was just a pile of burnt roof timbers and bricks. Kim parked up in front of it and turned off the engine.

"We can walk the rest of the way," Kim said.

"I can't go there," I said frantically.

"Of course, you can. There's something you need to see."

We walked beyond the caravan site and towards Filey Brigg viewpoint. I was dragging my feet, and Kim constantly stopped and turned to me to urge me quicken my pace to catch her up. She was acting really mysteriously, and I didn't like the vibe I was getting from her. I took out my phone and texted James as we walked.

> *Why is Kim taking me to Filey Brigg? Is she involved?*

> *Continue walking the path. All will be revealed to you soon.*

James' words did little to encourage me to go on. I could already feel the panic rising, and once we had reached the viewpoint, Kim stopped a few feet away from the place where Harry had lost his life and turned round to look at me.

"Look over the cliff," she said.

"I don't want to. Just tell me what your game is. Now," I replied sharply.

"Do it. And I'll tell you."

I slowly made my way over to the exact spot where Harry had died. It was plain to see how easily he could have lost his footing; the rocks were coated in seawater from the mist of the constant crashing of the waves thunderously buffeting the craggy cliff. The surface was as slippery as ice, and I took tiny steps to avoid falling myself. I looked over the cliff, as Harry had, and stared down onto the rocks below. I don't know what I was expecting to see, but any trace of what had happened had been washed away by the tide a thousand times since.

The ceaseless barrage of waves from the North Sea pounded against the indifferent cliff face overpoweringly. The wind was already picking up when I arrived, and it felt stronger the closer to the edge I got. I could barely remain standing against the blusterous onslaught. The wind brought with it a freezing mist of seawater that glazed my skin and was giving me goosebumps. The imperceptible salt lingering in the air made my mouth dry. I turned to Kim with a shrug. I was unable to figure out what she had driven me here for.

"I brought you here so you could stand in the same place as Harry did when he lost his life and hopefully tell me the truth," Kim shouted.

"Okay?" I yelled back.

"Harry didn't end his own life, Amelia. He was in love."

"I know he was in love."

"No. Not with you, Amelia. With me."

"What?" I shouted, taking a single step towards her.

"Harry loved me, not you. And he was excited about the future, not planning on killing himself."

"So, this whole time, it was you? You were the other woman?"

"No, Amelia. You were the other woman. We were going to live together and be happy. But you just couldn't let him go, could you?"

"He was mine!" I shouted.

"No, he wasn't. Years of you torturing him saw to that."

The only thing stopping me from racing over to Kim and trying to drag her over the cliff face was my woeful lack of confidence in my own footing. I thought Harry had decided to leave me of his own volition, but he was stolen from me, as I'd always suspected. This harlot was jealous of how strong our love was and decided to take it for herself. She had snuck in under my nose and started poisoning Harry's mind, and I couldn't look her in the eye any longer. I started cautiously, making my way over to Kim, who raised her hand to signal that I should stop.

"I'm going to have to insist you stay there, Amelia," Kim said matter-of-factly.

"You can't control me," I replied through gritted teeth.

"If you come any closer, I'll just walk away from this. And I won't tell you what I know."

"Spit it out then."

"You are insufferable. You've constantly played the victim and lied the entire time. I've been waiting for you to confess what you've done, but you won't! You won't even admit it to yourself."

"Admit what?"

"Your part in Harry's death. I can't keep the pretence up any longer."

"Kim, you are beginning to bore me."

"I reconnected with Harry again when he started his new job. It was the day after you broke his finger. Do you remember that?"

"Yes."

"Call it fate or coincidence, but it turned out I was his assistant. He was at the lowest point in his life, and I helped him through it. In the days after that, we started a relationship."

"You mean an affair?"

"No, a relationship. Because once he escaped you, we were going to move back here to Filey."

"Oh, and live happily ever after, right?"

"Something like that. Until you stepped in."

Kim had no idea what she was talking about. I didn't know the motive behind her decision to bring me down here, but I didn't think she knew either. All this time, she thought she had been manipulating me into making some shock confession that I'd taken Harry's life or driven him to suicide. But she didn't even know half of what was going on here. I would have kept up my own pretence longer, but the urge to tell her the truth and see her face in response was immeasurably irresistible. Kim clearly thought a lot about herself, but did she think I was this naive? My resting grimace cracked into a smile; I relaxed my shoulders and burst out laughing madly.

"Give it a rest, Kim. I knew he was having an affair," I chuckled.

"Like you keep saying. It was just your paranoia—"

"No, Kim. I *knew* he was having an affair. I got wind of it all as soon as it started. I just didn't know who with. Until now."

"What are you even talking about now?"

"All these little discoveries we made about Harry, I more or less knew about them all," I chucked, "Do you think that was the first time I'd been to his flat? Or visited Becky's house? I just wanted to figure out who he was cheating on me with."

"That can't be true," Kim sobbed in disbelief.

I loved Harry. I loved him more than anybody else, especially Kim. When Harry started acting suspiciously and all of a sudden began disappearing for hours at a time, I decided to take matters into my own hands and started following him. At first, I thought he was having an affair, but when I saw him go to the Broadheads with Steve, I knew something even more sinister was going on. Harry was a gentle soul, and I couldn't stand back and let people take advantage of him. What kind of wife would I be if I did? I didn't know the full extent of what had happened, but I knew he was getting involved in something that was bad news.

I was his loving wife, and I did what any loving wife would do. It was implausible for me to physically follow him around everywhere he went, so I put a GPS tracker on his car. When he took a detour on his way back from Filey to visit Becky, I had convinced myself that he needed the Broadhead money to fund an affair with her. I had no idea she was blackmailing him with a fictitious son. I just thought she was some tramp he'd started seeing. But I didn't confront him. I wanted him to man up and freely admit what he had been getting up to. But Harry became even more secretive and started being increasingly protective of his mobile phone. I could constantly hear it buzzing, but whenever I got the brief chance to check it, there were no messages. There was only one reason, in my mind, that he would be deleting the text messages. I became convinced he was having an affair with Becky, and I drowned the paranoia will pills and alcohol.

When I discovered that he was only going there for five or ten minutes, sometimes before work, I realised something else altogether different. But before I got to the bottom of it, Harry had stopped going. I later found out about the blackmail, and I hoped Harry had got wise to it and that he would stop the payments. The bigger issue was the constant trips to Filey and around Leeds. It was usually too far for me to follow and be able to ensure I'd get back before he did, so I had to rely on the tracker most of the time. Even though he told me he was going to nip into his old office or he had an errand to run for Steve, I could physically see he wasn't doing what he had said.

I began to get more and more agitated that he wouldn't own up to what he had been doing behind my back, and I started using the pills and drinking even more to compensate. After our little tussle when he'd started his new job, he became a new man overnight. Call me stupid, but I thought I'd got through to him. I thought I had the old Harry back, and he was the loving and affectionate man I'd married. We'd just moved into our new home, and as far as I was aware, he was ecstatic that we could potentially be parents. I thought I'd stopped him slipping away, but he carried on lying about his travels to Filey when he said he was going to work.

I had an epiphany, and I knew he wasn't going to stop.

And I couldn't have that.

"I'd been tracking him for months before you and he reconnected. I just never caught a good look at your face," I giggled.

The expression on Kim's face was every bit as satisfying as I thought it would be. I did suspect her at first, but I couldn't believe that Kim would have the gall to insert herself into my life with this little plan of hers. Kim had started to cry, probably because her whole pathetic plan was crumbling into dust in front of her. She had no idea who she was messing with. I'd often thought about what I would do to the woman who tried to take

Harry away from me. Most of it involved some form of gratuitous violence, but I never thought I would be inflicting it on Kim.

"You do realise he was using you, right?" I added.

"He wasn't. He loved me."

"Yeah, I don't think so. He was using you to get over me, that's all."

"He loved me. More than he ever loved you," Kim sobbed.

Apart from the constant spray of the sea pummelling my back, the heavens suddenly opened, too, and we were quickly soaked through. I could barely hear Kim, the little mouse, squeaking above the weather we found ourselves in, and it was enough for me to decide the time for talk was over. I started making my way over to Kim, and she stood her ground at first, but I saw the fright seize control of her eyes when I was only a few feet away, and she put her hands up in defence.

Not very ladylike, I know, but I punched her in the face as soon as I was within hitting distance, and she went down immediately. Her nose looked like it had exploded, and a crimson waterfall of blood started to run down her face. I grabbed her sodden, blonde bun and dragged her by her hair slowly towards the cliff face as she kicked and screamed violently. I lacked the physical strength to throw her from the Brigg by her hair, but it didn't stop me trying. I could feel the fistful of hair I was grasping, stretching and snapping as each strand gave way under the weight. After a few fruitless attempts, I decided to get on top of her and moved my hands down her face to her throat.

"Did you think you would actually get away with it?" I screamed in her face.

"Stop," Kim panted.

"If Harry killed himself, it's because of you. You got involved in something you didn't understand."

"Please," Kim gasped, uselessly grasping at my hands as I increased the pressure.

"You will pay for what you've done. For what you've done to Harry and me."

Kim mustered every shred of oxygen left in her blood to try and reduce the pressure on her neck, but she lacked the strength to break free.

The light in her eyes started to slowly fade.

XVIII

THE HIGH PRIESTESS

AMELIA - BEFORE

I told him I was sorry. I cooked his favourite meal. And after the night before, I could potentially be the mother of his child. Instead, he preferred to carry on lying to me. I wanted to follow him and be vindicated that my efforts had been appreciated, but he never arrived there. Instead, he drove to Filey once again. I wasn't content with just watching the tracking on my phone, and I needed to find out why he was going there, so I chose to follow him. I remained at a close distance the entire way there, still tracking him on my phone as I drove. I could see him bopping his head along to some music or the radio, and it was making me seethe with anger.

Who can lie like that directly to their wife's face? I'd given him ample opportunity to come to me with the truth, but he refused to. He pulled up outside a dingy set of flats and started looking around like he was there to meet someone for the first time. Was he cheating on me with multiple females? He saw a woman and pointed at her, and they both laughed and went inside. I imagined all the acts of depravity that were taking place in those walls involving my husband, and they were inside for at least an hour. The longer it dragged on, the more my anger turned to inconsolable grief. Had he been meeting random women on these trips to Filey to sleep with them? Was he trying to humiliate me?

I saw the woman leaving the block of flats with him, and she shook his hand, which I thought was odd. They were both dressed immaculately, and their exchange looked professional, more than anything. It dawned on me; she seemed like she was showing him around the place. Once Harry returned to his car, I got out of mine and slowly started following her. She got in her vehicle, and an estate agency was advertised on the back of it. I took a picture of the advert on my phone and watched her drive away.

In my ignorance of what had just happened between them, I found some relief. Maybe he wasn't cheating on me this entire time, and there was an innocent explanation for all this. But when I really thought about it, the real explanation was far more threatening. Harry was here to find somewhere to live when he finally plucked up the courage to leave me. It wasn't a heat-of-the-moment decision, and he was diligently planning it. It felt cold and calculated.

I couldn't believe I'd been so stupid. I thought the night before was a step in the right direction, but Harry never intended to take any other steps. He was nodding and smiling and telling me what I wanted to hear, but behind my back, he was planning his escape. I was still standing in the alleyway that I'd followed the estate agent down, and I dropped to my knees and started sobbing. Once I'd calmed down, I made a call to the estate agent's office. They didn't take much convincing that I was his wife, and they confirmed what I thought. I didn't know how to approach this with Harry. Why couldn't he just love me like I loved him?

I needed a drink.

I didn't know who or what they looked like, but there must have been someone else. Someone had got inside his head and contaminated him against me. Some jealous little bitch who wanted someone she couldn't have. Was it Becky? Or someone from his past? I bet he even had the blessing from his mother and sister, and they were all conspiring against us to try and split us up. I touched my stomach. If Harry's child was in there, I couldn't believe he would so readily give it up to be with some unknown tart. He might have set up his little love shack, but I wouldn't let him go that easily. I got back into my car and started the journey back to Manchester.

I kept imagining Harry sleeping with another woman. Or women. I wondered what it would be like to raise his child on my own whilst he galivanted off with his mistress. The farther I travelled away from him, the more my rage bubbled and boiled in the pit of my stomach. I began to hyperventilate, and I knew a panic attack was coming again. But instead of fearing it, I demanded it. That would show him if, on learning he was planning to leave me for someone else, I had a massive panic attack and crashed on the way home. I urged the panic attack to come on strongly and make me lose control of the vehicle, but it did neither. I couldn't even get that right.

I loved Harry, and I wished he could truly see just how much. I decided to give him one last chance to come clean. I needed to show him what he would be missing if he walked out on me. I had to get back to basics and remind him why he fell in love with me in the first place. When I got home, I made dinner again, like the dutiful wife that I was. I knew he would keep up the fairytale that he had been to work so he would be back home at the usual time. I spent hours slaving away in the kitchen. The roast beef was cooked to perfection and exactly how he liked it. It wasn't dry at all and even had a slight amount of pinkness in the middle. The roast potatoes were crispy and buttery. I'd even conceded to a long-standing disagreement and made Yorkshire puddings, which he incorrectly claimed were essential with a roast. I plated it all up, lit some candles, and waited for his return by the door with an opened bottle of beer.

An hour passed.

The beef had dried out on the plate and was stone cold. The Yorkshire puddings, once crispy and proud, had shrivelled up to a hard mass on the plate. I checked the GPS tracking on his car, and he was back at the office. He was probably with his assistant, the whore, "I was working late," he would then tell me. I'd had enough of the games. If Harry wasn't going to step up and tell me about everything that had happened, I had to do it for him.

I dispensed of the wifely niceties. I checked the time; he had another hour to make an appearance. I was going to sit Harry down and tell him everything I knew. Tell him that I'd been following him, and I knew all about the affairs. I was sick and tired of waiting in the background for him to have the courage to come clean himself, but against my better judgment, I wanted to give him a final opportunity to explain himself.

The food I'd prepared lay disappointedly on the dining table and the candle wicks had almost been drowned by the melted wax surrounding them. I'd put so much effort into it, and he had the nerve to stand me up. I did think about drinking the beer I'd opened for him and then drinking everything else I could get my hands on, but thought better of it. Harry didn't know it, but that was his last opportunity to do the right thing. I sat at the dining table, swirling the beer I'd opened for him aimlessly, with one eye still on the clock. I promised myself I wouldn't drink or get physical, but the temptation was almost too strong to defy.

Another hour passed.

That was it. Harry had missed my imaginary time limit. I didn't know if he planned on coming home at all, and for all I knew, he might have dumped his car and be shacked up with some slapper in his new flat in Filey. I took the bottle of beer in my hand and threw it into the fireplace. It smashed onto the hot coals in a cloud of bitter-smelling steam. He'd made his decision, and so had I. If he wanted to leave me, so be it. I was done playing the laughably oblivious housewife. I left the meal I'd prepared to rot in the open air and made my way to bed.

I heard him come in later that night, he crept into the bed, and I could smell traces of the whore's perfume that tainted his skin. It took everything I had not to leap out of bed and kill him there and then, but I kept my cool. I needed him to think I was none the wiser, just for a little longer.

"Where have you been?" I asked, pretending I'd just woken up.

"Sorry, I had to work late," Harry explained.

I knew it. Cliché.

"You work so hard for us," I swooned falsely.

"I forgot to mention that next weekend, we need to go back to Filey. Steve's having a party, and I said we would be there," Harry explained.

"That's the same weekend we will find out if we are going to be parents."

"I know, but he's had it planned for ages. I'd just forgotten to tell you, Ames, I'm sorry."

"It can double as a celebration! I'll follow you up there after the appointment at the clinic."

"Are you sure?"

"Of course. You should be with your friends," I smiled.

He was perfectly comfortable blatantly lying to my face in our marital bed, knowing exactly what his ulterior motives were. I didn't sleep a wink that night; I just gazed at a spot on the wall and started to plan my response to his betrayal. Every time I thought I was going too far, the scent of the woman he had been with all night wafted into my nostrils again, reigniting the rage. If I couldn't have him, no one else could.

The following days went pretty much exactly how I thought they would. He kept trotting out the same clichéd excuses. He would say, "I forgot something at the office," and then disappear for a few hours to later return with the same cheap stench coating his skin and hair. Or he would tell me he's going to work and then drive back to Filey.

Maybe he was going furniture shopping with his mistress, I thought. With each passing day, the more he treated me like a fool, the more crazed I felt. I'd removed the tracker from his car. I wasn't interested in where he was going anymore. Only where he would end up. I continued to treat him like a king until the morning of the clinic appointment. I was even making him a packed lunch for the trip. He was blissfully ignorant of my plans, just like he thought I was blithely unaware of his.

We got to the morning of the clinic appointment; it should have been one of the happiest days of our lives. But it wasn't. I had a splitting headache, and I thought I would vomit at a moment's notice. The more I continued my devoted wifely routine, the worse I felt. Harry was upstairs in the shower; I could hear the water rushing down the pipe outside the kitchen window. I heard something, and something within me snapped.

It was *whistling*.

Harry was in the shower whistling some merry tune, which was beginning to rub me up the wrong way. Just the simple act of him whistling made me realise that it was the day he was going to leave, and that's when I made my final decision. Harry should have felt exactly how I felt. He should have been mortified that our marriage was ending or desperate to reconcile things. But he had made his decision, and he was *giddy* about it. I knew what I had to do, but I'd take no pleasure in it,

I opened the kitchen drawer and got my tablets out; I could feel the anxiety burning a hole in my chest. The blood started to rush up my neck, and it swelled under the pressure, closing my throat just enough for me to struggle with every breath. I swallowed the tablets and closed my eyes. He was never going to tell me about the affair. He wasn't going to declare his love for me. A child wasn't going to fix everything. That day would be the last day I ever saw him.

He was going to leave me.

And there was *nothing* I could do about it.

From the cupboard I then retrieved the pestle and mortar in which I put two of the tablets. I ground them down into a fine powder and then added two more in. I continued the process until I didn't have any tablets left. I took the bottles of water I'd planned on packing for his trip and opened the caps carefully. I divided the powder between the two and replaced the caps. I was just placing them in the bag when Harry arrived from his shower, ready to leave.

"Not having any breakfast, Ames?" Harry asked, deceitfully shoving a fistful of toast into his mouth.

"I can't. I feel sick," I breathlessly replied.

"Amelia, whatever happens, we will deal with it," Harry started, "do you not want to try the old-fashioned way one more time before I leave?"

Not a chance in hell.

"Funny. No, I feel like I'm going to throw up."

"I didn't know I had that effect on you."

"It's just nerves about today."

"Are you sure you don't want me to cancel? We can always go up together tomorrow. I don't mind waiting."

"No, it's fine. I can't bear to see Yvonne's face if I robbed her of an extra day with her precious son."

"What's this?" Harry asked, pointing to the packed lunch I'd just prepared for him.

"Just a little survival kit in case you get hungry. A few drinks and snacks."

"You really are the most amazing wife in the entire world, you know that?"

Why are you leaving me then? I thought. I knew that the right thing to do was to be vulnerable and talk to him, but I couldn't bring myself to give him the satisfaction. Our marriage was broken beyond repair, and I knew that, but so did he. We were doing this little song and dance, both pretending to be happy but knowing the truth. He was positively bouncing around the kitchen like he didn't have a care in the world. If I had been ignorant of the truth, I would have guessed it was because of Steve's party or because he might have found out he was going to be a father. But I knew the truth. That day was the day he was going to leave me. I almost broke character but replaced my scowl with a smile before Harry caught on.

"I can't have my man going hungry, can I? Or eating questionable service station sandwiches. When do you need to set off?"

"I thought I'd go now; the car is already packed. I'm going to try to avoid the morning rush. Is that okay?"

"Of course. I love you; I'll see you tomorrow," I smiled falsely, leaning in for a kiss.

"I love you, Ames. Let me know how it goes."

Harry grabbed his bags, and I knew it would be the last time I ever saw him. There was enough Alprazolam in each of those bottles to kill anyone outright. If I got really lucky, Harry and his whore would both get thirsty at the same time, and they'd both be gone.

"Au revoir!" Harry shouted with his eyes crossed, lifting his top lip to expose his teeth.

I closed the door as he drove away and sat down at the kitchen island, contemplating what I'd just done. I didn't know how to feel. I hadn't twisted a knife through his heart or cracked his skull open with a blunt object, but I'd just murdered someone. Not someone, the love of my life. But love is meant to go both ways, isn't it? I felt strange, mainly because of the lack of guilt. Maybe I wasn't capable of feeling guilt anymore. I'd numbed myself with drugs and alcohol for so long that I didn't even know how I should feel. I thought about Harry constantly and wondered if those water bottles were still untouched. I wondered if he took a few sips on the motorway, lost all his faculties, and crashed. Maybe he would make it to Filey, and he would just fade away in front of all his family and friends.

I started to panic. I'd lost control of it all, and I didn't know what was going to happen or when. For all I knew, he could have discarded the bottles of water as soon as he left the house. I hadn't even considered my own life in all this, and if someone had found out what I'd done, I would be going down for murder. Although what I'd done was premeditated and calculated, I'd largely acted on impulse regarding the timing. I ran upstairs and vomited in the toilet until there was nothing else left to come up, and I started crying uncontrollably.

After the purge, I convinced myself that it wasn't my fault. None of it. Whoever Harry's mistress was, she was to blame. If that venomous snake hadn't slithered into our lives, Harry would still be breathing tomorrow. I was simply the delivery method of everything they deserved. I decided to try to put it out of my mind and pretend that it was just a normal day. I had an appointment to go to the clinic, and I should attend so as not to arouse suspicion. I didn't know whether I wanted the result to be positive or negative.

The journey to the clinic was a haze. I could barely concentrate on anything other than wondering what was happening to Harry. I listened to the radio as intently as I could in case there was a report about a crash or an incident, but there wasn't any. I parked up and looked at my phone, and he hadn't been in contact. I checked in and sat in the waiting room in a trance. I was surrounded by optimistic couples desperately waiting for some good news, chatting amongst themselves. My name was called, and I walked through to the doctor's office. I'd been in there many times with Harry, and I sat in my usual seat.

My attention is drawn to a small cut on his neck. It looked fairly recent but had scabbed over. It looked too large to be a shaving mishap, and I started to ponder what kind of implement would leave such a mark. My eyes lost focus for a second, and then I realised the doctor was speaking to me.

"Amelia?" he asked.

"Sorry, I was miles away," I uttered.

"Like it said, it's finally happened! The tests have confirmed you are pregnant. Congratulations!"

I didn't respond to the doctor. I simply stood up and walked out of his office. He followed me out in confusion, shrugging at the receptionist, but I left without a further explanation. I stood outside the clinic in the busy Manchester streets and screamed as loudly as I could, much to the alarm of passersby.

Wave after wave of regret crashed violently into me, knocking me off my feet. I was drowning in guilt and remorse whilst I gasped for air on my hands and knees on the pavement. My clarity returned, and I couldn't believe what I'd done. I'd killed Harry. He could be dead already for all I knew. I just wanted to scrub it all out and take it back, but I didn't know if it was possible. I got my phone out as quickly as possible and started dialling Harry's number.

"Hi, this is Harry. I can't come to the phone right now. Please leave a message," the phone played.

XIX

THE WORLD

HARRY - BEFORE

With any luck, that would be the last time I saw Amelia. Any possessions I cared about were packed in the back of my car, and I was on my way home to Filey. I didn't feel a single stab of regret in my subterfuge. The previous two weeks waiting for that day was total torture, but I was finally free. I pulled up in Manchester city centre and popped into the IVF clinic to officially withdraw my consent for further procedures. Anything that remained of my DNA would be disposed of, and Amelia wouldn't be able to use it against me again. I told them not to alert her, and they agreed. By the time she had found out what I'd done, Kim and I would be long gone.

When I was finished inside the clinic, Kim was waiting outside for me, with her bags packed too. Her entire face lit up when she saw me, and I hadn't found myself on the receiving side of a look like that for a while. I'd be lying if I said I wasn't questioning my decision in the morning, but once I saw Kim, I knew I'd made the right call. I was thrown back to when I first saw her on our first date many years ago. She was standing at the top of the stairs innocently smiling at me.

It was a beautiful moment for me, albeit a tad bittersweet. I knew that I'd made the right decision, but I was still upset. Amelia's mood in the morning reminded me of what we used to be like and what we could have been. She was sweet and caring, and even though I knew it was all an act, I still found myself missing her. Her former self, before the monster reared its ugly head and began clawing viciously at our marriage. If only she would have gotten the help she so desperately needed sooner, we could have been together. But the violent abuse wasn't going to stop, and I had to get out of there while I still could.

"Hi, Harry. Bit of a strange place to meet," Kim joked.

"Hi. Yeah, not the best place to have a date, I'll give you that," I said in jest.

"Are you ready to go home?"

"More than anything."

We both got in the car and started the three-hour journey to Filey. I'd left all my troubles back in Manchester, and it felt like old times. Throughout the journey, we chuckled and sang along to the songs on the radio. I had tears in my eyes most of the journey because of the sheer amount of laughter we shared. For the first time in months, I knew everything was going to be okay. From an outside perspective, it looked really rushed, but I fell in love again with Kim. She was the one. She always was. The biggest regret I had was letting my father's death get in the way of my relationship with Kim. If I'd have reacted differently, we could have been married with children right now.

And to state the obvious, I wouldn't have met Amelia. But the torment I'd endured from her was almost worth going through to finally sit in that car with such an amazing and kind woman. It didn't feel like a new relationship; it just felt like a continuation. It was then I realised just how strong of a connection Kim and I actually shared; several years and a failed marriage later, we could effortlessly pick it up where we left off. She was everything that I had ever wanted, and I was kicking myself for not gripping onto it with both hands all those years ago.

I planned to never set foot in Manchester ever again. Or anywhere near Amelia. I pleaded to whatever God would listen that she got a negative result at the clinic. Then, I would be truly free. I knew she would call me as soon as she left the clinic, but I turned my phone off in preparation. I had everything riding on a negative result at the clinic, but I was terrified that if Amelia was indeed pregnant, she would somehow force her way back into my life. And worse than that, that I would allow it.

The most important thing was that we were safe. I had first-hand experience of how dangerous Amelia was, and her violence was only escalating. Who knows what she was truly capable of? She was so volatile, and my previous transgressions paled in comparison to the latest. If she found out I'd left her, without even telling her, for another woman, and all whilst she was pregnant, there would be no telling what she might do. I'd told Kim everything, but I don't think she truly understood just how much danger we were in.

But I was trying to focus on the positives, and for a change, I was surrounded by them. We arrived in Filey, left our bags in the car, and went to the pub straight away. I decided pre-emptively that it was cause for celebration, and I tried to put Amelia at the back of my mind. I constantly imagined her smashing the house up because she couldn't get hold of me or furiously driving to Filey to check up on what I was doing. Steve was so happy to see us when we entered the pub, but the look of confusion on his face when I walked in with Kim was a picture.

"All right, Harry? What's going on here then?" Steve asked cheekily.

"Well," I started with Kim looking at me dotingly, "we are together. I'm leaving Amelia."

"About fucking time!" Steve roared.

I was a few drinks in, and the terror had started to fade. Everything began to feel right again. We shared stories and banter. I was surrounded by love and happiness. Kim could barely take her eyes off me, neither could mine off her. It was a glimpse of what my life was going to look like in the future: safe and in love. Maybe Kim and I would start a family of our own someday. I was getting ahead of myself, I know, but I couldn't help myself.

But I still couldn't fully enjoy myself; the fear of not knowing what Amelia's mental state was kept jolting me back to reality. Even though I knew I shouldn't, I couldn't help but feel slightly guilty about leaving Amelia in these circumstances. It was hard unbreaking those bonds that were once so strong, and I just wanted to call her and check if she was okay. The urge to do so was almost irresistible, but any contact with Amelia was likely to put Kim and me under threat.

As the evening went on, the likelihood of her having a violent meltdown increased severely. I imagined her going to the clinic and receiving the bad news, and I wouldn't be there to comfort her. I stopped drinking my pint and opted for a non-alcoholic one instead, just in case she turned up in a frenzy, and I had to deal with her. Kim had noticed my mood change and looked at me with concern.

"Are you okay, Harry?" she asked.

"Yeah, I just feel a bit weird about it all. What if she's actually pregnant? What happens then?"

"Then we will work it out. The most important thing is that you are out of there."

"I can't just leave her with our child."

"I agree. We need to go to the police in the morning and tell them everything. She shouldn't be allowed to look after children."

"You are right."

"I am. And she deserves everything that is happening to her."

"I know, but I still feel guilty."

"Do *not* feel guilty," Kim insisted, grabbing my hand with both of hers, "she drove you to this."

"I know she did. But I need to know what's going on with her. What if she is on her way here now?"

"Then we will deal with her."

"You don't understand how dangerous she is, Kim. What I've experienced so far is the tip of the iceberg."

"She isn't going to do anything with all these people here. Just relax, Harry, you're safe."

Kim was right; I wasn't responsible for Amelia's emotions anymore. She lost that right when she started being abusive to me. If the tables were turned and I had been beating Amelia, no one would blame her for leaving me. It was just so hard to let go, but I didn't know if Amelia had transplanted those feelings in me or if they were actually my own. I stayed on the non-alcoholic beer to keep me on my toes, and I watched all my friends get more and more drunk until they could barely stand. Once last orders were called, Steve announced that he was continuing the party back at his place, and everyone started making their way to his caravan park.

Kim drove us to Steve's place, and when we got there, everybody decided that we would stay outside to continue drinking, mostly because no one wanted to step foot in Steve's grim house. We lit a huge fire and had music playing. Everybody continued to laugh and drink until the small hours. It was so comforting being around so much happiness, and it started to calm my nerves. I was sitting by the fire with Kim, and I noticed her hands shaking slightly.

"What's up? Are you cold?" I asked.

"We are right next to a fire, Harry," Kim laughed.

"Obviously."

"I know you've had a traumatic few weeks, but I wanted to tell you something."

"What is it?"

"I love you, Harry," Kim smiled.

"I love you, too," I beamed.

"And I'm so proud of you for leaving her. It takes real strength to do what you did, and I just wanted you to know that," Kim said with tears welling up in her eyes.

"Thank you."

Kim had seen every part of me. She knew my past and wanted to be a part of my future. I had self-worth again, and I was excited to see what our lives together would be like. But even after such a wonderful moment, thoughts of Amelia were still scratching away on the back of my mind, and I knew she would be frantically calling my phone or even driving up here in a blind rage. I couldn't truly be in the moment with Kim, even though I desperately wanted to until I'd dealt with her. In some small way, I started feeling like my old self again, and the old Harry wouldn't leave Amelia hanging like that, no matter how she'd treated me.

"I'm sorry. I just need to make a phone call. It'll be ten minutes, okay?" I said softly.

"Okay," Kim smiled as I gave her a kiss on the cheek.

Physically leaving Amelia was one thing, but not anticipating the need to emotionally leave her was another. Even though she was over a hundred miles away, I was still firmly in her clutches. That wouldn't change until I faced her head-on and told her exactly what was going on. I owed it to myself and to Kim to finally end the relationship so we could all start to heal. I walked away from the party towards Filey Brigg and gathered all the courage and strength that Kim had instilled in me. I turned my phone back on, and the missed call notifications filled the screen. Along with all the calls was a single text message from Amelia.

> *I'm pregnant.*

The world stopped spinning. The wind had stopped blowing, and the grass ceased swaying. Every hope I held on to for a clean break with Amelia was left shattered. A child. I nearly launched my phone as far as the eye could see. I was hit by a tsunami of dread, fear and rage as the fantasy I'd held onto of never seeing Amelia again was crushed under the pressure. She would use the child as a way of forcing me back, and before I knew it, I would be back in the same position. Once she found out that I'd planned on leaving her, she was going to kill me. There was no question.

My thumb hovered over the call button, but I had no idea what I was going to say. Every slither of my being needed to tell her it was over and I wasn't ever going to see her again. I wanted to threaten her with the police if she ever came near Kim and me. I craved the catharsis of the breakup and to truly know that she knew it was over. I started to plan the conversation out in my head, but I couldn't form the words. I was so dumbfounded by the news that I could barely think straight, and I'd stopped in my tracks.

Kim was still looking at me from the fire, and I smiled back at her half-heartedly. I reminded myself of what she said. I was strong. I had courage. She was proud of me. The pregnancy would inevitably complicate things, but it didn't change the fact that my marriage needed to end. I'd be there for my child, but Amelia and I could never be together again. I felt strong for even coming this far, but I didn't know if I had the strength I'd need to follow this through, given the news.

I hit call.

And instead of a dialling tone, all I heard was a noise indicating the call couldn't connect. I tried again and again, but the signal was so spotty it wouldn't go through. The anticlimax left my mouth dry, so I grabbed a bottle of water from the car and had a quick drink before I started walking closer to Filey Brigg with the intention of finding more signal.

I continued to make one call after another, but I still didn't have any luck getting them through. I reached the Filey Brigg viewpoint, and I still didn't have any signal. I mustn't be as fit as I thought because I was out of breath even after the short walk. I put it down to the anxiety I felt for the call. In my stupor, I'd forgotten that I had the secret phone in my pocket, but I really didn't want Amelia to have the number. I turned it on, and it had a full signal. I almost finished the bottle of water in preparation and hit call, but I withheld my number. My heart was beating through my chest, and I was sweating buckets in anticipation. The phone rang ominously, and after only a couple of rings, Amelia answered.

"Amelia?" I said.

"Harry, is that you? What's happened? I couldn't get through to your phone," Amelia frantically asked. I could tell she had been sobbing.

"I don't have any signal. I've had to borrow someone's phone."

"Whose phone?"

"It doesn't matter."

"Harry, did you get my message then?" she agitatedly asked.

"I did."

"How are you feeling?"

"Not great."

"What's the matter?"

"I don't know how to say this, so I'm just going to say it," I gulped, "I can't do this anymore."

"I know you can't, but please don't."

"You know?"

"I know about the affair and the flat you've started renting. But I'm having your child, Harry. It's all going to be okay. Just come home. We can fix this."

I expected Amelia to become extremely angry and start screaming at me down the phone, but she was uncharacteristically calm about this. Just hearing her talk like that made me almost doubt what I'd planned on doing. But I forcefully reminded myself what she had done to me. The constant mocking and sadistic jeering. The perpetual threat of violence. Or the unending dread that one day she would take it too far, and I'd end up losing my life. More importantly, I reminded myself of what Kim had said. I was strong, and I could do this.

"No, Amelia, we can't fix it. It's never going to be the same again, and I have to do this. We won't ever be together again, do you understand that?" I said, starting to weep.

"Harry, I'm sorry for what I did. But it was because I love you so much," Amelia sobbed.

"I'm sorry. I've already made the decision. Goodbye, Amelia," I hoarsely whispered.

The phone slipped from my hand and down on the rocky outcrop below, bouncing towards the edge. Suddenly, I felt incredibly dizzy and unsure on my feet, and the scene around me started spinning. I tried walking over to my phone to retrieve it, but I could barely put one foot in front of the other. I got a few feet away, and I could hear Amelia shouting my name down the phone. I dropped to my hands and knees to retrieve my phone, but I ended up batting it even closer to the edge. I almost felt as if I was drifting in and out of consciousness. I reached out for my phone, but I was so uncoordinated I couldn't get a grip on it. It suddenly felt like my lungs had stopped working, and I was struggling violently for every breath. I put everything I had into getting back onto my feet, but I was so unbalanced that even the steady sea breeze was making me stumble.

I looked out towards the North Sea, and the bewilderment of my situation had cleared. I didn't know how she did it, but somehow, it was Amelia. She was always at least one step ahead of me, and in a pathetic attempt to hold onto control, she decided it was better to end my life than let me go. For the first time in a long time, I had hope for a brighter future. I fell in love again. Amelia had allowed me to have a miniscule taste of what my life could be before she violently snatched it away from me. In the end, the only thing she ever wanted from me was total submission. Once I'd escaped the control she had over me, she would have done anything to get it back. I didn't know whether her desire in my final moments to fix our marriage was genuine or it was a final, cruel trick she was playing on me. Even though I knew it was the end, I smiled faintly because my resolve had remained strong, and my last act towards her was one of defiance.

My heartbeat felt so powerful, and I could feel it in the back of my throat. But each beat slowly became further apart, and the strength started deteriorating. My vision started to fade to black, and my legs gave way. The last thing I felt was a vague sense of falling at speed.

And then, nothing.

XX

JUDGEMENT

AMELIA

Squeeze. Just a few more seconds and she would be unconscious. They say that your life flashes before your eyes when you are close to death, and I wondered what Kim was seeing. The romantic walks on the beach with my husband or the sordid liaisons when he should have been at home with me. She had taken everything from me, and it was all her fault. Harry's death and her own could be attributed to a grievous mistake that she made. The growing rage pushed me even further, and I dug my thumbs into her throat with all my weight. I saw the panicked expression on her face slip, and instead, I saw acceptance. Her arms and legs stopped flailing, as she was slowly fading away under my violent grasp.

I couldn't help but think it was only fitting that Harry's whore would die in the exact same place that he did. They couldn't be together in life, and they would have to settle for in death. I'd imagined this moment for so long, and I desperately wanted to savour every emotion. I kept on applying pressure without a single shred of remorse. She wasn't content with taking my husband from me; she felt the need to wedge herself into my life and start manipulating it from within. Tighter. I bared my teeth, and my hands started to ache under the constant strain I was putting them under. Even tighter. I could feel my fingernails almost drawing blood because I was pressing them so hard against her throat.

"Good riddance, Kim," I whispered.

Just as her eyes closed, I was grabbed from behind, pulled away from Kim, and thrown onto the rocks on my back. Kim immediately inhaled as much air as she could and started spluttering violently. When I turned to look at the person who grabbed me, I realised it was Yvonne and Poppy standing above me. Poppy was holding a can of pepper spray pointed directly at my face, and Yvonne ran over to Kim to help her back on her feet. Kim was fighting for every breath; if I had managed to hold onto her for a few seconds longer, I would have had my revenge.

"Fucking psycho," Kim gruffly uttered.

"Whore," I spat bitterly.

Kim looked like she was going to run over to me and start hitting me violently, but Yvonne restrained her and whispered something into Kim's ear, which seemed to subdue her slightly.

"She isn't worth it, Kim," Yvonne said loudly for my benefit.

"I didn't realise we were planning a reunion," I joked.

"Funny. You are finally going to tell us the truth. Stand up," Poppy ordered.

I rose to my feet and took a few steps back away from Poppy and her can of pepper spray. I remained standing and thought about the truth, which, honestly, I didn't know what it was. I tried killing Harry; that was true. But I never found out if he actually drank the poison I'd prepared for him. For the longest time, I couldn't face the thought that he decided to take his own life and step off that cliff face.

That would have been his decision, and he didn't *deserve* to choose.

I suppose the other version of the truth wasn't palatable either. The last exchange I had with Harry when he called me from the Brigg was so ambiguous that I'd replayed it in my head a thousand times over. For all I knew, he could have been standing on a slippery rock like

I was, trying to get a signal and fell. Or my drugged water took hold of him, knocked him unconscious as I planned, and he plunged to his death.

As soon as I found out when I was pregnant, I wished I'd never touched those bottles of water. I wanted to fight for him and in the right way. I bitterly regretted what I'd done, but in my mind, it was never confirmed whether he died by my hands or by his own. I was willing to let it go, but when James had told me his death was suspicious, I had to find out what truly happened. Partly out of self-preservation to keep myself out of prison, but I also needed to know what his final decision was.

However, in my quest of the whole truth, I'd bitten off more than I could chew. I started to find out the kind of man that Harry had become, and the more I dug into his past, the less I started to regret what I'd done. With each transgression I discovered that he'd committed, my remorse paled further into insignificance. By the time I was cornered by those three women on the Brigg, I was absolutely convinced that he deserved everything I'd done to him.

He was a liar, a criminal, and, worst of all, a *cheat*.

Harry plotted and schemed behind my back and didn't at least have the common decency to tell me to my face. In the end, my journey to uncover the truth had left me with more questions than answers. I'd gotten to the point where I didn't want to know anything else, and I would have gone home happily and never spoken a word about it ever again.

The three women standing in front of me were demanding answers. Poppy was already crying, Yvonne was tearing up, and Kim could barely breathe. As far as I was concerned, they deserved everything that had happened to them, too. They all had their parts to play in Harry's death. Regardless of whether I was the one to make the final decision, each of them had contributed to it in their own way.

Yvonne's constant underhanded scheming made Harry feel utterly hopeless and trapped, thinking he had a son that he didn't know about. He was terrified of telling me, so he didn't even come to me for help. When he found himself being blackmailed and taken advantage of, he probably didn't envisage another way out of the predicament he'd got himself into. Not to mention the way Yvonne had treated him his entire life and, on top of everything else, the inexcusable fact that she was responsible for his father's death, which was the most traumatic experience he'd gone through.

Poppy spouting her mindless optimism made Harry think he could leave me and have a better life without me. I must admit she just thought she was being supportive, but she should have known it would have caused an inner conflict within Harry. She ought to have given him the space to make his own decisions, but instead, she felt the constant need poke her nose into our marriage and, as a result, get involved where she was never welcome.

And last but not least, Kim. The final nail in the coffin. She was the lowest of all of them; she used her body to corrupt Harry, and when he was at his weakest, she went ahead and stole him from me emotionally. Even though he knew I was pregnant with his child, Kim's allure was too powerful for him to resist. She saw a husband and wife going through a rough patch in their marriage and decided to take advantage of that. I didn't feel sorry in the slightest for trying to take her last breath, as she knew she had taken everything else from me.

I openly admit that I'd made mistakes, too, but everything I did was out of my undying love for Harry and my desire to make our marriage the best it could be. Should I be blamed for loving him too much? No. Sure, my passion turned to anger on occasion, but it was born of frustration more than anything else. I could feel him slipping away, and I would have done anything in my power to keep him. I'd lost everything that I had ever cared about, and my unsuccessful attempt on Kim's life was witnessed by the manipulative matriarch and her submissive daughter. I glared at Kim, and the longer the deafening silence prevailed, the more upset she became. That should be me, I thought. I should be upset, but I wasn't. I didn't feel guilty about anything, and I was too busy thinking about how I could get away from this situation without facing any consequences. But that wasn't possible, and I'd finally lost control over my own life. And the only semblance of control I could keep hold of was not giving them the answers they so desperately pleaded me for. I had to give them something, so I decided to give them the version of the truth, which would keep me from behind bars.

"What are you yammering on about? What truth?" I said defensively.

"Did you kill my son?" Yvonne screamed.

"No, he killed himself. Because you all got involved in his life when you weren't welcome, you could have just left us alone to be happy."

"He wasn't happy!" Kim screamed, "You choked and pried every last gram of happiness right out of him!"

Anyway, I didn't think they deserved the truth. Only I deserved it, and if I couldn't get it, I'd make sure they couldn't either. I reached deep down inside, and instantly knew what would really hurt them. It was fictitious, of course, but I wanted Kim to suffer exactly how I suffered when he told me he was leaving me. I wanted her to have a taste of the despair and anger I experienced every single day. I needed to see her entire world implode because of something I'd whispered to her.

"In the end, Kim, he chose me. I spoke to him before he jumped. But he couldn't live with what he'd done," I explained coldly.

Kim looked stunned at what I had said at first but shook her head and managed a faint smile in disbelief.

Was she really that deluded that she could actually say, without a doubt, that Harry would choose her? Even I couldn't have made that assumption definitively, which is why I started this whole investigation in the first place. I could see Kim picking her words very carefully.

"Harry didn't kill himself. And he didn't choose you. He chose *us*," she said.

"Us?" I asked.

Kim looked down and gently patted her stomach, and I immediately knew exactly what she was getting at. Harry had gotten her pregnant. It took me months of trying and thousands of pounds worth of medical interventions, but to Kim, it had just happened. There was no feasible way that child was planned, and it was just an unfortunate after-effect of their grimy fumbling. I had fought with everything that I had to conceive my child. I did it for Harry, like I did everything. For this deluded whore to claim some kind of ownership over him because she got knocked up by accident made me feel a degree of fury I'd never before experienced.

Was it some cosmic sign that they should have been together? What if Harry and I were never meant to be, and I was always just kidding myself? No. I wouldn't let the paranoia get the better of me. Harry and I were in love, and I felt it in my bones. Kim had been sent to us as a test, and unfortunately, my husband was too weak to pass it. Kim began to nod triumphantly as she could see the penny dropping, and the wrath grew in me to a bursting point. I could feel the prickling at the back of my neck grow, but instead of fearing it, I used it. The adrenaline coursed through my veins violently, and every muscle in my body vibrated with a burst of rage.

I exploded into a sprint towards Kim, and Poppy was too slow to react as I knocked her to one side with ease. I just wanted to reach Kim and both of us be knocked from the Brigg to the rocks below. Yvonne wasn't as slow to react as Poppy and landed a punch square in my jaw. I lost my balance on the slippery rocks below my feet and careered off the edge of the cliff, only managing to cling on by my fingertips. Kim immediately grabbed my right arm to try and pull me back up, and Yvonne grabbed my left.

I didn't intend to fall on my own, but when I was presented with the option of letting go, I wanted to. And I'd take the truth with me. I wanted to be the second person they forced to their death at the Brigg, and I wanted them to feel the guilt for the rest of their lives. I released the grip from my fingertips, but they continued to hold my weight. Poppy joined them, and they dragged me from the cliff face and left me curled up on the floor a few feet away from the edge.

"You don't get to take the easy way out," Kim said breathlessly.

"You really think he would choose you just because you have his bun in your oven?" I laughed.

"He didn't know I was pregnant. He was dead before I'd found out. He chose me regardless."

"He used you. It was a bit of fun because we were going through a rough patch. That's all. You really think you could break up a marriage as strong as ours?"

"No matter what you say, Amelia, I know exactly how he felt. He loved me. He might have believed your gaslighting bullshit, but it won't wash with me."

Just the look in Kim's eyes made me believe her. She did love him, and she genuinely believed he loved her. But it was nowhere near as powerful as my love for Harry. I devoted my life to him, and I fought every day for him. It didn't matter what anybody else said, and no one else deserved Harry. Only me. The thought of him loving another woman wasn't something I could process, but the look in Kim's eyes was so intense that it started to chip away at my defences. I could see what she was doing. She was trying to force my emotions out and, along with them, my confession.

"You don't know anything about him," I dismissed.

"I know he wouldn't kill himself. And you know that too, don't you?" Kim hissed.

"No."

"Yes, you do. Because you killed him, didn't you?" she asked goadingly.

"No, he killed himself."

"Just admit it. You killed him, didn't you?" Kim shouted.

She wasn't going to stop asking me, and my patience was wearing thin. I didn't want to confess what I'd done, but she was backing me into a corner either. My confession was the only option I had left to hurt her, and I wanted her to feel exactly how I did. I wanted her to experience the dread of raising a child, knowing the father was dead. I wanted to know that she would never feel happiness again. If I could have physically thrown her from the cliff, I would have. But that option wasn't available to me anymore. Instead, I decided the only way I could destroy her would be to tell her the truth and watch her crumble.

"Yes," I whispered, "and I don't regret it."

I finally saw the light die in Kim's eyes, just like I'd wanted. Her face was a mixture of satisfaction and deep, primal anger. She walked away from us and started sobbing a few feet away. Poppy had tears rolling down her cheeks that she wiped away with her free hand whilst still holding the pepper spray pointed at me. Yvonne looked like she deeply regretted saving my life only minutes earlier, but was satisfied she had heard the truth from my lips. Kim stopped pacing and stood entirely still whilst staring at me in complete silence.

"How did you do it?" Yvonne asked heatedly.

"I laced his water with my anti-anxiety pills. He must have drunk it and fell off the Brigg. Whoops, clumsy wife," I said jokingly with a shrug.

"Why? Why would you do that to him?" Poppy cried.

"Because if I couldn't have him, no one else could."

"He was never yours," Kim said venomously.

"Of course he was! He was my husband!"

The frustration finally got the better of Kim, and she let out a scream, which must have been heard for miles around, and dropped to her hands and knees. She started pounding the rock with her fists, and Yvonne went over to console her. I could see that all three of them were starting to get very aggravated by me and my lack of empathy, but could they expect? For me to break down with them? Harry had been playing me for a fool for months on end with his infidelity and even exposing us to danger and extortion.

He *deserved* it.

"Now you know how I feel," I said emotionlessly.

Kim immediately rose to her feet again and thundered over to me, standing tall above me with her finger pointed in my face.

"Harry loved me. And I loved him. We were going to have a family together. In the end, he hated you."

"No, he didn't," I replied matter-of-factly.

"You broke his bones. And his spirit. Yet you have the audacity to think he still loved you. You killed him long before you poisoned him."

"I may have put the pills in the bottle, but you are the one who poisoned him. If you hadn't come into his life, he would still be breathing."

"I saved him. When he was at his lowest moment."

"You didn't do a very good job."

"You are disgusting," Poppy added.

"Pipe down, Poppy, let the adults speak. You don't need to get involved," I dismissed.

"Oh?" Poppy said, while taking out her phone and tapping on the screen. When she was finished, she put her phone away, and my phone beeped. She had a weird smile on her face as I took it out to look at the incoming text, supposedly from James.

> *I'm already involved, bitch.*

It was Poppy. The entire time. She had planted the idea in my head at the very start of this journey and continued to sway me throughout. I knew that my gut feeling, after finding his number in Harry's deposit box, was the right one. The only reason I dismissed it was because I received a text from James when Poppy was in front of me. I felt ridiculous for believing her for even a second.

"I knew it was you," I said knowingly.

"James was all of us," Yvonne added, "we knew you were involved the second we found out Harry had died."

"Why was the number registered to Harry?"

"It was his secret phone," Poppy started, waving the phone, "on the night of his death, we went looking for him. He had dropped the phone; it only had one call on it, and it was to you."

"When I asked you in that bar if you knew who Harry was trying to ring, you said you didn't. And that's when

I knew it was you. I just needed you to hear you admit it," Kim added in a quiet rage.

"So, what is this? Hijinks? A widow harassment club? Was Steve involved in all this, too?"

"Steve didn't want anything to do with this; he just wanted to move on with his life," Yvonne added, shaking her head, "Kim almost blew the whole thing when she led you to him. He would have exposed us."

"So you burned down Steve's house just to get to me? And I'm the psychopath?" I laughed.

"Steve got what was already coming to him. John had just asked the Broadheads to delay it until we'd dealt with you," Yvonne said.

"And that slag, Becky? The blackmail? Was that just for fun? Or did she know all about this?" I asked.

"Mum did that to try and split you both up after she found out about the abuse," Poppy argued, "we tried convincing Harry, but he wasn't having any of it."

"Yes, I made mistakes. But I would have tried anything to get my son away from you," Yvonne added angrily.

"Even sending me to the Broadheads? They could have killed me."

"Chance would be a fine thing," Kim said under her breath.

"They weren't going to kill you, Amelia," Yvonne said, "John just asked them to scare you."

"Why?" I said.

"In case you confessed," Poppy answered.

"Well, I'd say all your schemes backfired slightly, wouldn't you?" I teased ironically.

"Enough nonsense," Poppy said forcefully, "We have done all this to expose you and the way you treated Harry. You deserve to rot for what you've done."

"He got what he deserved," I affirmed.

"Harry was the kindest man I'd ever met. He made mistakes, but largely because you forced him into them!" Kim shouted.

"He was a cheat."

"No, Amelia. You just thought he was. You thought he was slipping away from you, but you were pushing him away the entire time."

"He was weak. He saw a younger blonde woman and didn't have the strength of character to say no."

"Harry was the strongest man I'd ever met. He was strong enough to leave you."

"He didn't leave me though, did he?"

"Come on, Amelia. I was with him that night. He walked off to make a phone call to you, but he had no signal, so he was walking to find some. When he finally got through, he told you he was leaving you, didn't he?" Kim said.

I'd already confessed to his murder, but that was one step too far. There was no way I was going to admit that. I wouldn't give her the satisfaction. Whatever she had planned for this revelation at the Brigg, it wouldn't include that. If she didn't have enough confidence in his love for her, I wasn't going to be the one to give it to her. She could live the rest of her life not knowing, just like I would have had to.

"I'm not playing this game anymore," I announced.

"It's not a game," Yvonne said, producing her phone from her pocket, which had been recording the whole thing.

"You are going to pay for what you've done," Kim said victoriously.

If they had recorded the entire thing, I was done. I would go down for his murder even if he didn't take a single sip of that water. I couldn't hide behind my dark humour and matter-of-factness any longer. That wasn't how my story should have ended: rotting in a jail cell. I was adamant that all of my actions were justified, given the context. I still didn't feel a shred of remorse for any of it, even after all their persistent yapping.

I just hated the feeling that these three weak women had conspired against me and led me down this path without me knowing. They had planned every step and watched me like a rat in a maze as they poked and prodded me to get me to this moment. I would have done anything to have my revenge on them there and then, but I wasn't in charge anymore.

The more I realised I'd lost control, the more the anxiety came rumbling back. I could feel my heart thumping through my chest and the familiar prickling at the back of my neck. I started hyperventilating violently, and instead of helping me, the three women almost started laughing as Yvonne stopped the recording. I crawled towards my bag to get my tablets, but Poppy kicked it further away. I could barely breathe anymore; all the anxiety and stress of the situation had hit me all at once. Poppy got her phone out and called the police, and I lay on my back, paralysed, waiting for them to arrive.

"I loved you, Harry," I whispered to myself.

In the end, I knew I wasn't the woman he left behind. It was *her*.

EPILOGUE

KIM - AFTER

"Harry? Come here!" I shouted playfully. Harry made his way over to me, giggling as he walked, but at the last hurdle, he tripped over, almost falling into the water of the pond I was squatting next to.

"Careful, Harry! You will hurt yourself," I said, ruffling his hair playfully.

Harry, completely unperturbed by the fall, simply stood back up and started running around again. I wanted to show him the frog that was sitting by the side of the pond, but he was more interested in stomping around in the mud beside it. Even at three years old, he looked so much like his father, and it was uncanny. I thought it would have been difficult looking into the eyes of my son and seeing my Harry in them, but I saw it as a beautiful reminder of what I once had. I decided to give my son Harry's name as soon as I looked into those eyes.

Not a single day went by without me thinking of Harry and the life we could have been living if *she* hadn't taken him away from us. I refused to use her name. On the rare occasions that I was forced to mention her, I would only refer to her using a pronoun. I wanted my son to live his entire life without ever hearing that name if I could help it.

I tried to remember Harry how he was that night before he lost his life, the hope in his eyes and the sheer happiness he felt. Or the brief relationship we shared, which was the happiest of my life. I tried to drown out the negativity and focus on the present. The thing that got me through it was our son; he was an endless supply of love and affection, and I adored spending every waking second with him.

"Mummy, come look!" Harry shouted.

I followed Harry, and he had found a frog on his own, a great big slimy one, casually chattering whilst sitting on a log. I held Harry tightly as we entered a staring competition with the frog on a log, and he gripped back onto me lovingly.

"Aunty Kim, what have you found?" Freya interrupted.

"It's a frog! And it's sat on a log!" I enthused.

"Wow! That's amazing!" Freya said with her mouth agape.

"Freya, come on, let's go and find more frogs!" Harry suggested excitedly.

They both started running down the path together, holding hands. It was such a privilege watching them explore the world together. We all made an effort to come here at least once a week and walk the coastal trail near Filey. In some small way, I wanted Harry to be closer to his father, and I wanted to feel closer to him, too.

"Don't go too far!" Poppy shouted from behind me.

"I don't think they're going to listen," I remarked.

"They are going to be trouble when they are older," Josephine laughed.

"They are trouble now," I jested.

Freya was the perfect likeness to Harry, too. They both had his eyes and hair, and you could tell they were siblings. My son didn't know about what happened to his father at the hands of *her*, and neither did his daughter. They were too young to understand that part. But we told them all the amazing things about Harry, and we spoke about him every single day.

After *her* confession at Filey Brigg, we took the recordings and all the evidence to the police. It was painful dredging it all back up again, but we finally got

Harry the justice he deserved. *She* had pleaded guilty and was put in prison for a very long time. It was ruled that she was unfit to care for a child, and after a lengthy legal battle, Poppy and Josephine happily adopted Freya. They were natural parents, and we all instinctively banded together and walked the journey into parenthood as one big, unconventional family. The shared trauma and grief between us could have had a negative effect, but we refused to let that happen. *She* kicked up a stink, obviously, but there was little or nothing she could do behind bars.

I moved back to Filey to have Harry; I wanted him to grow up in the fields and on the beach like Harry and I did. Yvonne was incredibly supportive and even helped me put a deposit down for a house on the seafront. We had an amazing life, and I felt truly blessed to have everything that I had. But one thing was missing, and it was the love of my life. I hoped he was somehow looking down on us, watching young Harry grow up, and he was proud of his little family.

We approached Filey Brigg viewpoint, and it still brought back bad memories for me, although I'd decided I wouldn't let *her* stop me from returning to such a beautiful place. It may have been the place where Harry lost his life, but it was also the place where he decided to start his life again with me. They had erected barriers since Harry's death in an effort to make it safer. Harry and Freya were leaning against them and looking into the North Sea.

"Can frogs go in the sea, mummy?" Harry asked.

"No, love. They prefer a pond," I answered.

"What if they use armbands like I do?" Freya asked.

"No, it's too salty for them," I explained.

We all leaned on the barrier and watched the waves crash against the rocks. I would have given anything for Harry to be here with us. It goes without saying, but I still hated what *she* had done to us, and not thinking about her required constant effort. Her jealousy and selfishness had done way more damage than she had realised. What she had done would affect us for the rest of our lives and the lives of Harry's children. I knew she was paying for her crime, but I couldn't help but think it wasn't enough.

We made our way back to the car, and we said our goodbyes as we split up to return home. We lived in a three-floor townhouse overlooking the beach. We were just getting into the holiday season, and the number of people visiting was starting to increase. I parked the car where I usually did, and Harry and I walked inside our family home together, hand in hand. When I opened the door, there was a letter waiting for me on the doormat, and Harry picked it up and handed it to me.

"Can I go and play now?" he asked.

"Wash your hands first, please," I instructed.

I opened the envelope, and there was a single piece of paper inside. It was a handwritten letter stamped by the prison in which *she* was currently residing.

There was once a whore from Filey,
Who was living the life of Riley.
But when his wife gets out of prison,
She'll realise she isn't,
And her survival was looking unlikely.

Her skills were slipping, and it didn't even rhyme properly. I'd received a poem from her every month since she was in prison, in addition to the occasional crazed rant scratched into a piece of paper. They were menacing at first because I had no idea how she got my address. But after a while, the menace faded, and I actually started being amused by them. They were a desperate cry for attention from a broken and lonely woman. Those little limericks she sent me were just to exert her control, even from behind bars, but I was determined not to let them work.

"What's that, mummy? One of those funny letters?" Harry asked.

"Yes, don't worry about this," I said, scrunching it up into a ball and throwing it in the bin, "I thought we were playing?"

I wished that Harry could have been here to see our son growing up. The older he got, the more the resemblance to his father grew. He always looked the most like his father when he smiled. That cheeky, signature smirk that Harry was famous for. I know he wasn't planned, but I knew that Harry would have been absolutely delighted, like I was. We spent the rest of the day playing like we usually did, and in the early evening, I put our son to bed. I read him his usual bedtime story, a captivating tale about a rabbit that played football.

"Did Daddy like football?" Harry asked.

"He did! He used to watch it at the pub with his friends!" I smiled.

"Can I see some more photographs of Daddy, please? I miss him," Harry asked with a smile.

Even though our son had never met Harry, I did my best to make sure he still knew who he was and what he stood for. As heartbreaking as it was, whenever my son said he missed his father, I knew I was giving Harry the respect he deserved. I had thousands of pictures of Harry through the years, mostly gifted to me by Yvonne from Harry's old room. It became a little ritual of ours, and we would go through Harry's childhood pictures and compare him to my son.

Even though it was a family of two, I loved my little family. I was hesitant to say it was incomplete because it never felt that way, but we both missed Harry immensely. I would keep him alive in his son's eyes with the stories of Harry's youth and the thousands of old photographs.

"Sure, but I'm not getting the albums out. Only on my phone, okay?" I bargained.

Harry clapped his hands together as I got my phone out. I hadn't noticed because it was on silent mode, but I had a text from an unknown number, along with about twenty missed calls from Poppy and Yvonne.

> *I'm coming for what's mine.*

THE WOMAN HE LEFT BEHIND

MORE FROM THE AUTHOR

THE DEBUT PSYCHOLOGICAL THRILLER FROM
PHILIP ANTHONY SMITH

RUN
FOR YOUR LIFE

HOW FAR WOULD YOU
RUN TO SAVE YOUR LIFE?

PHILIP ANTHONY SMITH

Would you risk your family, your marriage, and your life to earn some extra money?

Sean and his family are already struggling financially when he loses out on a much needed promotion. He is recommended a dubious app to earn extra money on the side, and keeps it from his wife. But it has secrets of its own...

Desperate to get fit and keep his family's heads above water, he starts running using the app. In the midst of their failing marriage, Sean finds a connection to a mystifying runner, who tests his commitment to his family.

A mysterious group of men begin to threaten his life, and he is left with a seemingly simple choice; **fight**, or **flight**. Sean continues to run using the app, but loses parts of himself on the trail. He tests not only his **stamina**, but his **morality**, and his **loyalty** to his wife.

Believe the hype. This relentlessly fast paced psychological thriller will have you racing to the end as you follow Sean's journey in finding the identities of the men behind the masks, and to the shocking twist at the end.

VISIT: **PHILIPANTHONYSMITH.COM**
FOR MORE INFORMATION

THE WOMAN HE LEFT BEHIND

A FREE BOOK

All my email subscribers will receive a free digital copy of my upcoming novella, '*Living To Forget,*' due to be released in June 2024.

Head over to my website and join my mailing list to receive it for free when it releases!

WWW.PHILIPANTHONYSMITH.COM

ACKNOWLEDGEMENTS

My first acknowledgement is to you. I'm basically an unknown author, and you decided to risk on your valuable time and pick up this book. I sincerely hope you loved it, and I'd love to hear your thoughts in the form of a review.

I wouldn't dare release a book without mentioning my amazing wife, Lindsey. She is the most supportive partner a husband could ask for, and this book just wouldn't have been possible if it wasn't for you.

I'd like to give a special mention to Domingo Alvarez, who painstakingly proof-read this entire book for me. Your edits and suggestions have been genuinely invaluable in making the book what it is, and I thank you.

Finally, I need to thank all the wonderful people who took an early copy of 'The Woman He Left Behind' to review and share their thoughts with me. I honestly take every word of your feedback on board, and it's been a pleasure working with you all. In no particular order:

Melina Rios - @melisbooked
Lauren Bustard - @books_withlaurenn
Shellie Waldron - @Yorkshire.Bookworm
Gail Kenyon - @gales.tales47
Katie Greenop - @katies_cosy_reading_corner

Anna - @Annamulreads
Rebekah - @bookish_beks
Caroline Reid - @caz.readz
Lou Whitmore - @Lollysbooknook
Zoe Ekin - @northyorkshirereader
Roxy - @roxyrecommends
Karen bail - @Lovetoread2023
Megan Bayes - @Megsbookshelf.x
Jen Morris - @jen.lifeinbooks
Sarah - @reading_happy18
Emma Gines - @emma.reads.thrillers.22
Julie Bradford - @juliereadzintherockies
Olivia Bradshaw - @_readwithliv_
Lauren Bennett - @readb.ylauren
Bethanie - @bethanies_bookshelf
Rachael Willmott - @rachaelsreads

TRIGGER WARNINGS

As a thriller author, I believe anyone should be able to pick up a book and enjoy it. I certainly wouldn't want any reader to come across something in one of my books that brought a dark memory back to the cold light of day.

In this book, you will find references and themes of the following:
- Death of a spouse.
- Domestic violence.
- Emotional abuse.
- References to suicide.
- Substance abuse and alcoholism.

Printed in Great Britain
by Amazon